"CYB MALFUNCTION!"

Ericho felt his whole body tense. "Alan, stop moving."

"Yes, sir."

In the control suit, Alan turned and began marching in a new direction.

"Alan, didn't you hear?" growled Rigel. "Stop moving."

The intern's reply chilled them. "I can't."

"What the hell do you mean you can't!" yelled Rigel.

"I can't stop moving. The suit's taking steps for me."

"Emergency abort. Use your manual thumb switch."

"I already tried—it's not working."

The cybersuit staggered toward the center of the bridge, and Alan yelled, "I'm fighting it, but I can't make it stop!"

Rigel ran up behind the cybersuit and tore open the real neck panel. Alan whipped around. A cybersuit glove fastened on Rigel's neck and lifted the tech officer up, strangling him. Ericho stared in disbelief. It was an impossible nightmare—a cyberlink with a man trapped inside. A cyberlink trying to kill them!

ANACHRONISMS

Christopher Hinz

A·SIGNET BOOK

NEW AMERICAN LIBRARY

PUBLISHED BY
PENGUIN BOOKS CANADA LIMITED

NAL BOOKS ARE AVAILABLE AT QUANTITY DISCOUNTS
WHEN USED TO PROMOTE PRODUCTS OR SERVICES.
FOR INFORMATION PLEASE WRITE TO PREMIUM MARKETING DIVISION,
NEW AMERICAN LIBRARY, 1633 BROADWAY,
NEW YORK, NEW YORK 10019.

This book previously appeared in a hardcover edition published by St. Martin's Press.

First Signet Printing, October, 1989

2 3 4 5 6 7 8 9

SIGNET TRADEMARK REG. U.S. PAT. OFF. AND FOREIGN COUNTRIES
REGISTERED TRADEMARK — MARCA REGISTRADA
HECHO EN WINNIPEG, CANADA

SIGNET, SIGNET CLASSIC, MENTOR, ONYX, PLUME,
MERIDIAN and NAL BOOKS are published in Canada by Penguin
Books Canada Limited, 2801 John Street, Markham, Ontario
L3R 1B4
PRINTED IN CANADA
COVER PRINTED IN U.S.A.

For my sister Lisa,
with love

The dry grief
of spectral gales
cloaking her spirit in dark design

Reason wilting; sequence betrayed by caresses of space
and a mind out of time
with homeland visions

The dry grief
of spectral gales
emptying her life of anachronisms.

—From *The Lytic's Lament*

STARSHIP
ALCHEMON
Control Network Major Systems

LEVEL 1
    SEN— Sentinels
    POP— Primary Operating Power
    PAQ— Primary Quantizer
    NEL— Nucleonic Engines
    SCO— Spatiotemporal Coagulators
    NAV—Navigation (Loop)

LEVEL 2
    PEH— Primary Ecospheric Homeostasis
    SOP— Secondary Operating Power
    SAQ— Secondary Quantizer
    EAC— External Airseal Control
    CON— Containment System
    MED—Medical System

LEVEL 3
    EPS— Elementary Probability Scanning
    GEL— General Library
    PYG— Primary Genesis Complex
    FWP— Food/Waste Processing
    GEN— Geonic Stability
    HYP— Hydroponics

LEVEL 4
    RAP— Robotics and Probes
    IBS— Internal Bio Scanning
    LIS— Lander Interface System
    ICO— Internal Communications
    SPI— Storage Pod Interface

LEVEL 5
    CYB— Cyberlink Network
    HOD—Holographic Display

SYG— Secondary Genesis Complex
IAC— Internal Airseal Control
ICS— Internal Corrector System

LEVEL 6

ETI— External Telemetry Interface
NUB— Nutriment Bath
LUM—Luminosity System
TEM— Thermometry Regulation
LSN— Luxury System—Natatorium
LSG— Luxury System—Gymnasium
LSD— Luxury System—Dreamlounge

Prologue

The Assignor knew it was going to be an unpleasant encounter.

The young woman wore loose trousers and an untucked gray pullover; the Assignor could not tell whether the clothing made her appear relaxed or whether she was faking it. He offered her a chair, then sat down behind his desk and clasped his hands together to hide his nervousness. He smiled. She did not smile back. He wondered if she already knew what he was going to say.

"Welcome to Pannis, Miss Frock," he offered.

"Call me Mars Lea."

He maintained his smile. "Mars Lea, we've just received a complete analysis of your test results from the Pannis Central Laboratory in Jamal."

"I know where it is."

The Assignor found himself nodding vigorously. "Of course you do."

Mars Lea leaned back in the chair. The Assignor heard a thumping noise; she was kicking the side of his desk with her flat heels.

He gently bit his lip to hide a grimace. He hoped someday to have enough seniority to avoid working with these people altogether. And this young woman in particular. . . .

"What does my analysis say?" she prodded.

She had long dark hair, hanging to her shoulders, untrimmed, grossly unfashionable. Her cheeks were as pale as the froth on a milkshake. The eyes . . . pale blue gems. Skinny. A long neck. She smelled of natural body scents and he did not care for the odor.

"Our test results are most interesting. . . ."

"Do I get a starship?"

He smiled, trying to match the woman's detachment, knowing he could not.

"Mars Lea, we at Pannis feel that a starship expedition

would, at this time, not necessarily be in the best interests of the Consortium."

"Afraid?"

He had been trained to ignore such a question. "The Pannis Consortium senses a slight cooperation problem."

"Haven't I cooperated with your tests?" she challenged. "I took two months out of my life. I practically lived in that laboratory of yours."

The Assignor wished he could detect anger or resentment in her words. He could deal with such emotions.

"We are certainly pleased by your cooperation during the testing procedures, Mars Lea. However, a year or more in a starship is a far cry from the lab."

"Yes, it is."

No sarcasm. Not a trace. He sighed, certain that the meeting was destined to get worse.

"Mars Lea, Pannis is willing to offer you any of a number of positions. In fact"—he switched on his desk monitor, moused through her file—"we are prepared to offer a choice of thirty-eight distinct assignments throughout the Consortium and its ancillary companies. The salary ranges are quite high. The benefits within a large consortium like Pannis are quite remarkable. I can assure you that—"

"What is the most exciting position you are offering?"

"Exciting? Why . . . I don't know." He scanned the screen. "Yes, here's one that sounds quite exciting. Archeo/geological assistant, digging up nineteenth century frontier cultures . . . a research project in the American Southwest."

"Blizzards?"

"Pardon?"

"Do you have anything with blizzards? I like storms."

"Storms?" God, these people were trying.

He accessed another sector of her file. "Yes, there is one job in the south polar regions available—an industrial classification—you would utilize your abilities to locate deep mineral deposits."

" 'Abilities'?" She laughed. "Is that what you think I have? Abilities?"

He felt his jaw tightening. "Abilities is a generic term, of course. Pannis certainly recognizes the inexactitudes of superluminal science, the lack of firm definitions, of clear guidelines and theories. We merely—"

"You merely use Psionics, you don't pretend to understand them."

He allowed himself a sigh. "If you wish to take the dimmest of attitudes, I cannot offer rebuttal."

She stopped kicking his desk. "Yes, I suppose that's true."

The Assignor came alert, sensing an echo of sadness behind her words. He could use that.

"Mars Lea, we at Pannis are not quite so coldhearted about all this as you suspect. We do recognize the extreme range of difficulties that citizens like yourself experience throughout the Corporeal. We do assist, wherever and whenever possible.

"The Pannis Consortium generally does not brag about it, but last year alone we awarded seventeen million to non-profit groups seeking to ease the burden of the Psionics."

"Ease my burden," Mars Lea whispered.

The Assignor did not hear her. "Pannis *is* concerned. We practice the Corporeal concept—functional satisfaction—that is our goal."

She regarded him silently.

"We at Pannis believe that you will meet that goal. At least one of these thirty-eight positions will pose a challenge to your unique . . . qualifications."

Mars Lea smiled.

Good. He was getting through to her. The Assignor smiled back.

"You don't have to make a decision right now. Take a few weeks to think it over."

"That won't be necessary. I've made my decision. I choose a starship."

The Assignor could not hide his disappointment. God, some days he hated this job.

He tried to explain. "Mars Lea, you must understand that a starship—"

The door opened. The Assignor stopped talking and stared at the immaculately dressed man strolling into his office. The man wore dark trousers with a matching headband. A pleated gray vest covered a turtleneck that rose almost to his chin. An icicle earring—a stylish sliver of frozen mineral water formed over a microrefrigerator—hung from his right lobe. The Assignor watched a droplet melt away and fall to the carpet.

The man was a senior official, a Pannis supervisor, a rank rarely seen on this floor of the office complex. The fact that the man was here filled the Assignor with dread.

A black mark, the Assignor thought bitterly. *I'm not handling this situation correctly and my promotion file will shortly reflect that fact.* The Supervisor had probably been monitoring their conversation, which meant that Mars Lea was even more important than her dazzling psionic ratings indicated. The Supervisor was here to rectify the Assignor's failure.

He won't come right out and criticize me. That was not the Pannis way. *He'll say that I've done a fair job under difficult circumstances. And then he'll see to it that I get a black mark.*

The Assignor wondered how many successes he would have to earn before Pannis considered erasing this failure.

The Supervisor sat down on the edge of the desk, facing Mars Lea. Another droplet slowly detached itself from the tip of his earring and splattered on the polished surface.

"You are being most uncooperative, Mars Lea," said the Supervisor, in a low, restrained voice.

"Yes, I am."

The Supervisor regarded her for a long moment. Then he turned to the Assignor.

"Access vessel departures. Look for a minor research mission—something leaving within the next few weeks."

The Assignor hid his surprise. *Is he actually thinking about putting this woman aboard a starship?*

The Supervisor wagged his finger at Mars Lea.

"Understand me clearly, young woman. You are not going to be given a major assignment. But if you insist, Pannis is prepared to gratify."

"Thank you."

The Assignor located vessel departures. He scanned the list, quickly narrowed down the possibilities.

"Starship *Bolero Grand*, two-and-a-half-year mission, nonplanetary, galactic physics research, crew of twenty-seven, including two Lytics—"

"Perhaps something smaller, a bit more intimate," suggested the Supervisor.

"Starship *Regis*, crew of six. Mission duration, fourteen months. A supply ship, bound for the Chartran Colony."

The Supervisor smiled brightly. "The *Regis* sounds perfect to me, Mars Lea. Will you accept such an assignment?"

"No. That sounds boring."

The Assignor was confused. Something was going on here that he did not understand. This Supervisor could not be this stupid—he would know that Mars Lea Frock was a difficult Psionic. If he had wanted her to accept the *Regis*, he would have pointed out the benefits of that particular ship, would have made the proposition sound far more attractive.

"Any other possibilities?" asked the Supervisor.

The Assignor nodded. "Starship *Alchemon*, nineteen-month mission to the LAL 21185 system. Planetary exploration. Crew of eight, including a Lytic."

The Supervisor frowned. "No, I don't think that will do."

"Why not?" challenged Mars Lea.

The Supervisor hesitated. The Assignor understood.

He wants her to accept this mission! He's leading her along!

The Assignor folded his hands on his lap. He did not know who was involved, nor why, but he had been with Pannis long enough to recognize a high-level setup.

It was just possible that he would not get a black mark after all.

The Supervisor asked the Assignor for more data on the *Alchemon* mission.

He nodded, read aloud the pertinent facts from the file. "They depart lunar orbit in eleven days. The mission is bioresearch oriented and will include a landing on the second planet of the LAL system: a world named Sycamore."

The Assignor accessed an auxiliary file. He kept his smile to himself.

"According to data from an unmanned probe, Sycamore is a very violent, unstable planet, locked in perpetual storms. Because of this factor, the *Alchemon*'s mission carries safety-risk classification.

The Supervisor shook his head. "Mars Lea, Pannis cannot, in good conscience, allow you to go on a mission such as this."

Her hands tightened into fists. "It sounds perfect for me. I want it."

The Supervisor pretended to consider her demand. He stared into the far corner of the office, narrowing his eyes, as if concentraing on alternatives. The icicle earring dripped two more times before he returned his gaze to her.

Tightened lips betrayed the Supervisor's dissatisfaction. The Assignor thought it was a good act.

The Supervisor spoke slowly. "If we were to grant your

request, Mars Lea, you would have to formally and legally absolve the Pannis Consortium from liability for anything that might occur. We could not be held responsible for sending you on a high-risk voyage."

"I'll do whatever is legally necessary."

The Supervisor produced a slight frown. "I'll have to clear this with my superiors, Mars Lea. I do not have the authority to send you on such a mission."

The Assignor knew that that statement was absolute nonsense—supervisors could send people just about anywhere they wanted. But Mars Lea Frock would not know that. Most Psionics remained relatively naive about the ways of the consortiums.

"Please wait outside," ordered the Supervisor.

Mars Lea stood up, turned quickly, and walked to the door with that stiff upright gait that seemed to characterize so many Psionics. The door closed automatically behind her. The Supervisor smiled.

The Assignor recognized that he was now faced with a potentially career-threatening situation: He was being forced to juggle two mutually exclusive sets of behavior. On one hand, he had to consider that he was involved in a high-level setup; fo reasons unknown, Pannis Consortium wanted Mars Lea Frock aboard the starship *Alchemon*. The Assignor would be expected to recognize the setup and not make waves.

But it was also possible that this entire affair was a test of *his own* abilities. Assigning a powerful, possibly unstable Psionic to a high-risk star voyage certainly fell outside the guidelines of normal policy. If the Assignor failed to question the Supervisor's motives and this was indeed a test of his own abilities . . .

I must be extremely careful.

The Assignor frowned while pretending to study the file. "Sir, I must point out that Mars Lea Frock is no ordinary Psionic. The Jamal Laboratory report classifies her in the upper one percent. And there are indications that she suffers periodic episodes of mild psychosis—"

"I've read the report," interrupted the Supervisor, with a wave of his hand. "I've heard of the *Alchemon*. That's one of the new ships, isn't it?"

"Yes, sir."

"Chronomute-protected?"

The Assignor checked the file. "Yes, sir. A full security package. Level One Sentinels and a quartet of warrior pups."

"Those are very safe vessels," the Supervisor pointed out. "And there's a Lytic on board." He shrugged; another bead of water fell from his earring. "This situation does not appear to pose any real problems. Remember: functional satisfaction. Pannis believes strongly in that concept. The mainstreaming of Psionics contributes to the overall good of the Corporeal."

It has to be setup, thought the Assignor. *But if I'm wrong, and this whole affair is a test of my abilities . . .*

The Assignor realized that he had no choice. He had to push the issue.

"Sir, putting this Psionic aboard the *Alchemon* appears, at least on the surface, to be an irregular procedure."

The Supervisor smiled tightly, then reached into his vest pocket and removed a three-inch-diameter flat disk. He rubbed his hand absently across the unit's dull plastic surface.

A safepad.

It was an antisurveillance device, capable of warping and transposing audiovisuals fed from the room's normal scanning monitors. If anyone was observing, they would see and hear two men carrying on a conversation. But that conversation would look and sound different from the one that was actually occurring. It was likely that the Supervisor had preprogrammed the safepad to substitute an innocuous discussion.

The Supervisor licked his lower lip. "We are entering a gray area here. It is best not to pursue this subject."

The Assignor nodded slowly, wondering what the safepad was displaying to the surveillance monitors. *Am I carrying on a normal conversation right at this moment, asking the Supervisor about tomorrow's weather?* Safepads could foil most eavesdropping gear, unless an alert observer happened to be watching lip movements on an analog camera. But that was unlikely. Digitized data remained the rule. Such data could be altered.

The Assignor also wondered whether the Supervisor had actually activated the safepad earlier. *Is there a record of any of this conversation?*

The Supervisor stood up and walked around the Assignor's desk. "Do you have any more questions?"

By igniting such a device, the Supervisor was technically

in violation of interoffice policy. The Pannis Consortium did not like interference with its employee monitoring.

"Sir, I believe that all my questions have been answered." *The less I know about this setup, the better off I'll be.*

The Supervisor rubbed his finger across the safepad, deenergizing the device as he slid it back into his pocket. He was wise enough not to risk a surveillance alteration for longer than necessary.

"You're doing a good job. I believe you're due for a promotional review next month."

"Yes, sir. I'm hoping to be transferred out of this section. Working with these Psionics . . . it can be very frustrating."

A distant smile crossed the Supervisor's face, as if he found the Assignor's words particularly humorous.

"Keep up the good work," said the Supervisor, as he exited the office.

"Thank you, sir."

The Assignor knew he should let the matter rest, but he could not resist another peek at the *Alchemon* data. He accessed the crew files, quickly scanned through the biocharts of the seven humans and one Lytic who were scheduled for the nineteen-month voyage.

On one of the charts, he discovered a special notation. He felt his guts tightening.

The Assignor was no expert on superluminal interaction, but he knew enough about basic Psionic categories to realize that a bad situation could develop if Mars Lea Frock was allowed aboard the starship *Alchemon*.

Nothing to be done about it, he rationalized. He had acquiesced to the Supervisor. He would look like a fool and possibly risk his job if he made waves at this point. If Pannis wanted this setup, that was good enough for him.

As he took one final look at the *Alchemon* expedition data, it suddenly occurred to him that maybe the purpose of the voyage had nothing whatsoever to do with bioresearch on the planet Sycamore. Maybe Pannis wanted to study something else.

He sighed. Whatever Pannis's intentions, it was best not to get more involved than he already was.

The Assignor slept uneasily that night. When he awoke the next morning, he remembered having been caught in the throes of some strange and terrible dream. But try as he might, he could not recall what the dream had been about.

1

The bridge of the starship *Alchemon* was hexagonal in shape, about eight meters across, with a high arched ceiling that lent openness to what would otherwise have been a crammed arena. The few segments of wall space that were not hidden by a mélange of monitors and data terminals caught Ericho Brad's eye as he entered through the southwest airseal: ivory voids, shadow traps throwing machinery panels into bas relief. These quiet spaces augmented the equipment, gave meaning to the glittering readouts that told how well the 200-meter-long ship was functioning. Much had gone into the planning and construction of the *Alchemon*. Only an artist's eye could hope to spot all the subtleties, but the careful spacing of the systems, the soft flowing lines where equipment melted into walls—these things were evident.

A hidden microcam tracked Ericho, projecting his picture onto one of the main screens symmetrically located along the perimeter of the room. *The lieutenant's jest, no doubt.*

The monitor went blank and Ericho was left with a mental image of himself: sea blue eyes, a savagely pleated brow curtained by stiff gray hair, carefully groomed beard and moustache, unadorned black formsuit stretched from neck to ankles. A proper enough appearance for a captain. He grinned at the thought.

From somewhere to his right came the voice of the lieutenant. "The color spectrum deserves our attention. Colors root us to the real world. Blues and reds, golds and greens—they serve as buoys in these forsaken times."

A chair, suspended centimeters off the deck and half circled by specialty consoles, floated out from behind an engineering rack. Lieutenant Tom Dianaldi's lanky frame rested awkwardly in the soft cushions.

"I was just gazing upon the rainbows." The lieutenant pointed to the HOD, the holographic display orb situated in the center of the bridge. "I never before took notice of the intertwinings, the glorious way they mold and shape one another, bringing new colors into existence and phasing out the old."

The HOD, a transparent sphere four feet in diameter, blossomed from the tip of a narrow spindle. Within the sphere, a trio of distorted rainbows wound together, forming an ever-changing array of swirling colors. The rainbow coloration indicated that the HOD was operable but currently programmed to receive no signals. Coherent light tracers lined the outer shell of the ship, ready to lock onto and project into the sphere a three-dimensional representation of any object within fifty thousand kilometers of the *Alchemon*. It was another design feature of the Pannis psychoarts department, for the telemetry scanners normally provided the computer with all the data the crew could conceivably use. The HOD reflected human need. It was sometimes nice to *see* what was out there.

Dianaldi's voice rose. "Rainbows are pleasing. Rainbows prove that the universe offers more than the extremes of black and white, of good and evil. Rainbows show that there is still hope for human beings."

The lieutenant had deeply tanned arms and a ruddy neck protruding from a pale green tunic. Sparkling brown eyes and a face kept free of facial hair belied his fourteen years of starcrossing. Ericho had met Dianaldi for the first time at the outset of this voyage, nine and a half months ago. His rank had surprised Ericho. The man still looked too young to be a lieutenant, second in command of a starship.

Another gravity-neutralized chair floated into view from the waist-high maze of control panels that ringed the HOD. The chair halted and the man occupying the contoured seat nodded perfunctorily to Ericho. Jonomy was the ship's Lytic.

A gray formsuit clothed Jonomy's thin frame, and the small chin, pursed lips, and soft oval eyes betrayed human ancestry. But beneath the bangs of black hair, where the brow should have been, was a large dark hole. A thick flesh-colored cable was attached to something inside his forehead. The umbilical cable hung over his shoulder, fell to the floor, and snaked across the deck for several meters before vanishing into an opening at the base of the HOD spindle.

Through that umbilical, and through a profusion of invisible laser relays, flowed information of such magnitude that

Ericho found it difficult even to imagine what it was like. Every system on the *Alchemon*, from external telemetry and corridor luminance to food processing and Loop navigation went directly into Jonomy's modified brain. Jonomy monitored, processed, controlled, and corrected the vast network; he allowed the *Alchemon* to maintain itself and injected his own signals into the system when it erred. He was a Lytic interface—state-of-the-art human cybergenetics—and the only crew member capable of fully understanding the vast intricacies of the ship.

Jonomy glanced calmly at the lieutenant, as if registering an erratic piece of equipment for later maintenance. At least that was Ericho's impression. Lytics, even more than normal human beings, often displayed cryptic facial expressions.

The lieutenant chuckled to himself.

Ericho sat down in his captain's seat, felt the chair sink slightly as the graviform projectors adjusted to his mass. He toggled a positioner on the chair's console, floated to a spot where he could observe both Lytic and lieutenant. "What's our status, Tom?"

Dianaldi smiled. "Our status, Captain, is still human."

"Ship status," Ericho corrected, vowing not to be drawn into another of the lieutenant's metaphysical whirlpools.

"We're maintaining prime orbit, normal attitude, geosynchronous to within point zero zero two of alpha base."

Ericho glanced at Jonomy. A barely perceptible nod from the Lytic indicated that Dianaldi's answer was correct.

A slight offset in his med profile—a secondary neurosis overlooked by the Pannis doctors, the problem compounded by the presence of Mars Lea.

That was how June Courthouse, the *Alchemon*'s crewdoc, had explained Dianaldi to Ericho early in the voyage, when the lieutenant's philosophical bent had first begun to manifest itself. And lately it seemed that Dianaldi's ramblings were growing more intense, more disturbing.

He reminded himself to have another talk with June about the problem.

Jonomy caught his eye. "Message from the lander, Captain."

"Feed it."

The Lytic hesitated. "Atmospheric disturbances again, Captain." Jonomy blinked rapidly, a sign that a mass of data was flowing into his artificially enhanced cerebral cortex. "Another storm epicenter has moved directly below us. It will take about two minutes to reestablish contact."

Ericho nodded. Like Dianaldi, the planet Sycamore often posed a challenge to clear communications.

They had been circling the cloud-veiled world for the better part of two weeks while the *Alchemon* telemetrically surveyed the planet. Yesterday, survey completed, Ericho had finally granted permission for a touchdown. Earlier today, four of the crew had piloted one of the landers down to the storm-ravaged surface.

The *Alchemon* was the first manned expedition to this star system: LAL 21185, an ancient red giant more than eight light-years from Earth and so old that it had been shining when the sun was still a collection of swirling gases. Current astrophysical theory held that such a star should not possess planets. It had four. Exobiologists universally insisted that no planet orbiting a red giant should be capable of supporting natural life. Three worlds succumbed to that dogma but the fourth, Sycamore, did not. A computerized probe had been sent here several years ago and the probe's discovery had set the stage for the *Alchemon's* closer look.

In the Pannis Consortium's grand scheme of cosmic exploration and development, the original probe's twenty-month round-trip had been relatively minor. Pannis had set up a new Loop: a physically created transpatial corridor that cheated the relativity laws and rendered light-years mere irregularities. In essence, a Loop was an invisible doorway connecting Earth and the solar system with any particular star its builders chose. Loop travel was, for all intents and purposes, instantaneous, but due to the unstable nature of Loops, they had to be built at the outer reaches of planetary systems. It took months—sometimes years—to travel to and from Loops toward one's final destination.

Creating a Loop was notoriously expensive, even for a wealthy Consortium like Pannis, and most Loop investments failed to return even a fraction of the money spent. More than a hundred Loops now existed, linking Earth to a diversity of star systems, but only a handful had led to planets capable of supporting human life and less than 1O percent produced substantial cash returns by way of raw materials. Alien life had been found on a dozen worlds, but none to compare with the rich Gaia of humanity's home planet. And no life form approaching human intelligence had yet been discovered.

The LAL 21185 Loop had been constructed rather late. All of the neighboring systems had already been explored and it was only because Pannis's forty-year franchise development rights were about to expire that they had undertaken the expensive and complex task of building a transpatial corridor. If they had not built a Loop, their claim would have expired, the Corporeal would have placed the SOL/ LAL 21185 rights up for bid again, and one of the competing consortiums probably would have snatched the scientifically devalued franchise for next to nothing. And so the Loop had been built and the standard unmanned probe sent through, and it had returned with the astonishing news that the second planet in the system supported a primitive and unknown form of bacterial life.

The Sycom strain lived in an environment that would sequentially electrocute, bake, and suffocate an unprotected human. The microorganisms apparently lived in perfect harmony with their violent world, at least according to the most recent data. The expedition's science rep and three crew members were down on the surface hoping to learn why that was so.

"Message coming through," said Jonomy.

The baritone of Hardy Waskov, the Pannis science rep, emerged from the bridge's hidden speakers.

"Captain Brad, we have completed our studies here at alpha base. We are preparing to lift off for an area approximately two thousand kilometers to the north. We will re-establish contact at that time."

Ericho felt a muscle tighten in his jaw. "You know the rules, Hardy." *On a virgin planet, there are to be no unnecessary communication breaks.* The science rep knew Corporeal exploration policies all too well. That fact did not discourage him from trying to circumvent them whenever possible.

There were times when the rules had to be ignored—Ericho realized that. But Hardy Waskov literally seemed to grasp for situations that violated common precaution. The science rep had been a thorn in Ericho's side since they had left lunar orbit nine and a half months ago and their relationship was made even more complicated by Hardy's lateral command privilege. True, there were only certain situations where a science rep could overrule a captain, but Hardy always seemed to use those occasions to fullest advantage.

Hardy's reply was icy. "I believe, Captain, that in light of our most comprehensive studies of the planet, an exception can be made. We have discovered that the Sycom strain has been migrating slowly southward. Initial calculations suggest that the organisms originated from a common source about two thousand kilometers from here."

"What is the migration rate?" Jonomy asked.

Ericho sensed hesitation at the other end of the audio link. Hardy had just made the discovery and he obviously did not want the Lytic, with total computer access, to upstage him with some instantly formulated theory explaining the migration. Normal humans had to withdraw facts, check and correlate, and then input their data back to the computer for analysis. A Lytic could do it all at once, often in the space of microseconds. Scientists tended to be a bit jealous of Lytics.

Hardy finally responded. "The migration rate suggests that the Sycom strain has been moving southward for about half a million earth years. However, my initial data could be faulty—I strongly suggest that we wait until more concrete information is forthcoming before attempting to formulate theories."

"Of course," Jonomy said calmly. The Lytic had probably already run the data and obtained an answer. No one but another Lytic could know for certain.

Ericho said, "If this bacteria's been there for half a million years, then a few extra days of ground travel shouldn't make any difference." The lander could operate like a tank, crawl at a reasonable speed across the surface to its new destination and, more importantly, remain in communication with the *Alchemon*. If they took off into Sycamore's violently unstable atmosphere, the electromagnetic anomalies would make it impossible to maintain contact. They had learned that fact only this morning when the lander had first entered the planet's ambience.

Hardy sounded furious. "Are you officially ordering us to waste several days in transit when we could lift off and land in less than three hours?"

Perhaps Ericho was being overly cautious. But Sycamore was a bizarre place, especially the atmosphere: a physicist's den of iniquity, with elements gyrating madly between mass and energy. The less time the lander spent aloft, the better he would feel.

"That's an order."

Hardy replied calmly. "In that case, I must refuse. As you know, Captain, evidence of superluminal interaction precludes minor safety regulations. Our Psionic believes she had made a contact."

That got even Jonomy's full attention. The Lytic stared across the bridge.

Ericho kept his voice even. "Made contact with what?"

There was a long pause.

"The contact is very vague, but she is quite sure that it is not originating from one of us. We have reason to suspect that it originates from the source of the migration."

Ericho half entertained a notion that Hardy was making up the story just to get his own way. But it was difficult to imagine the science rep distorting the truth to that degree. "Mars Lea must have some idea of just what this contact is?"

Hardy sounded exasperated. "Captain, you know full well that Psionics is not an exact science. Mars Lea has felt something and we believe that an immediate investigation is warranted. Now either you grant us your official permission or we will move out on our own."

It was a hollow threat. Ericho's tech officer, Rigel Keller, was the lander pilot. Rigel would not move the craft unless he received authority from the *Alchemon*.

"Put Mars Lea on," Ericho demanded.

"I can't. The contact is so intangible that I had to ask her to don an isolator hood. If she removes it, we may lose the contact altogether."

Ericho took that in stride. "What makes you so certain that this contact is originating from the source of the bacterial migration?"

There was a loud sigh. "Because Mars Lea experienced it at the exact moment that I discovered the probable source of the migration. As you should realize, Captain, coincidences are prime indicators of Psionic interaction."

He realized it. That did not make a decision any easier. The very concept of Psionic crew members was disturbing. He had served with them on several interstellar expeditions over the past fifteen years and not once had their abilities proven beneficial.

The use of Psionics aboard exploratory voyages had become common about twenty years ago. At that time, one of the gifted humans had *experienced* the primitive emotive patterns of a spindly-legged creature found on the planet Nickalon 2. That telempathic contact had opened the doors of scientific inquiry into that creature's theretofore mystifying behavior. Since then, the consortiums had been scouring Earth and the settled planets, searching for those rare humans possessing strong extrasensory abilities.

Mars Lea Frock had been added to the *Alchemon*'s roster just ten days before departure, an unusual event in and of itself, since crew assignments were generally finalized months prior to takeoff. She was actually under Hardy's direct command, which was fine with Ericho. One weird crew member—the lieutenant—was enough of a responsibility.

"Should I assume your silence is the go-ahead to lift off, Captain?" Hardy quizzed.

Mars Lea's contact was probably some sort of false juxtaposition of superluminal impulses; the woman could very likely be receiving telempathic imagery from Hardy or one of the others. Then again, there could be some life form down on Sycamore that had thus far eluded their detection.

Jonomy caught Ericho's eye and the Lytic gave a slight nod. *After all,* the nod seemed to suggest, *exploration always carries an inherent risk.* Ericho had not risen to a Pannis captaincy without taking calculated chances. But an upsetting flow of juices in his guts spoke to him on another level. Things did not feel right.

Dianaldi chuckled. "Ah, Captain. A decision requiring a clear choice—black or white. No in-between solutions. No rainbows."

Ericho sighed.

The lieutenant continued. "Have you ever read the *Book of Parallel Thirst,* by the lunar philosopher Bal-Kur? He came to all the decisions in his life by remembering that the universe remains shrouded in duplicity."

"I see." Ericho glanced at the Lytic, but Jonomy had turned away to study a set of enhancement screens. It was easy for Lytics. The somewhat other-than-human social status afforded cybergenetic beings enabled them to ignore circumstances not directly related to their functions. As captain, it remained Ericho's responsibility to deal with the lieutenant's spiraling thoughts.

"Officers of the *Alchemon*, I await your reply." The sarcasm was practically crusted onto Hardy's words.

Ericho nodded slowly, made peace with the inner turmoil of mind/body discord as he had done a thousand times in the past. "All right, Hardy. You have permission to lift off. But I want full contact reestablished every hour. That means you make the trip in short jumps."

"Agreed," said Hardy triumphantly. "We will attempt to restore transmission at those times. Waskov out."

"Attempt to restore" was one of those quaintly optimistic phrases used regularly by scientists and politicians. Ericho was not really concerned, however. With Rigel Keller piloting the lander, Ericho's orders would be carried out.

Dianaldi folded his bare arms and grinned. "A wise decision, Captain. And if you had said no to Hardy, that too would have been a wise decision. Duplicity encompasses both black and white."

Ericho was sure of one thing. When they returned to Earth, he was going to do everything in his power to prevent Tom Dianaldi from getting another starship assignment. The lieutenant was simply too neurotic for the closed psychological environment of a deep-space vessel. Ericho was no philosopher, but in practical terms he believed that human beings imposed their own value systems onto the frameless neutrality of a random universe. Dianaldi struck him as a man doomed to search hopelessly for meaning out there in the nothingness.

2

━━━━━━━━━━━━━━━━━━━━

The planet was a nightmare.

It was daybreak in their new locale, and the sounds of morning were amplified into Mars Lea's heavy shieldsuit: a violent cacophony of crackling and hissing, interspersed with faraway explosions of volcanic gas. High above them, thundering energy storms tore holes in the upper atmosphere. Fierce winds scoured the surface, wild currents raging across the bleak landscape like parasites trying to suck the last bit of nourishment from eroded bedrock. According to Hardy Waskov, a Sycamore morning was the mildest part of the day.

Everything was sporadically perceived here. The smooth windswept hills, where visible, blended into a sky so dark and brooding that Sycamore's sun remained a pale green halo at its clearest. Clusters of blue liquid, the consistency of mercury, licked at the ground, fighting endless battles against invisible forces trying to align them into windwhipped strands of airborne plasma. Thick billowing fog, propelled by the random wind currents, sometimes limited sight to less than three meters. Then abruptly, a gust would slice the fog and a narrow valley of pimpled bedrock would become sharply outlined as it flowed toward the distant horizon of volcanic peaks.

Why did I travel across light-years to come here? What possessed me to demand a starship assignment?

Mars Lea had asked herself those questions nearly every day for the past nine and a half months.

Life on the *Alchemon* had been . . . *unreal.* This planet was unreal. Standing at the base of a hill, feeling the aqueous motion of Sycamore's ground through her shieldsuit sensors, she wondered just how conscious she was of this place. Her awareness remained crisp. She was alert to the fog, the unstable blue droplets, the occasional flashes of pale lightning spiraling down from the dark heavens, turning

28

patches of sky bloodred. But there was more here, hidden behind a veil of psionic interference the way the mountains hid behind the fog. True consciousness—the holistic blend of thought and feeling—seemed on the verge of disintegration.

I'm losing touch with myself.

"Are you all right, dear?" Elke Els moved to her side and Mars Lea stared at the young, faintly oriental face lit by directional lumes embedded in the helmet's faceplate. The petite blond scientist looked monstrous in the shieldsuit, a conglomeration of tubular radiation pads and scarred armor protecting her from the violence of Sycamore's ecosphere. It was a necessary but unpleasant distortion of the human form. Mars Lea was glad she could not see her own reflected image.

"Mars Lea?" Elke repeated.

"I'm fine." She forced herself to smile. Trapped within this bulky machine on the unstable surface of an alien world, expressions felt like caricatures.

This voyage has changed me. I don't know how, or exactly why. But it has happened.

Elke grinned. "I have to confess, I'm beginning to share Hardy's enthusiasm for this place. The very instability of this planet is enticing. Think of it! Life exists on Sycamore, and it has adapted itself extraordinarily well to this ridiculous ecosphere. The Sycom strain is like nothing we've ever discovered."

Mars Lea saw genuine excitement in the scientist's dusky green eyes. Elke was Hardy's assistant and, at twenty-nine, closest to Mars Lea in age—a year older. In temperament, however, they remained far apart. What Mars Lea perceived as ugly, Elke found wonderfully alien.

"Any new perceptions?" the scientist asked casually.

Mars Lea shook her head. That question had been put to her more than a dozen times since their touchdown in this new area four hours ago. Elke and Hardy had tried many variations. *Any telempathic messages, Mars Lea? Do you detect something, Mars Lea? Are there superluminal impulses dancing through your mind, floundering in your body, tickling your soul?*

No!

How many times had she tried to explain it to them? Her ability to sense the radiance of other life forms was not some precise interception of thought, like a transmission from one data terminal to another. Back on Earth, at the Jamal Research Laboratories, they had divided her so-called abilities into neat little arenas of expertise, assigning quantitative values to each, computing numeric comparisons with other humans possessing telempathic skills. She was a Psionic of the highest caliber, they had concluded at the end of two months. They had informed her of that fact in a way that suggested they had learned something.

Fools.

She kept her smile intact. "Nothing new."

Elke sighed. "Well, dear, I wouldn't worry about it. I'm sure the contact will come back to you in its own good time."

Yes. In its own good time.

Hardy Waskov's booming voice cut through their helmets. "The probes haven't found anything yet, but we're definitely within the area of greatest bacterial concentration. Rigel just received computer confirmation from the *Alchemon*—all the surveys match up perfectly. The Sycom strain originated near here; I have no more doubts."

Mars Lea stared upward at her helmet's inner control panel and tried to make sense out of the complex 3D directional grid. Hardy appeared as a moving yellow blip, somewhere behind them.

"Can we pinpoint the area of origin any closer?" Elke asked.

"No. Too many energy patterns in the atmosphere. Tight-range instrument inaccuracies."

"Geophysical changes? Subsurface increases in ambient radiation?"

Hardy cleared his throat. "Nothing. But if my theory is correct, we're within a five-kilometer square of the focal point of the original bacterial migration. A half-million years ago, the Sycom strain spread out from this area to infest the rest of the planet. There simply has to be an anomaly of some sort."

Mars Lea shivered. Off to her left, a cluster of the thick blue droplets abruptly aligned themselves into a shimmering chain, zigzagging through the fog like some slow-moving beam of light. She spoke hesitantly. "This blue liquid . . . that's where the bacteria lives?"

"Yes, most of it," replied Hardy. "The strain certainly

propagates within the liquid, and I suspect we'll learn that it also derives some nourishment from the droplets."

She shook her head inside the bulky helmet. "I still don't understand what makes it so different from earth bacteria?"

Hardy's voice took on a singsong quality, as if he were speaking to a child. Once, Mars Lea would have been angered by his patronizing attitude. But now . . .

"This strain draws nitrogen from the atmosphere, and in that respect is similar to earth-based microorganisms. But it appears able to synthesize a wide range of elements for its metabolism, rather than having to exist solely on carbon."

Elke cut in. "And its ability to exist in this heat puts it several steps above solar bacteria."

Mars Lea glanced at the temperature readout on her helmet's lower control panel. Outside the suit, it was 190 centigrade.

"I'm not even positive it is a form of bacteria as we know it," concluded the science rep.

Elke frowned. "Well, it certainly looks like a bacteria."

"Yes, that's the heart of the puzzle. And if it truly is a bacteria, then I'm virtually certain that it was brought here. I cannot imagine how such a microorganism could have originated within an environment of such intense subatomic interaction."

Mars Lea stared into the fog. There was still much she did not understand and probably never would. Hardy, Elke, and the others had been nurtured in a culture of sophisticated technical elegance, trained to master science at an early age. She felt a familiar stab of bitterness. For many years, the Corporeal, out of fear, had practiced subtle discrimination against Psionics, treating them as lowerclass citizens. Times were changing, but Mars Lea had been permitted only a basic and mediocre childhood education. She knew she would never catch up.

But she was glad she could still feel anger about something.

"At any rate," Hardy continued, "we should be able to keep the samples alive for the return trip without the need for special ecospheric arrangements. The strain has been surviving quite well within a variety of standard cultures—"

A husky voice broke in. "One of the probes found something—a piece of rock that does not appear indigenous to the planet."

The voice belonged to Rigel Keller, the *Alchemon*'s tech

officer and their lander pilot. He was monitoring their explorations from the relative security of the tiny ship, two kilometers to the south.

"Location?" Hardy demanded.

"About seventy meters east of Elke and Mars Lea. That's about half a kilometer from you, Hardy."

"I'll meet the two of you there in a few moments," Hardy said firmly. "Under no circumstances are you to attempt an examination before my arrival."

Elke grinned at Mars Lea. "Affirmative, Hardy. Hey, Rigel, you getting a video feed from that probe?"

One of the tiny screens within Mars Lea's helmet came to life. She stared in silent fascination at a smooth stem of colorless stone angling from the base of a small hill. The resolution was not good; Sycamore's atmosphere played continual havoc with video transmissions.

Elke giggled. "Jesus, Rigel, it looks like a giant cock."

Rigel did not respond.

"Measurements?" inquired Hardy.

"About two meters long, half a meter wide. The probe is still feeding composition data, but the outer surface is made up of the same general elements as the bedrock—silicon, calcium, lots of suspended nitrogen."

"Inner layers?" Hardy asked excitedly.

"Definitely. There's massive structural changes a few centimeters in. The probe's still correlating."

Elke pointed to a gentle rise off to their left. "Well, let's go take a look."

The scientist began walking: The huge automaton that was her shieldsuit vanished into a layer of swirling fog. Quickly, Mars Lea turned to follow. The others knew how to travel easily in shieldsuits, but despite having spent hours practicing during the voyage, Mars Lea still found the process difficult.

You did not exactly walk. You raised your foot as if you were going to take a step forward and then the shieldsuit's inner sleeve of sensors translated the force and direction of your movement into mechanical energy. The heavy boot took the step for you. Very little human energy was expended by a person inside a shieldsuit, unless you counted the concentration it took to operate.

Elke slowed when she noticed Mars Lea was having trouble. "Sorry, I forgot." The scientist twisted her neck sharply;

the helmet swiveled, panning across the dark sky. "You know, this atmosphere has an overabundance of electromagnetic radiation—everything except good natural earthlight."

"Earthlight?" Mars Lea was not really interested. It was hard enough concentrating on walking without having to absorb trivial comments.

"A metaphor, dear. There's really no such thing as earthlight. But you know what I mean—blue skies, real shadows, the way the horizon turns gold after the sun sets."

"Oh." She was close enough now to notice that Elke wore a faint smile.

"I think you would have to agree that what makes this planet particularly repulsive is its lack of earthlight."

Mars Lea did not agree. There were means of perception far stronger than the visual. Sycamore was alien in more fundamental ways.

They moved through the fog in silence, ascending a series of gentle slopes, circling the base of a steeper hill. Elke navigated—she knew how to read the complex array of readouts inside her helmet. Mars Lea had learned basic shieldsuit functions but most of the control panel's numerals and patterns remained enigmas.

I'm almost helpless here. The thought chilled her.

They angled around the base of one more hill and came to an abrupt halt as the fog parted.

The strange wind-scoured stump protruded from the hill directly ahead of them. It stood nearly vertical, as tall as a person, and possessing a fine craggy texture similar to the surrounding bedrock. A few meters away, a floating exploration probe, the size of a large melon, blinked senselessly in the thick fog. The probe was one of a batch that Rigel had sent out from the lander.

The tech officer's voice burst into their helmets. "Well bless the little shrimpfuckers! Get this: I transmitted the probe's latest data up to the *Alchemon* and the computer says that within the stump there are carbon-based multicellular structures—"

"Organic!" shouted Elke.

"You got it. And surprise number two: There's evidence of current metabolic activity."

"Don't anyone touch it!" Hardy commanded, his voice suddenly strained.

"Alive," murmured Elke.

"There's more," said Rigel. "Jonomy measured the thickness of the outer layer, which appears to be coagulated rock, and compared it with the buildup of similar coatings on other planetary surfaces. The computer estimates that the stump has been here for about half a million years."

Hardy's voice was almost a shout. "A direct correlation! The Sycom could have originated with the living matter inside this rock."

"Maybe," said Elke.

"That's not all," continued Rigel. "Jonomy ran a preliminary scan through GEL. Based on the probe's scant data, GEL says there are no organic comparisons."

Mars Lea nodded to herself. GEL—the General Library. All of the *Alchemon*'s major systems carried three-letter designations. The library was one of the few systems she had become familiar with during the voyage.

She glanced at her helmet grid, saw the blip that represented Hardy moving toward their position. Elke stepped closer to the stump.

"Does the living part extend into the ground?" she asked.

"No," said Rigel. "It's solid rock underneath. The goddamned whatever-it-is has a layer of coagulated stone on the outside and is as lively as a spring chicken on the inside. Don't ask how it's carrying on metabolic activity. The computer has no idea what it could be synthesizing, unless it's somehow absorbing nutrients from the surrounding rock. Which should be impossible."

Elke stretched out her hand, touched the surface. "It looks and feels exactly like the ground."

Mars Lea felt a sudden unease. Gingerly, she walked her shieldsuit closer to the scientist.

A dull throb touched the base of her spine, seemed to trickle up the back of her neck, sending a wave of feeling into consciousness. The strange sensation brought on a word/thought—*tragedy*.

It was the same feeling she had experienced earlier, at the time Hardy had first announced his discovery of the source of the bacterial migration.

Tragedy in the past? she wondered. Or tragedy in the future? Like most of her psionic imagery, the experience offered no simple interpretation.

She turned to Elke, debating whether to inform the scientist of her latest psionic contact. But Elke appeared transfixed by the rock, her eyes wide open, childlike with wonder, and Mars Lea decided to say nothing.

The scientist's voice emerged as a whisper. "It's one distinct life form, isn't it, Rigel?"

"The probe doesn't have the instrumentation to ascertain that for certain, but EPS says it would be a fair guess."

EPS. Mars Lea had heard Jonomy mention that system. It had something to do with calculating probabilities.

She gasped as an airborne shape tore out of the fog ten meters away. An instant later, recognition brought a sigh of relief—it was Hardy Waskov. The science rep rocketed toward them, a meter off the ground, a stream of particles pouring from the back of his shieldsuit. He slowed; his boots touched bedrock and he shut off his propulsion module. Wisps of jetstream smoke dissolved into the fog.

Mars Lea had been warned that controlled shieldsuit flight was a dangerous way to travel, that it took years of practice to master. The warnings had been unnecessary; walking remained enough of a challenge.

Hardy's puffy face seemed to leer at her from within the helmet. His complexion was dark, the lips wide, almost feminine. Shaggy eyebrows dominated tiny eyes. All but a few strands of hair were hidden by a gray skullcap.

"Mars Lea, do you perceive anything?"

She shook her head.

"We may ask you to wear an isolator hood again when we return to the lander. It's a shame there's no way to adapt a hood to the inside of a shieldsuit. At this distance, the psionic impressions should be fairly strong. That's assuming, of course, that this living rock is the source of your contact."

She shrugged, feeling the thick shoulderpads elevate in response to her movement.

"Rigel, have any of the other probes located similar objects?"

"No. And we're beyond the original grid scan. If you want me to extend the search radius and cover more area, I'll have to move the lander. I'm having a hell of a time maintaining communications with the probes as it is."

"How far out are they?"

"Some of the probes are at the seven-kilometer range."

"No other anomalies?" Hardy asked.

"Nothing. What you see is what you've got."

"Very well, Rigel. Recall the probes. I want you to establish a full sensor array out here as soon as possible. What we don't have aboard the lander we'll get the *Alchemon* to shoot-chute down to us. Oh, and you had better break out one of the turboshovels."

"Excavation?" Elke wondered quietly.

"Quite possibly. Of course, we certainly won't risk removing the object until we've run the full range of tests."

Elke frowned. Her face seemed to flush. "We should be extremely careful. If this thing is truly alive and has been here for half a million years—"

"Yes," said Hardy excitedly. "Can you imagine the stir this will cause when we return it to earth? Nothing like it has ever been found."

"We should be careful," Elke insisted. "We shouldn't just rip it out of the ground. It may turn out to have some complex interrelationship with Sycamore's ecosphere. We could destroy it."

Hardy grinned mirthlessly. "We'll use our best judgment."

Mars Lea knew that Hardy intended to bring the object back with them.

A loud screeching noise suddenly filled her helmet. Sheets of emerald green fire lanced across the sky and lightning bolts cracked against the surrounding hills. For an instant, it seemed as if everything were illuminated beneath a ghostly light. Then an awful jolt split the heavens and the strange rock seemed to perform some energy counterpoint, feeding shafts of red lightning back up into the sky. The ground shuddered and a tremendous explosion shook them. Spittles of bedrock fell out of the air; Mars Lea instinctively threw her hands up to protect her face. The quick movement of her arms, translated into mechanical energy by the shieldsuit, almost threw her off balance.

The bombardment ended abruptly. The normal background of crackling and hissing returned. There were loud releases of breath. Mars Lea felt beads of perspiration rolling down her forehead.

"Jesus," murmured Elke. "What the hell was that?"

"Check your suits," Rigel ordered.

Mars Lea shivered. Elke's face looked pale inside the thick helmet.

"Look!" Hardy shouted. He pointed to the rock.

Wisps of light smoke poured from the object, swirling

into the fog. The stump looked different, as if it had been whittled down and coated with glossy steel-blue paint. For a moment, Mars Lea thought that the smoke was causing strange reflections. Then she realized that the dark mass was pulsating with life.

Hardy's voice trembled. "The outer layer of rock has been vaporized. I've never seen anything like this! Rigel, are you still receiving data from the probe?"

"No. The lightning must have nailed it—the main sensor package is fried. I'm getting imagery from your suit cameras, though. Now listen: That was one hell of a nasty power discharge. I want the three of you to doublecheck your shieldsuit status."

"Incredible," Hardy whispered. "It appears to be one distinct life form, definitely complex. I can just make out some protrusions beneath its surface, perhaps some sort of a bone structure. The upper end is slightly thicker. The entire mass has a gelatinous quality."

"Your suits," Rigel insisted. "Check your suits."

"Yes, I'm fine," said Hardy. "Green all the way." He turned to Elke. "How about you?"

The scientist kept staring at the gently pulsating mass.

"Elke?"

"What? Oh, yes. All green."

Mars Lea turned her attention to the tiny rows of trouble lumes within her own helmet. Each tiny light represented a particular shieldsuit function.

"All green," she offered. The phrase seemed to suggest that everything was all right. She felt a gurgling in the pit of her stomach. Everything was *not* all right.

"I just talked to Jonomy," said Rigel. "The computer indicates that the particular type of energy transformation you witnessed occurs only rarely on the surface. EPS says that the possibility of lightning nailing that stump and knocking out the probe without touching the three of you is beyond the realm of reasonable calculation. Jonomy suspects that the three of you may have served somehow as ʒ catalyst."

Hardy pivoted. "Mars Lea—any perceptions immediately prior to the lightning?"

There had been that one vague sensation, when Elke had touched the rock. *Tragedy*.

Mars Lea decided it was not important. It was not what they were looking for. She shook her head. "Nothing."

"Is a psionic catalyst possible?" Elke wondered.

"I'll ask," said Rigel.

Elke extended her hand so that the heavy shieldsuit glove was only centimeters away from the pulsating surface. "It's relatively cold. Palm sensors read it more than a hundred degrees below surface temperature."

Hardy frowned. "We're in an oven down here. Maybe the vaporized crust somehow protected it from harsher environmental effects—"

He trailed off. The two scientists exchanged intense looks.

Elke's eyes widened. "It might die now that it's exposed!"

Hardy nodded. "Rigel, I want an ecocapsule sent out here immediately. Never mind the internal adjustments—just make sure the coolers are set at least a hundred degrees below planetary norm. And inform Captain Brad that he should begin making basic preparations to the *Alchemon*'s containment. Naturally, we'll be bringing the organism up."

Rigel's reply was cool. "I'll pass your request on."

Hardy glared into the fog. "Of course, Rigel. Request the captain's opinion, but kindly make it clear that Pannis would be most unhappy if we discovered an obviously developed life form and failed to return it to the solar system."

There was no response.

Elke dropped to her knees in front of the organism, examined its base. Gently, she pushed her glove into the dark blue mass. "You're right, it's gelatinous. There appear to be vessels and darker lumps beneath the surface; I can make out vague patterns." She moved her hand slowly upward. "A skeletal structure, perhaps? I can feel what almost seems like a human ribcage, although the spacing is all wrong. The bones are too far apart . . . five of them, maybe six—"

Hardy nodded. "Rigel, ask Jonomy for constantly updated probabilities regarding the temperature range that the organism might survive in. And please have him relay all the data into the containment system."

Mars Lea folded her arms across her chest, wanting to hug herself. The shieldsuit's heavy armor made the action impossible. She might as well have laid two huge branches across the thick breastplate.

She knew what the others only suspected: It was her own

presence here that had caused the violent energy display and the life form's subsequent release. She knew that to be true, though she could not have explained why.

Rigel spoke. "Ecocapsule's on its way out to you. And I talked to Jonomy. He says that a psionic catalyst might be possible. However, GEL has no record of any analogous situations."

Mars Lea felt a shiver race up her spine.

"Jonomy says that the energy discharge might also have been caused by the natural electromagnetic leakage from your suits."

Hardy frowned. "Yet EPS maintains that the probabilities are beyond reasonable computation? On what does our Lytic base his suspicions?"

There was a long pause. "He calls it an educated guess."

Anger blossomed across Hardy's face. "Kindly inform our Lytic that we would prefer that he stick to his primary function—computer interpretation. As scientists, we—"

"Look out!" screamed Elke.

Mars Lea did not know why the scientist had yelled. But she instinctively took a step backward and flung her arms away from her chest. With a sickening realization, she sensed that her movement had been too rapid and that the shieldsuit would now translate her panicked lurch into violent motion.

Her left leg jerked out from under her and she lost her balance, fell forward. In the instant before her breastplate hit the ground, she saw the reason for Elke's warning. The organism had begun to bend in the middle, like some impossibly huge snail. As the upper end of it dropped toward the scientist's head, Elke scurried out of the way. The top of the pulsating blue mass planted itself on the bedrock. Like a misshapen toy slinky, it upended itself.

Mars Lea crashed face forward onto the ground. Sirens wailed in her helmet and a whole row of trouble lumes flashed amber. Blue droplets splashed against her faceshield, clinging to the transparent plastic like dew on spring flowers. She heard excited voices but they seemed to melt away from her, becoming vague, incomprehensible: melodies in the distance.

An image seemed to form within her: faintly glowing threads hanging within a deep and utter blackness. The threads intersected one another and she sensed patterns, as if she were seeing the delicate outlines of some vast endless spiderweb. She had no idea what the luminous strands were or what they might represent. But the blackness . . . that was a place she knew. She had been there before.

Mostly in her nightmares.

She screamed.

Awareness sheared back into the present. Urgent voices surrounded her.

"It's okay, Rigel," she heard Elke say. "Only her stabilizers went amber. There's no external suit damage."

Mars Lea shuddered uncontrollably.

"Relax, dear. Relax."

The scientist's voice was soothing and Mars Lea felt her muscles begin to untense. Arms gripped her, helped her to stand. Leg motors whined softly as the shieldsuit completed the process of righting itself.

Elke smiled. "Really, dear. You must confine your acrobatics to the ship's gym."

"Yes, you must be more careful," said Hardy, sounding unconcerned. He was staring fixedly at the upended organism. They followed his gaze.

"I wonder why it came at me?" asked Elke.

Hardy shook his head slowly. "Perhaps it sensed a cooler environment—your suit, the refrigeration gear. Its reaction might have been a basic survival instinct."

"Ecocapsule should be coming over that nearest hill in another minute," offered Rigel.

"Good," said the science rep. "The sooner we get it protected from this environment, the better chance we'll have of keeping it alive."

Mars Lea wanted to be away from this place. "We should go back." Her throat was dry and her voice came out as a whisper.

Again, Hardy addressed her as if he were speaking to a child. "Yes, don't worry. We'll be going back soon."

She swallowed. "We should go now."

Elke smiled gently. "It's all right, dear. In a little while, we'll be safely back aboard the lander."

We should go now! she wanted to scream. The frightening image remained just on the edge of consciousness: a web of glowing strands floating in that vast and terrible place.

The blackness. She had been there before, and not just in her nightmares. On several occasions as a child, she had been thrust into that omnipotent well of utter dark. To this day, the blackness represented a source and repository for all her fears, a locus of dread, as real as Elke's *earthlight*.

"A half million years," murmured the blond scientist. "Could this thing have actually been alive and trapped within the rock for that length of time? It shouldn't be possible."

"Some form of molecular stasis," mused Hardy. He scowled; lines formed along the edge of the thick lips, betraying his age. He was the oldest member of the expedition, surpassing June Courthouse, their crewdoc, by several years.

Above them, a thick white cylinder with tapered ends soared out of the fog. The ecocapsule descended gently, landing upright a few meters away from the organism. The top flipped open, revealing an inner shell lined with gossamer-thin strands; a delicate webwork strong enough to cradle and protect even the most massive life forms. The ecocapsule squatted there in the fog, like a kettle waiting to be filled.

"Well," said Elke, "I suppose we could try goading it. Maybe the creature will do a few more somersaults for us."

Hardy nodded vigorously. "If we can get it close enough, the ecocapsule's elevation modules should be able to lift it into the web. Rigel, what's the organism's mass?"

"Heavier than it looks—about two hundred kilograms."

Elke shook her head. "I don't know. With that kind of weight, the elevation modules might cause internal damage when they lift it. That bone structure seems delicate. We could break the ribcage if we're not careful."

"How about a tarp?" Rigel suggested. "There's three varieties stored in the base of the capsule."

Hardy nodded. "Yes. We can wrap it in a tarp, provide an exoskeleton of sorts, equalize load stresses. That way, the elevation modules—"

The creature abruptly tilted itself again. With three slinky somersaults, the organism tumbled over to the capsule. On its last flip, it pushed violently off the bedrock, became airborne, vaulted over the container's lip, and plopped down into the cushioned interior. The ecocapsule's top automatically sprang shut. An external readout panel went green, indicating a correct pressure seal.

For a while, no one spoke. Elke finally broke the silence. "Perhaps it sensed an environment similar to its previous one?"

"Yeah, maybe," muttered Rigel. "And maybe the son-of-a-bitch *wants* to go with us."

"We must not leap to any conclusions," Hardy warned. "We have no idea what we're dealing with here. For now, we must simply accept these actions without coloring them with the spectrum of our preconceptions."

Rigel's voice dropped lower. "That sounds nice, Hardy, but there're too many coincidences going on here for my peace of mind. I don't trust anything that's this fuckin' cooperative."

"Merely our preconceptions," Hardy reaffirmed.

Mars Lea felt drained, as if she had gone through some emotional crisis and was now in a state of withdrawal. Something had passed her by here, and she did not know what it was. There existed a psionic word to describe her state: *Ta-shad*—experiences that remained out of reach, trapped on the mythical event horizon beyond consciousness.

"I think we should go back," Elke said quietly.

Mars Lea nodded. She had a sudden desire to be with Jonomy.

3

This was Ericho's twelfth deep-space expedition and his fifth as captain. His commands had included a three-man Loop reconnaissance flight, a major exploratory voyage boasting a crew of forty, and a colony vessel carrying eight thousand settlers. The *Alchemon* had nine crew members including himself, which should have made for a fairly easy reign. Instead, the last few months ranked among the most difficult of his career.

Seven of the crew were experienced starcrossers; only Mars Lea and young Alan Ortega, their Pannis intern, were on virgin flights. But even with two inexperienced crew members aboard, things should have been going more smoothly.

Low on the psychosynchronicity scale, June Courthouse had explained, meaning that the crew was unable to mesh together into a tightly functional unit. Star voyages lasting over a year always produced greater stress levels, and when individual capabilities were higher than average—as with the *Alchemon*'s crew—tensions brewed. It was June's belief that a profusion of experts rarely contributed to the common good.

Ericho agreed with the crewdoc's diagnosis. He would certainly have preferred to command a crew with intelligence levels just on the plus side of competence. Then he could have acted more like a captain, helped mold them into a frictionless group.

The thought amused him, brought back memories of his adolescent fantasies of starship command: Ericho Brad, leader, making bridge decisions of great import. Unrealistic as those fantasies were, they had been powerful enough to propel him into a career.

Most of the consortiums utilized computer-generated psychological parameters to match crews with particular missions, a practice that the majority of starship captains were lobbying to have changed. Ericho, too, favored more direct input into crew selection. In the closed environment of a deep-space voyage, minor psychological problems tended to blossom; a statistically acceptable quirk in a person's behavior at the outset of an expedition could produce, nine and a half months later, a mentally disruptive Tom Dianaldi.

Lobbying efforts had led to some gradual changes. Under specific conditions, and subject to consortium approval, a captain could now choose some of his crew. It was a minor victory, but it had enabled Ericho to have two people he could count on assigned to this voyage: June Courthouse and Rigel Keller.

The bridge came to life: An aggregate of green lumes on his chair's control panel turned amber; a series of low-frequency notes howled out a warning. Ericho recognized the pattern and spun his chair to face the Lytic.

"Level Six, Captain." Jonomy blinked rapidly as his own chair floated around the perimeter of the HOD. With the computer umbilical attached to the Lytic's forehead, the illusion was that of a man dangling at the end of a snaking rope.

Tom Dianaldi, seated on the opposite side of the bridge, popped his eyes open.

"It's a backup vaporizer feeding Moe engine," said Jonomy. "Module Seventy-eight-A. It's a cold short—I believe we have a break in one of the cryogenic lines."

Ericho nodded. "Give me a schematic."

The Lytic did not reply but Ericho's armrest display monitor lit up into a mass of labeled geometry. Bright red patches indicated the areas of trouble. As he watched, internal repair systems closed in on the problem and the red patches began to shrink. Only one stubborn clump of meandering scarlet refused to go green.

"Captain, I've notified RAP for manual correction. A repair pup is being dispatched into that tube. Duplex circuitry is handling the load without any problems."

Ericho turned off his display. There was no need for him to do anything; this problem was just one more in a series of minor malfunctions that plagued a ship as large and complex as the *Alchemon*. He felt particularly useless in such situations, knowing full well that the computer and the Lytic were easily able to handle them.

The captain needs to master that the master's not the cap-

tain. That was lesson number one at Pannis command school and the dialectic saying was so inbred into Ericho that it floated into his awareness whenever trouble occurred. He had long ago adjusted to the true nature of starship command.

Jonomy killed the alarm system and the bridge grew silent again. Audio dampers absorbed the most blatant sounds of ship operation and only a faint rumble remained—the distant growl from the *Alchemon*'s three mighty engines. Even though the ship was still orbiting Sycamore and the engines were not firing, their complex maintenance systems remained operational.

"Captain, the robot has arrived in the trouble area. RAP estimates about an hour for repairs."

RAP was Robotics and Probes, the Level 4 system that controlled the maintenance robots—the *Alchemon*'s pups. The small probes were dispatched to handle repairs that could not be dealt with by the computer's internal correctors. Hundreds of pups slavishly patrolled the kilometers of access shafts that wound mazelike through the ship, an entire domain where size prohibited human intrusion.

Dianaldi giggled. "Ah, its voice was like that of a storm and its breath blew like a hurricane—"

Within the HOD, the contorted pattern of rainbows disappeared, was replaced by Dianaldi's favorite hologram. It was a transparent face, colorless, an elongated triangular skull-like image sketched by 3D wand. There was a scribbled, amateurish quality to the hologram. The entire face seemed to have been drawn with one unbroken line, twisting and weaving back and forth to form the features.

"Override it, Jonomy," Ericho ordered.

The hologram dissolved back into rainbows. Dianaldi's face soured like a child deprived of a toy.

When not externally activated, the HOD could display representations from the computer via any of the bridge terminals, including the lieutenant's. Ericho knew of captains who permitted personal fantasizing on the bridge. He did not.

"Lieutenant," the Lytic suggested, "there is no one in the dreamlounge at present."

"Ah, Jonomy, you are a gem of the evening—slashing fusion with an unkempt soul, a light melting the night."

Jonomy turned back to his data panels.

"No more HOD-play," Ericho warned, knowing he would

have to repeat the order a few days from now. Dianaldi always orchestrated the same image: the skull-like face drawn by an unbroken line. Sometimes the lieutenant created a background for the face, superimposing it over a glittering starfield.

Dianaldi chuckled. "Captain, I am, for now, yours to command!"

Maladjustment, mused Ericho. *Half this crew redefines the word.*

For pure strangeness, the lieutenant easily led the pack. But Hardy Waskov was not far off his pace. Besides being an unyielding bastard, the science rep had little consideration for safety standards. Four months ago, shortly after coming through the Earth/Sycamore Loop, Hardy had proposed dumping a large supply of their fusion batteries out of the storage pod in order to set up an enzyme fabrication experiment in deep space. It was a pet project, totally unrelated to the impetus of the mission, and an experiment that could have cost them all dearly if a major breakdown had later occurred. Fusion batteries provided a backup power system; during an emergency shutdown of the main engines, the batteries could very well save their lives. To deliberately subvert the use of a critical backup system, light-years from home, signified to Ericho a deep instability.

And then there was Mars Lea.

Jonomy caught his attention. "The lander has cleared the atmosphere, Captain. We've reestablished contact. They've achieved orbit and should be docking with us in about eighty-five minutes. Hardy is demanding your decision on the creature."

My chance to act like a captain. And I don't know what to do.

Hardy wanted the creature brought directly into the containment, the ecospherically shielded area of the ship that theoretically could safely house any life form. But based on the information beamed up from Rigel, and Jonomy's extrapolations, this creature was a unique and bizarre find. It was difficult to imagine something being alive and trapped inside a layer of rock for half a million years, and then being abruptly released at the moment of its discovery. And he had seen the video of its capture. The way it had hopped obediently into the ecocapsule would make even a cautious man paranoid.

The creature would have to be returned to Earth. A primary purpose of interstellar missions was the acquisition of alien life forms—and Pannis would have his job if he failed to carry out that obligation. But he did have a choice in the method of transport. If Ericho felt that the creature posed too great a danger, it could be carried outside the *Alchemon*, locked within a larger version of the ecocapsule and linked to the ship through one-way umbilicals.

But then he would have to spend the next nine and a half months with a disgruntled science rep, for Hardy's study of the creature would be severely limited outside the containment. And if it later turned out that the creature was harmless, the Pannis science department would greet Ericho with something less than sympathy. The scientists would not appreciate the fact that almost a year of potential study had been lost due to a captain's caution. Despite occasional misgivings, Ericho liked commanding starships. He intended to continue doing so.

"Any new probabilities on the creature?" he asked.

Jonomy rubbed his hand across the umbilical, caressing it as if it were a part of his body. "Regarding potential danger, there is nothing to add. EPS maintains that the ratio of clear data to quirks in the creature's composition and behavior remain too lopsided for substantial projections. The highest probability—8.3 percent—suggests that the creature should be kept outside the ship for the duration of our mission. A negligibly lower figure—8.1 percent—suggests that the creature should be brought into the containment."

There were times when a Lytic could be a great help. This was not one of them. Jonomy was fully aware of the political implications of Ericho's decision and he would be wary of giving advice.

Ericho tried another approach. "Over the next nine and a half months, can you project the creature posing an increasing danger to us?"

The Lytic blinked. "Such an assumption connotes a negative bias, Captain. In normal situations, it is likely that the more we learn about a life form, the less of a threat it will become."

"Do you see this as a normal situation?"

Jonomy licked his lips. "Difficult to say, Captain. Would you like me to run some projections along those lines?"

He sighed, aware that he was wasting his time. He could

bandy probabilities with the Lytiç for hours and still come no closer to a rational decision. "Is the lander within visual range?"

"Yes, Captain."

The HOD darkened; the silver white winged lander became visible against the blackness of space. The lander appeared motionless yet in reality was approaching the *Alchemon* at better than five thousand kilometers per minute. In the lower part of the hologram lay Sycamore, a gray ball wrapped in swirling layers of cloud, its atmosphere shrouding primordial violence.

Jonomy magnified the projection and the tiny ecocapsule carrying the creature became visible, clinging to the underside of the lander like a sucking infant.

Dianaldi got up from his chair, gave them a mock salute, then marched to the southeast airseal. It slid open as he approached. "Blister me well, for the panacea of ostracism will certainly be my epitaph." Hands flashed to his cheeks and he rubbed them into a smile. He turned and dashed quickly through the airseal. It slid shut behind him.

"He is not improving," said Jonomy.

That was an understatement. Dianaldi was turning into a walking malfunction.

"Captain, Hardy insists on speaking to you. He sounds impatient."

The science rep always sounded impatient; that did not mean Ericho had to talk to him. Hardy would be back aboard the *Alchemon* all too soon, bombarding him with petty grievances. Perhaps, though, with his precious creature to study, Hardy would not be as much of a bother.

Ericho realized that he had made a decision.

"Tell him that the containment is ready."

—From the papers of Thomas Andrew Dianaldi

His name is Renfro Dackaman.

He's a Pannis headhunter, one of those icy-assed errand boys that the Consortium unleashes when the home office is having trouble at one of its corporate outposts. His job is to hire and fire and do whatever is necessary to bring the outpost back into the Pannis fold. Headhunters solve labor problems, restructure management, and generally straighten out all the kinks, make things right again, make things profitable. No one likes headhunters. Everyone reacts to their arrival about the same way they might react to an impending lander crash: If you're lucky, you might get out alive.

And Renfro Dackaman really enjoys his work.

We were returning home on the Theodoris, a relatively short cargo/passenger run via the Earth/Karama Loop. The journey was three and a half months each way, and Dackaman was hitching a ride back with us after straightening out some problems at the Pannis headquarters on Karama. The ship was cramped; about forty extra passengers had been added for our return trip. Most of these passengers were ex-Pannis employees—the so-called problems that Mr. Dackaman had straightened out.

To say that feelings were running hot on the Theodoris would be an understatement.

The man who was sharing my cabin turned out to be a Dackaman victim, and every day I had to listen to bitter stories of terminated employment contracts and forced resettlements. In the beginning, I naively assumed that this Pannis headhunter couldn't possibly be as bad as my cabinmate suggested.

I changed my mind after meeting Dackaman. He was calm and cold and utterly obnoxious—but in a quiet, restrained sort of way. His mannerisms suggested that he considered himself the natural superior of everyone on board, captain included. And there was something menacing about him, some subtle facet to his personality that remained diffcult to put a finger on, even later, after the incident.

I tried to rationalize that Dackaman was none of my business. After all, this was my first voyage out as a junior lieutenant—a genuine officer—and I was thoroughly enjoying my new status. I resolved to put the headhunter out of mind; I politely requested of my cabinmate that he refrain from discussing Dackaman in my presence.

That was a mistake, and one that I'll live with for the rest of my life.

We were just about to pass through the Earth/Karama Loop when my cabinmate tried to kill Dackaman.

The headhunter had a predilection for combat shieldsuits; he performed a daily workout routine, in the Theodoris's gym, wearing one of the two units that Corporeal regulations required us to carry. The day before we looped, my cabinmate donned the second combat shieldsuit and followed Dackaman into the gym. There is no doubt in my mind that my cabinmate entered that gym with murderous intentions.

Still, we'll never really know for certain what happened in there. Our Lytic could not monitor the gym—it was a designated privacy area. The combat shieldsuits were supposed to be disarmed, but someone removed the weapon restraint linkages from both units. Personally, I believe that my cabinmate challenged Dackaman to a duel, and that one or both of the men then armed the suits.

Dackaman says it was self-defense, and no one doubts that the board of inquiry back on Earth will clear him. He said that he had not even realized the suits were armed until my cabinmate entered the gym and started shooting at him. The headhunter professed that his reactions at that point had been purely instinctual. He had done what was necessary to survive.

What he did was literally blow my poor cabinmate to pieces—chopped off his arms and legs with lasers, then blasted holes in his face and guts with mag projectiles.

Part of the tragedy is my fault—I should have been more sensitive to my cabinmate's state of mind. I can't help thinking that if I'd acted a bit more compassionate and had tolerated the man's constant tales of woe, there would have been no confrontation in the gym. But I forced him to repress his feelings in my presence; I deprived him of an outlet for his emotions. And I think that his anger eventually brewed to the point where he could no longer contain it.

But what will stick in my mind forever is watching Dackaman calmly emerge from the gym, moments after the killing. The headhunter leaned against the wall, closed his eyes, and grinned.

I truly hope that the board of inquiry does clear Dackaman. Because someday I'm going to get the son-of-a-bitch myself.

4

The entrance to the containment lab was located in the southwest quadrant of downdeck, in a section of corridor bounded by airseals at both ends. Past the southern lock, toward the stern of the *Alchemon*, escape doors led to lander number three's hangar and the twin storage pods that hung beneath the ship. Beyond the north airseal lay the main expanse of downdeck; the various shops and specialty labs, the natatorium, the freefall gym, the medcenter, and the social rooms.

Eight geonic elevators, spaced throughout the ship, ascended to updeck, where the bridge, crew cabins, dining areas, and gardens provided for a more settling ambience. Mars Lea felt reasonably comfortable up there. Down here, standing before the containment lab's imposing airseal, she felt small and powerless.

She rubbed her palm across the door's smooth surface. Cool to the touch. Inexplicably, that seemed proper. According to Jonomy, this airseal was the strongest one on the ship, excluding the external locks.

The lab door is formed of quadruple plates of geonically desensitized metal, she recalled Jonomy saying. The plates sandwich layers of bacterially neutralized air, pressurized so that any breach will blow the air inward. Walls surrounding the containment and lab are similarly shielded. The door itself contains a fully independent open/close system for emergencies. Sensor arrays surround the containment and are programmed to call for help in the event of a mishap; all sensors are tied directly into Level 2—second highest echelon of the computer's six-tiered control network.

Mars Lea did not understand all the ramifications of Jonomy's explanation. But his words made her feel safer.

The door was the only way into the lab. And the only way into the containment itself was via a long chute, angling through the bowels of the ship to a special airlock nestled between the two storage pods. That was where Rigel had temporarily docked the lander upon their return from Sycamore. There the ecocapsule had been detached, guided into the lock, and inserted up the chute into the containment. Rigel had then carefully maneuvered the small craft around the huge gray slab of the *Alchemon* to one of the north hangars.

Upon the lander's arrival in the docking bay, decontamination probes had swarmed onto the craft, blasting the outer hull with liquid and gas neutralizers. Thirty minutes of safety scouring had been necessary before medical probes were permitted inside.

Inside. The personal decontamination that followed had been one of the worst experiences of Mars Lea's life. Melon-sized robots with pincer arms had ordered them to strip and a full hour of indignities commenced: ultrasound and electromagnetic scanning, antigen sprays, a sizzling spongebath with a foul-smelling yellow cream, a stifling shower of thick orange gas. Needles pricked her arms, robots casually inserted microprobes into her bodily orifices. All modesty dissolved in the first five minutes and outright fear blurred awareness when she realized that tiny unattached probes were inside her body, exploring, searching for signs of contamination.

Contamination. Even now she felt strange inner tinglings as flesh recalled the passage of invaders.

Why did I come on this mission?

She remembered the meeting with the Pannis Assignor, ten months earlier. *I told him I wanted a starship assignment. I told him I liked storms.*

She had been angry. As a Psionic, she remained an outsider to the mainstream of Corporeal life. People were afraid of Psionics, afraid of having their thoughts known or their feelings read. Of course, Mars Lea knew that such fears were mostly unfounded; telempathic contacts usually did not occur in such simplistic forms. But fear overrode reason.

The Corporeal itself could not be blamed for the plight of Psionics, no more than you could blame a vast cold ocean. No single group or organization was responsible for the second-class status of psionic humans.

But those facts did nothing to temper Mars Lea's rage.

When Pannis Consortium had offered her employment in

exchange for submitting to their tests, she had eagerly accepted. She would take their money and become a guinea pig at the Jamal labs. But she would make life miserable for them. She would punish them; in the name of all Psionics, she would make them pay for her life of social injustice.

A bitter laugh escaped her. Her mother, who had also possessed mild telempathic prowess, had once told Mars Lea that a Psionic was a person who could never be sure of what was important in life. Her mother had committed suicide when Mars Lea was fifteen.

Angrily, she smacked her fingers across the door's typer, keying in the entrance code. With a speed that seemed to make it simply disappear, the airseal flashed open.

The containment lab was 300 cubic meters of benches, floor-to-ceiling equipment consoles, and racks of modular electronics. Canisters and cabinets hung from plain gray walls. Shadowless illumination came from sheets of white lumes mounted beneath the translucent floor and above the ceiling.

A gentle draft touched her face as she entered the lab. The door, sensing she was clear, blasted shut.

Hardy Waskov sat at a circular workbench just inside the room. Bare chubby arms matted with dark hair poked from a sleeveless lab shirt.

"Mars Lea, I thank you for coming." The science rep came to his feet. His double chin perked into a smile.

"We both thank you, dear," said Elke, emerging from behind a cabinet. The petite blonde wore a white smock and skintight black pants.

Hardy asked, "Have you ever been in here before?"

Mars Lea nodded. The captain had given her a complete tour of the *Alchemon* a few days after they had left lunar orbit.

"Fully recovered from decontamination?" quizzed Elke.

"Yes."

Hardy beamed. "That's good." He crossed the lab to stand beside Mars Lea. "We are now fairly certain, by process of elimination, that it was your presence on the surface that triggered the events freeing this creature from its estimated five hundred and ten thousand years of entombment. We're also reasonably certain that this life form is unique to the planet."

"Rigel left a batch of probes on the surface," Elke added,

but they haven't found anything yet. And we've clarified the bacterial migration patterns and have run some initial tests on the creature."

Hardy laid his hand across Mars Lea's shoulder and squeezed her affectionately. She wondered what he wanted.

The science rep continued. "More than a half million years ago, we believe this creature entered some sort of suspended state. Gradually, windborne specks of dust coagulated on its skin, eventually forming a rock shell completely encasing it. But before that happened, some of the creature's natural microorganisms escaped from its body and managed to adapt themselves to Sycamore's ecosphere."

"The Sycom strain," said Elke. "One tough little bacteria."

Mars Lea nodded. "Where did the creature come from?"

Elke's eyes lit up. "We think that it was brought to the planet. And that means that there is—or was—other intelligent life in the universe!"

"An absolutely incredible discovery, in and of itself," murmured Hardy.

Elke shrugged. "But exactly how it arrived on Sycamore and for what purpose . . . at this point, your guess is as good as ours."

With his arm around her, Hardy walked Mars Lea toward the back of the lab.

"There is much for us to learn about this creature. We have planned some basic experiments that we would like to implement as soon as possible. Naturally, you'll play a primary role in our testing program."

She wished he would let go of her shoulder.

They came to the back wall, which was totally flat and devoid of cabinets and equipment. Elke touched a nearby control panel. The wall became transparent.

The gelatinous creature behind the reinforced glass looked a darker shade of blue than Mars Lea remembered. It looked . . . healthier. But what really surprised her was the containment itself, which bore an uncanny resemblance to Sycamore's surface. Billowing clouds danced across a mock surface of the planet; blue liquid occasionally aligned itself into shimmering strands, tearing from one side of the ten-meter-wide cell to the other. Thick fog seemed to hang from the ceiling. Mars Lea almost expected to see Sycamore's dull sun peeking through the mist.

"How did you . . . do this?" she asked.

Elke chuckled. "Modern science."

Hardy withdrew his arm from her shoulder. "The containment is not merely a place to hold alien life forms; it is a sophisticated arena for duplicating alien environments as well. We programmed it, fed in samples taken from the Sycamoran ecosphere, including the bacteria, and supplied the requested raw materials. The containment system did the rest.

"Our earlier worries about the creature being harmed by temperature changes appear to be unfounded. It's as hot in there as it was on the surface—almost two hundred degrees centigrade—yet the creature's biosigns are stronger than ever. We've attempted to use the containment's probes to select skin and tissue samples from the creature, but . . . we're still having a few technical problems with those experiments."

Elke grinned. "I'll say! The tissues incinerate."

Hardy nodded. "The tissue samples self-destruct once they're removed from the body. The probes slice off a tiny bit of tissue and it burns to a crisp before the probe can even get it into a protective jar."

"Because of the heat?" Mars Lea asked.

"No," said Hardy. "It's certainly an oven in there, but the tissue shouldn't burn up so quickly. No, some other process is at work here. We suspect that some sort of accelerative decay mechanism takes control once the tissue is removed from the body of the creature.

"The creature could be generating some sort of invisible energy field, which surrounds and shields it from external environments. This hypothetical field may also stagnate the natural aging process." The science rep shook his head in wonder. "Think of it! A life form totally unlike anything yet discovered! I quite honestly believe that this creature will prove to be the greatest scientific discovery of our age. In numerous ways, it defies the tenets upon which our theories of universal biology are based. This expedition could prove to be truly historic."

Elke mirrored his excitement. "There are processes at work here that are unique!"

Inside the containment, the creature suddenly wobbled. It looked as if it was going to upend itself again, but instead it straightened, and assumed a rigid stance.

Mars Lea took a step backward. "Can it . . . see us?" The

question was not right—the gelatinous organism had no eyes, no apparent sensory organs. And yet she felt as if it was watching them.

Elke shook her head. "The glass is one-way, if that's what you're asking. But we do believe that it can sense us. And telempathically, we think that it can sense you."

Mars Lea shuddered.

Behind them, the airseal opened. The captain and Rigel Keller strode into the lab.

Hardy spoke with mock formality. "Well, Captain—we're honored to be graced by your presence."

The captain ignored him. He walked to the containment wall, halting a meter in front of it, his attentions focused on the creature.

Mars Lea found herself, as usual, fascinated by the captain. The black formsuit seemed to accent his six-foot frame and the trim beard and mustache gave his face a sense of controlled power. She often felt she could discern a deep wisdom in Ericho's piercing blue eyes.

The tech officer invited no such comparison. Rigel Keller was taller than the captain and more broad-shouldered; his upper arms resembled the knobby roots of an unearthed tree. Short brown hair topped a wide chiseled face. He winked at Mars Lea. She turned away.

Ericho frowned. "Jonomy examined your experiment roster. We have some misgivings."

Hardy grimaced to Elke. "See, just as I suspected." He faced the captain. "To begin with, I resent your Lytic breaching the science section. He has no right—"

"He has every right," Ericho countered.

"I would certainly have made the experiment roster available, once it was clarified. Since the schedule has not yet been finalized, I would appreciate it if you would hold any of your objections until that time. And at any rate, Captain, your job is to get us safely home, not to interfere with my programs."

Ericho shrugged. "If it concerns ship safety, I have every right to ask questions."

Elke unfastened her lab smock, threw it into a disposal bin. "I have some work to do up in the east garden. Mars Lea, do you want to come along?"

The captain shook his head. "I'd like Mars Lea to stay. Some of this concerns her."

Elke turned to Rigel, smiled "How about you? Want to come?"

"Later."

Elke ambled toward the door, hips swaying. Rigel's eyes followed.

Hardy spoke coldly. "Well, Captain, what displeases you?"

Ericho kept staring at the motionless creature. "Item 43 on your experiment agenda concerns the placing of a fusion battery inside the containment."

Hardy nodded. "Yes, we must learn whether the creature can tap into raw power sources. It appears to be generating some sort of protective field or barrier, yet we still have no idea what it is synthesizing, using for energy. We should be able to accurately measure any fusion cell power drain, even if the amount is microscopic. That should tell us whether the creature is capable of direct energy absorption."

Rigel leaned against the glass and withdrew a tiny capsule from his shirt pocket. He jammed it up his nostril, inhaled gracelessly. A stimulant, Mars Lea assumed; one of the on-duty drugs that Pannis regulations permitted.

Ericho pointed his finger toward the containment ceiling, hidden behind the swirling fog. "You're aware of the tracking lasers up there?"

"I'm aware of basic physics," Hardy snapped. "You don't seriously think I'd be foolish enough to allow the lasers to be activated with a fusion cell in there!"

Rigel grunted. "If that hunk of meat tries anything weird, those lasers are going to carve it into kitty litter. And if one of those beams touches a fusion cell, you've got one hell of a hot-'n'-nasty shitstorm down here."

Hardy's anger turned to exasperation. "The *Alchemon* isn't stupid enough to blast a fusion cell with one of its own lasers. The ship is intelligent enough to use some discretion and would not risk vaporizing a part of itself."

Ericho gave a reluctant nod, acquiescing. Hardy was right; according to Jonomy, the fusion cell experiment had a wide safety margin. Ericho actually had no problems with item 43; it was the experiment with Mars Lea that really bothered him. He had only raised the fusion cell issue in order to allow Hardy a victory. Give and take. Ericho had given the science rep item 43. Now he was going to take.

"Item 132 on your agenda concerns—"

"I know what numbers my experiments refer to!" Hardy

snapped. Then abruptly, his face softened. "Really, Captain, there is no need for this constant battle of wills. Our primary mission has been successful. We are returning to Pannis with not only the bacteria, but with an alien life form. Both are safely contained. I wish you would be willing to trust me in these matters."

"Item 132 appears to be a bit extreme," Ericho said evenly.

"You will note, Captain, that the experiment you refer to is not scheduled to take place until an exhaustive range of other tests have been performed. At that time, the safety factor will undoubtedly be more than acceptable."

Rigel flashed a grin at Mars Lea. "How about it—the safety factor acceptable to you?"

She shook her head, confused.

The tech officer laughed. "Hell, he hasn't even told you."

She looked from Hardy to Ericho. "Told me what?"

Rigel looked amused. "Hardy intends to put you into a shieldsuit, send you outside the ship, and have you crawl up the containment chute. And then, once you're standing inside, next to that blob, he'll have you remove your suit. That's so you can get physically close to the creature, make direct body-to-body contact with it. Naturally, the containment's environment will have been adjusted to the point where both you and the creature can coexist." The tech officer smiled at Hardy. "I don't know how she's going to breathe that shit, though. There's not a hell of a lot of oxygen in there."

"She'll wear an airmask!" Hardy snapped.

Rigel laughed. "Oh, yeah. Good idea. Of course, Mars Lea, let's hope that our weird little friend in there doesn't get any funny ideas while you're trying to psionically arouse him. 'Cause it'll take you at least a couple of minutes to get back into your shieldsuit and move your ass back down that containment chute." The tech officer paused. "Still, that should be plenty of time to escape, so long as blue blob isn't trying to eat you or fuck you."

Hardy bristled. "There's no reason for such talk." The science rep threw a protective arm across Mars Lea's shoulder. "He's just trying to frighten you—"

"Damn right!"

"Mars Lea, if and when we ask you to be part of the experiment that Rigel has so inelegantly outlined, I can assure you that we will have ample safety measures. There will be no danger."

She squirmed uncomfortably, wishing again that Hardy would take his arm off her shoulder. "Why would you . . . want me to go in there in the first place?"

His heavy hand patted her back. "As you well know, superluminal impulses are inversely proportional to distance. The closer you physically come to the creature, the greater the strength of the telempathic contact."

She shuddered. And once she exited the containment, she would no doubt be subjected to another unpleasant session with the decontamination robots. *No, I won't do it.* There was no way Hardy could force her. He might nag and sternly remind her that it was her duty, that she was aboard the *Alchemon* for the express purpose of utilizing her psionic abilities. But they could not make her do it.

There was no need to make trouble right now, though. When the time came, she would refuse. She faced the captain. "This should be my decision."

Hardy thumped her on the back. "That's the spirit!"

For a long moment, the captain regarded her silently. Then he shrugged. "Just so you're aware of the possible dangers."

Hardy beamed. "Yes, Captain, I believe you've made her most aware of all that could possibly go wrong without spelling out the obvious benefits of this experiment. Now, if you please, I would appreciate your departure. We have much work—"

Hardy stopped in mid-sentence, turning to stare at Rigel. Mars Lea followed his gaze.

Rigel had dropped to his hands and knees and was looking into the containment from near floor level.

"What's wrong?" Ericho asked.

Rigel didn't reply. He straightened and jabbed at the controls of the closest intercom. "Jonomy, are you monitoring?"

The Lytic's voice erupted into the lab. "Yes, Rigel, I saw it. I was just about to call you."

"Saw what?" Hardy demanded.

Jonomy spoke calmly. "The creature momentarily exhibited some geonic activity. For a period of about four and a half seconds, it elevated and suspended itself several centimeters off the floor."

"Damn right," Rigel added.

Ericho frowned. "Are you certain?"

Mars Lea wondered the same thing. The fog swirled thickly around the floor of the containment, making it difficult to see the base of the creature.

"I'm telling you," said Rigel, "I saw the son-of-a-bitch elevate."

"He's right, Captain. Several of the cameras are phased to penetrate the fog. I recorded clear video from two sources. It lifted itself up off the deck."

Ericho turned to the tech officer. "Anything like this happen on the surface? When it somersaulted and bounced into the ecocapsule?"

Rigel shook his head. "No, that looked like a physical trick, nothing more. Hard to say for sure, though."

"I've checked for malfunctions," the Lytic added. "There is nothing out of the ordinary—no geonic or magnetic anomalies detected anywhere within the ship. I ran the data through EPS. Probability is high that the creature possesses its own form of geonic nullification, possibly of a biological origin."

"Any correlates for something like that?" asked Ericho.

"None."

Mars Lea glanced at Hardy. The science rep's face remained passive but she saw the closely guarded excitement in his eyes.

The captain looked unhappy. "Jonomy, you scanned this thing. Are you sure there's no evidence of internal cybernetics, that we're not dealing with some kind of machine here, possessing a living shell?"

"Absolutely not, Captain. This creature is one hundred percent organic."

Rigel scowled. "I don't like this one bit. If blue blob can do gravity tricks, there's no telling what it's capable of. If something happened, we might not even be able to blow the bastard out the airlock. It could resist sudden decompression."

"The vacuum would probably kill it," the captain mused. He did not appear too certain.

Hardy stared at the creature, seemingly oblivious to the conversation. Mars Lea felt a bit sorry for the science rep. The others were talking about ways to destroy the creature; Hardy at least wanted it kept alive.

Tragedy.

The psionic image hit her again—a word/thought climbing the base of her spine, a wave of feeling breaking into awareness. The psionic impression was the same as the one she had experienced on the surface, except that now it was stronger, somehow *closer*.

And beyond the feeling she sensed glowing threads, intersecting, forming patterns in that awful place of complete and utter dark—the blackness.

She swallowed. "May I go now?"

Hardy nodded, his face lost in thought. She was glad he was too preoccupied to see her discomfort.

But the captain noticed and he stared at her with a puzzled frown. He looked ready to speak, but then apparently changed his mind, abruptly clamping his mouth shut as if to hold back the words.

She broke his gaze and forced herself to walk calmly to the door. Only a concentrated effort of will kept her from bolting from the lab in total panic.

5

June Courthouse leaned back in her desk chair and took a sip of milk from an open beaker. "Tom Dianaldi is warped by a variable delusional system, characterized by states of near rage and intense psychotic distortion. There are moments of coherence—fluid consciousness—but they are not of a communicatory nature. He perceives himself most clearly at these times but is nevertheless unable to accept outside emotional guidance."

Ericho sat across from the crewdoc. "What does that mean for us in simple terms?"

A faint smile crossed June's face. "In simple terms, it means we've got a crazy lieutenant on board."

June's private cabin was dark and cool, lit only by a pair of golden lume panels on the north and south walls. Soft light shadowed the age lines on the crewdoc's black skin; mute testimony to a departed youth. A disciplined bubble of white hair seemed to sit so perfectly on the top of June's head that it could have been mistaken for a wig.

"Do you think he's dangerous?"

Gray eyes sparkled. "That's a very relative term, Ericho. Anyone who's been in space for more than six months would probably fit my definition."

"You know what I mean."

June nodded. "At this point, Dianaldi's personality quotients have drifted so far off the Corporeal norm that I doubt even a primal lab could reach him. I would say he's approaching the point where irrational actions could result."

"Should I remove him from active duty?"

June hesitated. "I think that would make things worse. He is the lieutenant. That role is one of the few links that he is still maintaining with the real world. As long as he's carrying out his duties, I would not remove him. Needless to say, he should be watched."

Ericho agreed. "Jonomy's been observing Tom on the

bridge and when he's in corridors or rooms that have surveillance monitoring. But even Jonomy has to sleep." That was true, though Lytics could remain awake and alert for days on end.

June gave a thoughtful nod. "And Jonomy can't monitor the designated privacy areas."

"That's half the ship," said Ericho. "The crew cabins, the dining and social rooms, the gym, the pool—"

"The gardens and the dreamlounge," June concluded.

Ericho had no quarrel with the rule of limited surveillance aboard starships. It was a good idea, initiated decades ago when Lytics were first assigned to long voyages.

Back then, crews had not taken kindly to being constantly watched. It had been bad enough prior to that time, being observed by computers and machines, but Lytics were in a class by themselves. Cybergenetic humans had never been very popular and their intrusion into the regulated life of starcrews brought about marked increases in shipboard paranoia. Surveillance equipment was sabotaged, computer terminals were wrecked, and in a few cases, Lytics were actually murdered. The Corporeal had reacted to the growing problem by demanding that the consortiums introduce designated privacy areas on starships.

June asked, "Isn't there a way to get full surveillance in special situations?"

"Sure. A Sentinel-override. But that's Level One and it takes a major problem to wake up a Sentinel."

June shrugged. "Then I guess you'll have to settle for watching Tom when you can. I wish there was something more I could offer, I really do. But aside from putting him under somnolence beams—vegetating him for the rest of the voyage—there's not much I can recommend."

"Do you think it'll come to that?"

"I hope not. We wouldn't be helping Tom by putting him to sleep for nine and a half months. But if he gets much worse, I'd consider it as an option."

June finished her milk and dropped the empty beaker into a disposal chute beneath her desk. "When we began this voyage, Tom Dianaldi was well within the standard psych parameters, although borderline in a few categories. Still, his profile was acceptable for this starcrossing—at least until Mars Lea was added to the crew."

Ericho nodded. "You said that you suspected she might be psionically disturbing him."

"It's no longer just a suspicion. I've been doing some research. Are you familiar with the basic psionic categories?"

"Not really. Three different types, aren't there?"

"Uh-huh. Projectors generate superluminal impulses, receptors receive them, and conveyors relay the faster-than-light signals, functioning sort of like a com satellite between two distant points.

"Now we've known for a long time that most humans possess at least some telempathic ability, however slight, in one or more of those categories. But what makes Mars Lea so special is that she is powerfully gifted in all three—a socalled Renaissance Psionic. She can superluminally project her own thoughts and feelings, she can receive signals from other sources, and she can convey the impulses between strangers. I located a declassified portion of the Jamal Laboratory report on her in the library. The report concludes that she is one of the most potent Psionics ever studied."

"And Dianaldi?" Ericho asked.

"Tom has no measurable ability to psionically project or convey, but he's a substantially endowed receptor. That means he's being constantly bombarded by superluminal impulses from his environment. And since psionic signals geometrically increase in amplitude the closer one gets to the source, within the relative confines of this ship, Dianaldi is being literally blasted by Mars Lea. Since he possesses no ability to pass along—convey—these signals, and no ability to project his own impulses, I imagine these superluminal signals sort of just float around inside him, intermingling with Tom's own thoughts and feelings. After ten months, it's not surprising that his personality has been altered."

Ericho nodded. "Would it help to keep Tom and Mars Lea at opposite ends of the *Alchemon?*"

"It wouldn't hurt. At least make sure they don't remain in the same area together for extended periods. But I doubt Dianaldi will get any better even if he's quarantined from her. You'd have to get them a couple million miles apart at this point to begin to undo the damage. I believe there's been what they refer to as a 'telempathic bridge' established between Tom and Mars Lea—her thoughts and feelings are flowing into him along this superluminal conduit. And once such a bridge has been built between two people, it's very hard to tear down."

Ericho asked, "How about that isolator hood that Hardy uses on Mars Lea to enhance her psionic contacts? Is there any sort of device that has the opposite effect? Something that can shield Tom from this constant bombardment?"

"We're dealing with faster-than-light signals here," the crewdoc replied. "There is no known method for preventing superluminals from traveling where they please."

Ericho frowned. "The *Alchemon* generates superluminals. The Sentinels—"

She held up her hand. "Yes, I know—the *Alchemon* produces its own superluminal impulses and they're prevented from escaping the boundaries of the computer system. But the Sentinels are artificially generated by the ship and they're very different from organic superluminals."

June shook her head. "The problem is that Psionics is still such an infant science. There are literally hundreds of theories as to how the impulses bridge the gap between living organisms, how they interact with the brain's neuronal structure, why some people have powers and others don't. No one knows for sure. Until the actual discovery of the superluminal spectrum, about fifty years ago, Psionics wasn't even considered a science. Before that, they had a hundred different names for it—parapsychology, mindreading, voodooism—it has antecedents reaching back to the dawn of recorded history. But there's still too much we don't know.

"We can mechanically generate a limited, controllable type of superluminal—a Sentinel—and we can measure the three basic categories found in humans. We can say that an individual with a strong projector ability will likely exert an influence on the personality and behavior of someone who's a strong receptor. But the basic laws that govern Psionics— those we're still not sure of."

Ericho felt a flash of anger. "Maybe not, but Pannis shoud have known enough to be a bit more careful. Someone should have realized that putting Mars Lea and Tom together on this voyage could cause problems."

"You're right. The Assignor who put together the crew for this mission really fouled up. Frankly, I'm still at a loss to understand how Tom and Mars Lea could have gotten aboard the same ship. Pannis usually doesn't make such bad mistakes. And even if the Assignor screwed up, someone—a Supervisor, maybe—should have caught the error."

Ericho forced down his anger. Gross incompetence. There

was nothing to be done about it now, but when they returned to Earth, a Pannis exec board was going to hear about this.

Another thought occurred. "What about the rest of the crew? Is Mars Lea bombarding all of us?"

June regarded him silently for a moment. "That repeating dream you told me about a while back. Are you still having it?"

He sighed. "Yes. Almost every other night, it seems." He looked at her sharply. "You think Mars Lea is causing my dream?" He had never really considered the possibility.

"Most everyone in the Corporeal possesses at least some degree of psionic ability," June answered. "In normal situations, though, Dianaldi is the only one of us whom we would expect to be seriously affected by a strong telempathic presence. The rest of the *Alchemon*'s crew has negligible psionic talents. Alan Ortega is even below the line—he has absolutely no measurable telempathic abilities.

"But this is not a normal situation. Mars Lea . . . as I said, she's very powerful. Some of the scientists at the Jamal Laboratories maintained she was such a strong psionic presence that they doubted they could even come close to documenting the full range of her abilities.

"It would not surprise me if Mars Lea is the cause of your dream."

My dream, Ericho thought.

I'm piloting a lander down through the cloudy atmosphere of some planet—Earth, I think, though I'm never quite certain. I'm in a weird, very fast, spiraling descent, which is all wrong, since I know that such a flight path should be vaporizing the heat shields. Outside the window, I see a shimmering energy display—rainbow blades of controlled lightning seem to be flanking the craft, and I am vaguely aware that this strange spectrum of flashing light is somehow protecting the lander from the effects of a dangerously fast reentry. There are other people in the craft, seated behind me, but I cannot tell who they are.

He shook his head. "The same dream, over and over. I must have experienced it at least fifty times since the voyage began. Pretty boring, actually." He laughed grimly. "And I always wake up before the lander touches down. I never know if we make it or not."

"Mars Lea could be the cause of your dream," said June. "She could be unconsciously bombarding you with some thought or feeling that is leading you to experience this same dream over and over. That sort of psionic interaction has been documented."

"And if Mars Lea has formed one of these telempathic bridges with me," Ericho frowned, "then I could have this same dream for the rest of my life."

"It could be worse," June pointed out. "It could be a nightmare."

Yes, he thought, *it could be worse.*

"There's one other aspect that we have to consider here," June said slowly. "That organism in the containment—according to what Jonomy told me, this . . . creature, this—"

"Blue blob," suggested Ericho. "At least that's what Rigel's been calling it."

She grinned. "That sounds like a Rigel name. Anyway, my point is, it would appear that this blue blob is also telempathic, perhaps in ways we can't even imagine. And the events on the surface would seem to indicate that this creature has some sort of psionic interaction going with Mars Lea."

June stared at him gravely. "And I have to tell you something, Ericho. I've been getting a very unpleasant feeling myself over the last day or so when I think about that creature. It's almost a sense of . . . something bad that has happened . . . or is going to happen. Some terrible tragedy." She drew a deep breath and folded her arms across her chest. "Anyway, this blue blob—it could be having some sort of telempathic effect on me, perhaps through Mars Lea."

"Jesus," muttered Ericho. "Nine and a half more months to Earth—"

"I know. And that worries me even more. It's not just Dianaldi we've got to be concerned about. I believe we may be trapped in a psionic whirlpool out here. We could all be affected and it could get worse."

She turned to her desktop terminal and typed in a series of commands. She spun the monitor so that Ericho could also observe. "Look at this."

A representation took shape on the screen: an elongated triangular face, drawn by black pencil on a white background. The mouth appeared overly large and there was little forehead; the eyes were located near the top of the skull. Ericho noted that the entire face was drawn by a single unbroken line, twisting and winding back and forth to form the features.

"Dianaldi's 3D image," he mused. "Or a two-dimensional version of it." Ericho read the tiny words printed beneath the sketch: "Its voice was like that of a storm and its breath blew like a hurricane."

He laughed uneasily. "That's Tom's handiwork, all right. Did he send this picture to you on the terminal?"

"No. I found this in our library. Ever since you told me about Tom's infatuation with this image, I've been researching GEL for corollaries. Yesterday, scanning through an old art file, I finally got lucky.

"It's an image of Humbaba, an ancient Babylonian demon. This particular representation comes from the Colorado Museum of Ancient Cultures, circa twenty-first century. Humbaba is a mythological giant out of the *Gilgamesh Epic,* which is probably at least three thousand years old."

June's eyes narrowed; she stared at the screen and a delicate smile crossed her black skin, expanding from forehead to cheekbones. "Notice how the entire face is formed from one solid line. See the way the mouth seems almost to be shaped out of entrails, and the way the whole caricature seems to resemble a human fingerprint. It's as though the artist deliberately tried to contain all aspects of an entire being within this face."

She shook her head. "I don't know. Perhaps this image carries no importance—just a random fetish that Dianaldi latched onto. But maybe there's more to it than that."

Ericho felt abruptly uneasy. "Babylonian demons. Jesus!"

"I know. The whole thing's kind of scary."

"Is there anything—anything at all—we can do to lessen Mars Lea's effect on Tom?"

June stared at the far wall for a long moment. "There is . . .something. Research findings indicate that most of these Renaissance Psionics, who are powerful in all three telempathic categories, are sexually repressed. Mars Lea certainly fits that scenario—I don't believe she's had sex with anyone on the *Alchemon.*"

"Is she a virgin?"

The crewdoc shook her head. "No, but she does avoid the subject of sex like the plague. I understand that Rigel tried to come on to her early in the voyage and that since that occasion, she has barely even spoken to him.

"The point is, there is a definite, but unclear, relationship between psionic prowess and sexual repression. Studies suggest that Psionics who become more sexually open may unconsciously reduce their telempathic output."

Ericho chuckled. "Are you saying we should get her laid to cut down on her powers?"

June gazed at him.

"Me? You've got to be kidding!"

She reached across the desk and drummed her fingers playfully on his hand. "It would be for the good of the mission—"

He pulled his hand away. "I'm sorry, but I've got a personal rule—I only get involved with one sexual partner at a time. Things tend to remain less complicated that way." He paused. "And I'm very content with my present partner."

June smiled. "I'm honored you feel that way, Ericho. I truly am. But I would understand it if you—"

"No, I won't do it. Besides, Mars Lea doesn't appeal to me at all. And she's so overly sensitive—and I don't mean just psionically—that even if I managed to seduce her, she would probably be aware of my real feelings, would know that I was just trying to manipulate her."

June folded her arms on the desk and leaned forward. She regarded him warmly. "Any other candidates you can think of, who'd be willing to do the deed?"

"Dianaldi's out, of course. And Rigel seems to have already rubbed Mars Lea the wrong way. I wouldn't begin to know how to approach Hardy about such a thing . . . he seems so very formal when it comes to sex."

"How about Alan? He's young and, according to Rigel, perpetually flesh-hungry. And since he has no measurable psionic ability, he would probably be unaffected by physical/emotional closeness with Mars Lea."

"He sounds like a good choice. When are you going to ask him?"

June burst into laughter. "Well, I suppose that such an odd request would normally fall under the domain of the medical department. But in this instance, I'm afraid I'll have to defer to the captain."

"I was afraid you were going to say that." He grinned. "Any advice on how to broach the subject?"

"Be subtle."

6

Mars Lea awoke.

She lay on her back at the edge of the swimming pool, her knees dangling over the padded lip, feet submerged in the cool liquid. She opened her eyes, squinted at the curving wall of ultraviolet reflectors that surrounded the natatorium. The glazed dome enclosed three-quarters of the pooldeck, a suspended hemisphere tinted pale blue at its concave summit. The dome was supposed to resemble an earth sky.

She readjusted a shoulder strap on her one-piece bather. Her body felt weak and only an intense thirst forced her to overcome sluggishness and struggle to her feet. In the water, several figures splashed noisily. She ignored them. Stumbling past the small garden behind the pool, she came to a dispenser nestled in the wall. A gentle touch of the water button caused a thin sensorized hose to snake from a slot and nestle itself snugly between her lips.

She sucked eagerly, drank until her belly felt bloated. A time/date clock above her—two perpendicular lines of varying lengths—indicated that she had been asleep down here for almost seven hours. She felt as if she could use seven more.

"Mars Lea!" The male voice came from the water, was instantly followed by a loud splash. She stumbled back to the rim and stared at the two figures swimming toward her.

Alan Ortega hopped from the pool, shaking his head, sending a spray of water from his long brown hair. The intern was a bit taller than Mars Lea, slim and deeply tanned, and naked except for a fluorescent green crotch pad. Alan broke into a grin; baby-fat cheeks swelled, making his twenty-year-old face look even younger.

"Get wet—we need a third for waterball."

"I'm tired," she explained, wishing he would go away. There was something strange about young Alan. In a way, she liked him; he was one of the few people on the ship who did not always seem to want something from her. Yet, there was some facet to his personality that remained disguised . . . or missing. He lacked a center, a place where he connected with the real world. She saw him perpetually out of focus.

"Come on, Mars Lea," the intern urged. "Play with us."

Elke Els used the walkway to step from the water. "Yes, dear, play with us." The scientist laughed and yanked off her bathing cap. Long blond hair fell to her shoulders. Her wraparound orange bather was contoured to lift her bosom, making her large breasts appear larger.

"I'm tired," Mars Lea repeated.

Elke moved to stand beside her. "Not afraid of the fish, are you?"

She shook her head. The pool was dual-functional, used for swimming and as a reservoir for the *Alchemon*'s carefully maintained biosystem. Occasionally, the water became so oversaturated with nutrients, plankton, and tiny fish that swimming became next to impossible. Then some complex feedback mechanism would trigger a host of warning signs and the pool would be drained and refilled with clear, fresh water. Nutrients, plankton, and fish would vanish into the bowels of the ship, later to emerge elsewhere in a transformed state. Most of the crew's fresh food, air, and potable water came from such complex metamorphoses.

Right now, the water remained fairly clear, marred only by a few minnows and a clump of algae in the deep end beneath the diving board.

"The fish don't bother me," Mars Lea said.

"They don't bother Rigel, either," remarked Alan, breaking into a fresh smile. "He likes to swim when the water's overflowing with fish. He likes to catch 'em with his teeth and eat 'em raw."

Elke flashed an amused grimace. "Rigel's disgusting."

Alan sat down on the deck, crossed his legs. "Mars Lea— you coming to the Homebound?"

"What's that?"

Elke licked her lips. "It's a special time that you save yourself for . . . so that you can lose yourself altogether."

"Tomorrow, at twenty-one hundred hours," said Alan, "in the east social room. Rigel says that the captain's going to allow a full array of ingestors." The youth paused. "Captains aren't supposed to do that, but Captain Brad does what he wants. He's no Pannis lackey."

Mars Lea did not answer. Jonomy had explained that the consortiums maintained certain rules for shipboard behavior, rules that they fully expected captains to ignore. "Concessionary regulations," the Lytic called them. Such regulations were in place for the sole purpose of granting starship commanders "options for disobedience." Psychologically, captains were believed to feel more in control if they had certain rules that they could break. Mars Lea suspected that the use of ingestors—consciousness-altering drugs and devices—fell under that heading. She did not think Alan quite understood.

Elke offered an exaggerated smile. "I hope the captain doesn't get himself in trouble."

Elke understood.

"The Homebound is our chance to let loose," continued Alan. "It's tradition. Whenever a starship heads for home, they have a Homebound."

"We're going home?" Mars Lea asked. She wished the idea would make her feel better. It did not.

Alan hopped to his feet. "We left Sycamore's orbit two hours ago. We're heading out of this system, toward the Loop. That means it's time to celebrate. We're all going to a Homebound and we're all going to get blasted."

"This is Alan's first Homebound," Elke explained.

"Damn right!"

Mars Lea smelled something—a heavy odor, almost sickly. Her mind struggled to translate the smell: wet flowers on a muggy riverbank.

She turned, gazed at the carefully maintained bed of roses and hyacinths behind the pool. She sniffed. No, the natatorium flowers possessed their own particular olfactory brand, easily distinguishable from this other smell.

And wet flowers on a muggy riverbank was not quite right. This odor was . . . different. More pungent. She could recall no exact corollary.

"Do you smell that?" she asked.

"I smell the flowers," Alan offered, following her gaze to the bed of roses and hyacinths.

"No. Something else."

Alan sniffed, then shrugged his shoulders. "I never had a good nose."

Elke frowned. "What do you smell?"

"Like flowers . . . but only much stronger . . . and different, somehow."

Abruptly, the odor grew in intensity, became overpowering. Mars Lea covered her mouth and nose but the odor just kept coming on, growing stronger, and she knew that it was not real, that it was of psionic origin.

She doubled over, almost retching from the sheer intensity of it. She heard distant voices—Alan's and Elke's—concerned mumblings—and then someone uttered two words in a voice she did not recognize: *Sentinels obey.*

The psionic attack ended; the odor vanished, as if cut off by a switch. She straightened, met worried frowns.

"You'd better go to the medcenter," insisted Elke. "Right now."

Mars Lea shook her head. "No . . . no . . . it wouldn't do any good."

"Was that a psionic experience?" asked Alan, his voice full of wonder.

"Yes."

"Wow."

Elke was still frowning. "Are you sure you're all right?"

"I'm fine."

Alan probed. "What was it?"

"It wasn't important. Just . . . a strong smell. Things like this happen to me sometimes. They're not important. You shouldn't worry about them."

"But, dear, we do worry. Why don't you run over to the medcenter. June might have some drugs—"

"Drugs won't help."

Alan grinned. "You think not, huh? Well, you just wait until tomorrow night." He moved next to her, put his hand on her arm, gently rubbed her flesh.

"Mars Lea, if you come to the Homebound with me, I promise I'll help you forget all about this psionic stuff. Trust me. We'll have a good time. I promise."

"I don't think so."

"Come on—take a chance!" He threw his arm across her shoulder and squeezed her tightly. She felt her body go tense.

"Mars Lea, I've got it. Stroke lenses! Have you ever worn them?"

"No." *Let go of me!*

Alan grinned madly at her. "Bloody black spatial! You won't believe what you've been missing. Try 'em with me tomorrow night. Stroke lenses are nicer than drugs, 'cause if things get too weird, you can always take them off. With drug ingestors, you have to pop an antidote."

Let me go!

Elke gently pulled Alan away from Mars Lea. "C'mon, Alan, can't you see she's not interested?"

The intern grinned. "You've got to learn to relax, Mars Lea. You've got to allow yourself to have some fun. You can't spend all your time thinking about blue blob." He winked at her. "Besides—he's not as sexy as me. That's guaranteed."

"For your information," Elke reproached, "blue blob is not as sexy as you because blue blob happens to be female, and naturally more in control of her urges."

"Really? That thing is a woman? Wow."

"And you'd better not tell Rigel," Elke warned.

Alan frowned. "Why not?"

Elke sighed. "It's a joke, Alan."

The intern laughed. "Oh, yeah. Rigel goes after all the women. I got it." He wagged his finger at Mars Lea. "Tomorrow night, we won't think about Rigel or blue blob. It'll just be you and me, okay?" With a mad grin, he twisted around and dove into the water. His body knifed cleanly into the pool and he swam the length of it submerged.

Elke shook her head. "Well, that was weird. He usually doesn't act so pushy. This Homebound's really got him excited."

Mars Lea did not respond. She decided that she was not going to go to any Homebound. They could not make her.

Elke stared at her gravely. "Are you sure you're all right?"

"I'm fine." She hesitated, remembering the strange odor and the unknown voice: *Sentinels obey,* the voice had said.

"Elke, I've heard people mention Sentinels. What are they?"

The scientist hesitated. "They're Level One computer functions. I don't know much about them. You should ask Jonomy."

"Level One . . . that controls everything, right?"

"Sort of. There are six levels of control, each level more sophisticated than the one below it. Level Six, for instance, controls most of the luxury systems, like this pool. But it gets more complicated than that, because the pool is also a part of FWP—Food and Waste Processing, which I believe is a Level Three system. Plus HYP—Hydroponics. Then there's GEN—Geonic Stability, also Level Three. And the natatorium must have a breathable atmosphere, so a Level Two system—PEH—Primary Ecospheric Homeostasis, has some control. Plus most of the power is routed from Level One—POP and NEL: Primary Operating Power and the Nucleonic Engines. Then there are the backup systems—" Elke stopped. "Confusing, huh?"

Mars Lea nodded.

The scientist chuckled. "Well, I wouldn't worry about any of it. Starships are so complicated these days that no one but engineers and Lytics really understands them. Just accept the fact that the *Alchemon* takes care of us and keeps us alive."

Mars Lea reminded herself to ask Jonomy about the Sentinels.

Elke glanced at the clock behind them. "I should get going. Hardy has another batch of experiments scheduled in an hour." She grinned. "He gets really testy when I'm late."

"Elke, wait . . . this creature . . . you said that it's a female?" Mars Lea found the idea repulsive.

"Definitely female," said the scientist. "We found evidence of a barely formed vagina. As you saw for yourself, there are no external body openings, but underneath that outer blue membrane exists the morphogenetic beginnings of an advanced, probably intelligent, life form. There's a head, complete with eyes, ears, a nose, and several sensory organs that we can't identify. A central bone structure is present and Hardy believes he's located a quartet of unformed appendages. Two arms and two legs, probably. A spine runs through the body, culminating at the base of the head. The brain, in its present undeveloped stage, possesses what appears to be a phylogenetic variation of the tripartite human brain—four distinct sections instead of three, each one evolving over, and encompassing, its forerunner.

"Most of its internal organs are also unformed. There are, however, some tantalizing resemblances to a human kidney and a valved heart.

"The creature appears to be almost in a fetal state, but even that doesn't exactly explain things, because blue blob is somehow bypassing the normal entropy processes inherent to all living organisms. It bears all the hallmarks of an evolutionary creation, yet it is not evolving."

"Could it be human?" Mars Lea asked.

"No, there are too many structural differences. We're sure it's not of our species, although it could have come from an ecosphere similar to earth's."

"Has it . . . elevated itself again?"

Elke's voice rose in excitement. "Yes, as a matter of fact, several times. Five or six hours ago, it suspended itself in the center of the chamber for almost twenty-five minutes. It's the strangest thing you can imagine: The damn thing just lifts itself up and floats." She shook her head. "Who knows? Maybe it just pretends there's no gravity. Until now, real organic geonic nullification was thought to be an impossibility. We have simulated gravity on the *Alchemon*, of course, but that's based on sophisticated pressure tricks and subatomic fields that grant us artificial polarity in relation to the ship. We're tricked into believing there's an up and down. But blue blob—she ignores our tricks."

"We should return this creature to Sycamore," Mars Lea blurted out.

Elke turned to the pool, watched Alan begin yet another lap underwater. "Maybe you're right."

—From the papers of Thomas Andrew Dianaldi

Renfro Dackaman.

I turn the name over in my mind almost every day now, trying to look at it from different angles, trying to see this perversion of a human being from different perspectives. I know that he has become an obsession with me, but I'm powerless to do anything about it. I'd like to kill him, but I don't have the courage.

The board of inquiry that investigated the Theodoris *events found Dackaman innocent, of course. No great surprise there; the outcome was never really in doubt. Good headhunters are too valuable to waste. If he had been a tech officer, for instance, or maybe a mere ship's liutenant, he'd probably be doing time in a lunar prison right now.*

Moral: If you're going to get into a combat shieldsuit and blow away another human being, make sure that you're of some importance to your employers.

Bastards.

7

The east social room was the largest single area on the ship. Over thirty meters in length from north to south airseals, and encompassing both decks, the hall blossomed with architectural oddities. A double row of thick crystal-facaded pillars ran the length of the room, sprouting from the carpeted floor and vanishing into the dark recesses of the ceiling. On the west side, a third airseal had been holographically augmented to resemble a Greco-Roman arched portal. A transparent geonic chute rose beside it, climbing the dark side panels to connect with a terminated updeck corridor, eight meters above. The zero-G elevator blazed with its own spectrum of color: an inner sleeve of red, amber, violet, and chartreuse lumes outlining glass-sheathed electronic circuitry.

The social room's main lighting swept downward from the ceiling, and was directed so that the pillars threw deep shadows onto the east wall. There, plastiform paintings of former earth emperors hung at regular intervals. Unstable luminescent pigments gave the portraits a deceptive three-dimensional quality. The better ones looked almost as good as holograms.

"I feel luscious!" exclaimed Elke.

Ericho, leaning against a pillar and nursing his third orb of Toraz lime brandy, smiled at the scientist. From neck to ankles, Elke had encased her body in a low-intensity natal suit. Sensations of touch were magnified; the skin became sensitized to the degree where even a gentle breeze might feel like the finest massage. Ericho had often worn natal suits in his younger days.

He reached out, touched her shoulder, watched with amusement as she moaned with delight.

A hand touched Ericho's own shoulder and he turned slowly. Tom Dianaldi stood there, wide-eyed, bare-chested, a glittering emerald hanging from his left earlobe.

"Two who bleed for humanity, who transmit urine and children with the graceful ease of the laser. Artisans of recreation. Tongues tasting both sides of the equation under skies of dark excitation."

Elke grinned madly. "A poet of the night."

"A synthesizer, dear Elke. A revitalizer of entropy, awaiting the web of existence to shred my spirit. A spirit prepared, with fear and lust, for the coming of the night."

Elke licked her lips.

"And you, Captain. Wearing a white officer's cloak to this Homebound celebration is excruciatingly subtle—an action/reaction toward purity of soul." Dianaldi stepped back, pouted like a child. "Ah, but you are alone in your perfection. Come with me, and taste caverns of blood. Allow your passion to mingle with the beauty of God."

Ericho chuckled and took another sip through his straw. Toraz lime brandy was the finest in the Corporeal. Smooth going down and no unpleasant aftertaste. More important, there was just enough alcohol in it to make whatever the lieutenant had to say bearable.

He felt good, better than he had in weeks. They had all needed this Homebound; the *Alchemon* had more than its share of tensions and a few hours of abandon seemed the perfect remedy. Ericho knew that he could even get drunk if he desired, although he had no intention of doing so. Jonomy was minding the ship—the *Alchemon* would be taken care of, no matter what its captain decided to do. Still, Ericho felt a sense of propriety. He would drink a bit and soften the edges, relax in preparation for the nine-and-a-half-month journey back to Earth. But he would not completely lose himself.

Besides, someone had to keep an eye on Dianaldi.

The lieutenant took a curious step backward, pivoted to face him. "I see, Captain, by your expressive sobriety, that you've allowed only minimal chemical input. Either one *participates* or one merely enjoys—a choice between enervating bliss and rampant boredom."

June had prepared a list of safe drugs for the Homebound, making certain that none of the heavier psychotropics and amphetamines were available. The limitations had been imposed on everyone; that seemed the only way to guarantee that Dianaldi would not have access to any ingestors strong enough to throw him over the edge.

"What are you using?" Ericho asked.

"Using?" Dianaldi's voice rose in pitch and he burst into laughter. "Oh, Ericho, rich Ericho! You are not, perchance, a Lytic? Approaching reality with a cybernetic consciousness and lacking wickedness for a soul?"

"Someone has to mind the ship."

Dianaldi's grin melted slightly, and for once he looked serious. "Yes, they do indeed."

Elke cupped her breasts, inhaled with pleasure. "It's all food for the spirit, Captain. Peerst needles, trancs, synthetic coke—"

"Or poison for the soul," Ericho countered.

Elke laughed.

Dianaldi struck a rigidly comic pose, body twisting to one side, hands delicately rubbing his bare chest. He allowed a long dark hair beneath his right nipple to curl around his forefinger. Then he yanked on it, wincing as he tore the hair from his skin.

He held the hair up until it caught the light. "With this, I mark my passage—my habitual nature, twisting under the guise of intellect."

He dropped the hair to the floor. "Let me tell you what I am using, rich Ericho. Let me tell you of cannabis extracts and Q-sensualizers. Let me tell you of my penis, which will soon be one with God!"

With a crazed laugh, Elke hurled herself at Tom. He opened his arms, caught her. Feet tangled; hands pawed as they stumbled across the hall, finally collapsing inelegantly to the floor. Limbs thrashed as they rolled across the carpet like crazed puppies. It seemed to Ericho that they were trying to devour one another.

June Courthouse and Hardy Waskov were seated on cushions near the south airseal, their attention riveted on the highly animated tech officer standing before them. Ericho sat down next to June.

Rigel was telling a story.

" . . . and my dada used to say: 'Son, there is no such thing as the unknowable, no matter how alien. Our universe has certain characteristics. Life forms obey rigid principles. Intelligence procreates only under very specific harsh conditions. Modes vary, but all behavior processes share a common genesis. Understanding what is alien becomes simply a function of time.' " Rigel grunted with laughter. "So I said: 'But, Dada, I don't want to be an exobiologist, like you. I want to be a professional soldier.' Then Dada would get red as blood and mumble about Mama's ancestry and finally stomp off to his study in a fit!"

Rigel withdrew a palm-sized orb from a side pocket of his gray vest, plunged a needle-tipped stabstraw into the thin plastic container. "Actually, back then, I really didn't know if I wanted to be a soldier. But I sure as hell didn't want to be an exobiologist. Dada spent too much time not having fun.

"What I really wanted to be when I was very young was a Lytic. I remember being real upset when I first learned where Lytics came from. I was pissed. You couldn't go to school for it. You had to be born into it, raised in a lab. So I said to hell with it all and I went out and enlisted in our glorious Corporeal Armed Forces. Five fuckin' years in a CAF combat unit." He put the thin straw to his lips, shuddered slightly as he drew and swallowed. "I fought in several of the Antigenesis uprisings. Man-to-man in combat shieldsuits." He stared into space. "Fuck the army."

"Yes," interrupted Hardy, "the Antigenesis uprisings did substantial damage to many scientific disciplines. Research was halted in many fields."

June Courthouse wore a distant smile. "I was planning to study planetary engineering at the Walkabout University in Central Australia. They were supposed to have the finest curriculum on the planet.

Rigel took another bitter gulp. "Walkabout University— weren't they nuked during one of the Antigenesis uprisings?"

"Vaporized in microseconds." The crewdoc pulled a handkerchief from her pocket and delicately wiped a layer of sweat from her black forehead. "Some of the finest minds in the Corporeal died that day."

Rigel nodded in sympathy. "So you became a crewdoc."

"No, not right away. Actually, I got mated to a lovely boy from Luna, and spent a couple of inglorious years trying to become his mother." She laughed. "What an emotional mess that was, for both of us."

Alan Ortega wandered out from behind a pillar. His long brown hair was ringed by a braided snapcloth. A transparent black disk was pasted over each eye and a pair of thin wires trailed from the lenses to a small transmitter hanging from the belt of his white jumpsuit.

"I have reached . . . parabolic velocity," he said simply. His thin frame erupted into laughter.

"I'm fuckin' impressed," grunted Rigel.

"I've seen things," said Alan, with a touch of awe in his voice. "I've looked into my own consciousness and I've seen myself there."

"Very shrewd," offered June, turning to Ericho with a smile.

Alan reached up and adjusted one of the disks. "I don't care what any of you think. Stroke lenses are a way to really expand yourself.

Stroke lenses, thought Ericho; sensory modification devices that augmented what the eye naturally perceived by feeding back random information from the brain. Some called them mirrors into reality, but Ericho knew that they simply reflected and refracted perception until nothing was real.

Rigel stabstrawed a fresh orb. "You should try one of these, boy. You wouldn't waste your time staring into your own shit."

"What is it?" the intern challenged.

June answered, her tone clinically precise. "Rigel is drinking bit-o-scosha, an acetic liquor distilled from the vines of the same name on the planet Peliprime. It is a depressor of the central nervous system as well as a mild aphrodisiac. There is substantial evidence that continued use leads to synaptic dysfunctioning in certain areas of the cerebral cortex. It is also carcinogenic, concentrating on the throat and stomach membranes."

Rigel roared with laughter. "Nothing a transplant and some cellular regeneration won't cure!"

The crewdoc smiled politely.

"Give me some," Alan demanded. Rigel threw him his orb, pulled a fresh one from another pocket.

Hardy leaned forward. "Did you know that the Cybernetic Analytic Foundation expressly prohibits Lytics from using drugs and liquors of any sort?"

"That's probably why Lytics are so boring," Rigel quipped. He threw his head back and spoke toward the ceiling. "And, Jonomy—just in case you're listening somehow—no offense."

Alan giggled.

Hardy wagged his finger at the tech officer. "But we're fortunate that Lytics are under such proscriptions. After all, the fact that Jonomy remains alert allows you and the captain to enjoy the luxury of this celebration."

Ericho doubted that the science rep had taken any drugs.

Rigel shrugged. "Starships were fairly automated before Lytics came along."

"True," admitted Hardy, turning to Ericho. "But you have to admit, Captain, that you have less real work to do than your predecessors did thirty or forty years ago."

Ericho admitted it.

"Look!" exclaimed Alan, pulling off one of his stroke lenses for a better view.

They followed his gaze to the geonic chute. Tom Dianaldi and Elke Els were floating upside down in the middle of the transparent shaft, naked bodies squeezed together in a tangled embrace. The lieutenant pushed off one of the side ladders and the lovers rocketed feet-first up the freefall tube. They passed the updeck airseal. Tom's outstretched foot compressed against the padded roof of the shaft, checking their motion. Then he kicked violently, rocketing them headfirst back down the chute. No sound came from the acoustically sealed tube, but from their expressions, they appeared to be howling with laughter.

"Hell of a way to do it," grinned Rigel.

Alan replaced his stroke lens, gazed trancelike at the two figures. "They just turned blue—pure shiny blue. And it almost looks like there are three of them in there."

Ericho whispered to June. "Are you sure it was a good idea to let Tom get involved in all of this?"

"No," said the crewdoc, with a touch of annoyance in her voice.

He looked at her with surprise. "I wasn't being critical."

She sighed. "I'm sorry. I know you weren't. But, Ericho, please believe me—I'm fresh out of ideas. It's possible that the ingestors and a night of undiluted fun might throw him over the edge. But it's just as possible that a good dose of really mad activity might help Tom, allow him to see himself a bit more lucidly. Frankly, I don't think we have much to lose at this point. I believe that it's only a matter of weeks before we're going to have to put him to sleep, vegetate him for the rest of the trip."

Ericho nodded. "He's been getting worse, all right. This morning I caught him wandering around one of the mech repair shops. I asked him what he was doing and he looked at me kind of funny and said that he didn't know."

June shook her head sadly. "I feel bad for him, I really do. It must be awful, being caught in this superluminal bombardment, not knowing whether your thoughts and feelings are your own or someone else's."

"At least Mars Lea isn't here," Ericho said. "I was actually relieved when she said she wasn't coming to the Homebound."

June's sad expression melted into a grin. She whispered: "Afraid to see your matchmaking abilities put to the test?"

Ericho glanced at Alan, who was still staring at Tom and Elke in the geonic chute. "I tried, I really did." He chuckled. "I convinced Alan that seducing Mars Lea was for the good of the expedition and ultimately, for the greater glory of the Corporeal. I told him that he was going to have to be brave about it."

June laughed.

"I don't know what went wrong. I haven't had a chance to debrief him yet."

Tom and Elke continued to perform madly. Alan pulled off both his stroke lenses. "It's not fair."

"What's not fair?" quizzed Rigel.

"The balance aboard this ship. There are six men and only three women."

June smiled. "Sounds fair to me."

"It should be more equalized," the intern insisted.

Rigel gave Alan a hard slap on the back. "You just have to be a little more aggressive, boy."

"Balance is not always a matter of numbers," offered June. "For one thing, there are some males aboard the *Alchemon* who do not possess overly strong sex drives. Jonomy, for instance. Lytics, with more direct access to their neuronal structures, are supposed to be able to bring themselves to a climax that is far more intense and satisfying than what a normal human is capable of experiencing. They do it all internally. They don't need women."

June stared at the lovers in the shaft. "Also, the *Alchemon* has one female crew member with unusually strong drives."

Rigel grunted, "Elke's a fuckin' nympho, all right."

Alan was still not satisfied. "Too bad there's only one of her."

"Life's tough," agreed Rigel.

8

Mars Lea passed silently through the gentle S-curves of downdeck's west corridor. At one time, she had believed that the odd winding symmetry in this area of the *Alchemon* was a design feature of the Pannis psychoarts department; a deliberate attempt to escape the right-angled, straight-line approach that delineated most of the other passageways. Jonomy had corrected her. It had been necessary to bend this corridor to conform to the shape of large engineering machinery located in this section.

Human access areas constituted less than five percent of the ship's available space. The rest was machine. The machine took precedence.

A dark labyrinth of narrow service shafts lay beyond these walls; another world, watched over by an army of tiny service probes: the *Alchemon*'s pups. Jonomy had explained that pups did most of the general repair work aboard the ship. Mars Lea thought that a pup was a silly name for a robot.

An airseal detected her, whisked open. She crossed into the section of corridor bounding the containment lab entrance, halted in front of the huge lab portal. She was reaching for the access keyboard when the door abruptly slid back. She jumped.

Jonomy stood inside, smiling.

"That wasn't funny," she chided, entering the lab. "You scared me."

The door snapped shut.

"How did you know I was out there?" she demanded. "I thought you could only monitor our whereabouts from the bridge."

The Lytic wore gray trousers and a white cotton pullover with thick red horizontal stripes. She knew he had carefully chosen his attire; the stripes made him appear broader, helped disguise his thin frame. Several times, she had tried to persuade him to eat more, gain some weight. He invariably refused, preferring to remain skinny.

"I can monitor certain basic systems from anywhere on the ship," he explained. "I have a built-in RF/laser relay up here." He patted his temple. His dark bangs were trapped behind a strip of maroon cloth, and the headband also served to hide the umbilical opening in the center of his forehead. "I'm tied directly into PAQ—the Primary Quantizer, Level One. I used that system to reach Level Four, Internal Bio Scanning. IBS transmitted an infrared image of you coming down the hallway. You looked very warm."

Mars Lea matched his smile. "I learn something new about you every time."

"That is proper."

There was an innocence to Jonomy, something about his face; a childlike sense of wonder, as if he were continually amazed by the reality of the universe. He had not yet grown cynical, like the others.

He was, after all, a Lytic, regularly assimilating vast conglomerations of data, absorbing knowledge far beyond the capacity of mortal humans. And it was that ability that made Jonomy and his kind outsiders to the mainstream of Corporeal society. Lytics and Psionics had much in common.

She asked, "Is the Homebound over yet?"

"No."

She glanced between several equipment racks to the rear of the lab. The back wall was opaque, the creature in the containment out of sight. She wished she could eliminate it from her awareness just as easily. "Why do we have to meet down here?"

"There are limits to what I can monitor via my relays. The containment and this lab are not merely physically isolated from the rest of the ship, but somewhat isolated in terms of data flow as well. I promised Hardy that I would keep an eye on his creature. Since you didn't want to come to the bridge—"

"I don't like it up there. It's so . . . formal. Of course, this isn't much better." She gazed at the equipment cabinets and racks of instrumentation. To their left, Jonomy had turned on one of the monitors. It was flashing through pages of data at blinding speed.

"You can read that?" she challenged playfully, knowing that he could.

"That's the status readout on the condition of our creature."

"Is it floating again?" she asked. "No—never mind. I don't want to know." She pouted. "I suppose you have to keep an eye on that monitor at all times."

Jonomy put his hand beneath her chin and gently stroked. "As a Lytic, I'm accustomed to multiple tasks."

"That's not very romantic, Jonomy. Can't we go somewhere else?"

He shook his head. "It's either here or the bridge. I would be derelict in my duties if we retreated to one of the cabins."

"All right. But you'll know if Hardy or one of the others returns? Right?"

"Of course." Again, he patted his forehead. "Don't worry. This time I'll pay much closer attention. I'll see someone coming well in advance. No one will walk in on us again."

"Is that a promise?"

Jonomy pulled her to him.

The sudden warmth was like a shock to her system. She drew a deep breath, threw her arms around his waist, squeezed. His mouth suckled at the dry skin above her collar; small delicate hands cupped her breasts. He led her to a graviform chair behind a rack of consoles, his fingers releasing her just long enough to make an adjustment at the chair's control panel. The seat's motors hummed softly as it flattened into a small couch.

Jonomy guided her down. She ran her nails across his back, clawing desperately. He slipped off her pants. She wanted him to go slower, wanted herself to go slower, wanted to prolong, knew it was not possible. They were always like this together.

A deep feeling overcame her: gratitude. Moments like these made her life bearable. Passionate lovemaking seemed to shrink the psionic universe, shield her from its constant bombardment, grant her a temporary respite. Moments of near-freedom. This whole expedition was awful enough; she could not imagine what things would have been like without Jonomy.

He enveloped her. Thoughts dissolved into wet warmth.

She awoke naked, her head on something soft—his thigh. It was boyishly smooth, marred only by a few hairs and a series of infinitely tiny birthmarks. She ran the tip of her nose across the flesh, then twisted her head to look up at him. He was awake, his gaze intent upon the status monitor. She pinched him firmly. He smiled down at her.

He had removed his headband. Mars Lea stared at the thumb-sized orifice in the center of his forehead—his third eye, his Lytic brand—the place where the umbilical cable was physically connected when Jonomy was on the bridge. The opening did not seem as revolting as usual, though she still preferred for him to keep it covered while they were making love.

She examined the orifice more carefully, noted the way in which the flesh turned inward, becoming a granular funnel, ending in a studded plate several centimeters beneath the skin.

His smile widened. "I'm glad you're awake. My leg was beginning to experience paralysis."

Lazily, she rolled over, sat up, rubbed her eyes. "How long have I been asleep?"

"Two and a half hours."

She felt better than she had in weeks; fully rested, so unlike her recent awakenings from long sleep periods. She sensed a great distance separating Mars Lea Frock from the psionic universe—that whirlpool of alien feelings, thoughts, and sensations that had been a part of her for as long as she could remember. It lay dormant, unfocused; she was alert, attuned to the present, locked into the real world. She cherished such times, however fleeting.

She got up from the couch and slipped on her pants and blouse, crossed to Hardy's desk, sat down in front of his terminal. After lovemaking, an intense desire for knowledge always seemed to expand within her—an intellectual longing, a hunger simply to learn. She laid her hands on the keyboard, stared at the monitor.

Jonomy understood. "What's today's lesson?"

"I want you to teach me more about the *Alchemon*—about the computer."

Jonomy sat down beside her.

She stared at the complicated array of multicolored keys, wishing once again that the *Alchemon*'s terminals were voice-activated, like most of the computers she had been accustomed to on Earth. But as Jonomy had explained, the perfect tonal-command system had never been designed—one that would respond accurately to the varied inflections and emotive patterns of human speech. For clarity, the typer remained the preferred method. Unless you happened to be a Lytic.

She moved her finger across the blue tabs of the typer's command section, randomly halting on a key labeled I.S. "What does this one do?"

"I.S. stands for intrinsic search. That command informs the computer that the following data entries are to be handled purely within its own local boundaries. For example, if we were orbiting Earth, within telemetry range of millions of other computers, and you asked a specific question that our computer couldn't answer, the *Alchemon* would naturally transmit your query to all these other starships or earthbound data centers in an attempt to find the answer. The intrinsic search command would override that process, limiting the data hunt to the confines of our own computer."

She interrupted. "I thought the *Alchemon* knew everything."

He smiled patiently. "We have a vast library, but there will always be specialized or new data that is not contained in our system. That is why all the computers are tied together. That is why there is such a thing as the Corporeal."

She nodded, pointed to another key. "How about this one?"

He pulled her hand gently away from the keyboard. "If you really wish to master the ship's terminals, there are better teaching methods. A more organized approach would enable you to learn at a rate far beyond—"

"No, I don't really want to know all this. I guess I was just trying to lead up to a question."

"It must be an important question."

"I . . . I had a psionic impression yesterday. It was . . . a smell, a powerful sickly sweet odor." She swallowed, feeling her guts tightening with fear.

She chided herself. *You're stupid, Mars Lea! You're feeling better than you have in weeks, and now you're going to ruin it for yourself!*

Jonomy perceived her growing discomfort. He laid a hand on her shoulder.

She sighed. *Fear or no fear, I have to know.* She finished quickly. "Anyway, this weird smell—right afterward, I heard, or sensed, the words: Sentinels obey. I figured it must be related to the *Alchemon*'s Sentinels. I want you to tell me all about them."

"Ahh. The Sentinels. They seem to fascinate everyone, but there is really no great mystery. They are, in essence, a safety feature designed to protect the *Alchemon* from dangerous programming commands, from the hostile assaults of another computer, or from human malevolence.

"SEN is Level One. It functions as an overseer to the rest of the system. A direct threat to the integrity of the *Alchemon* awakens a Sentinel, which means that SEN generates a superluminal control current and feeds it into the system. In simple terms, this faster-than-light current—this Sentinel—outspeeds all of the normal circuits, which are limited by the velocity of light. In that way, the Sentinel overwhelms and effectively countermands the adverse programming." He reached for the keyboard. "I'll give you an example."

The screen came to life as Jonomy typed.

COMMAND 006A6TY7488:

LEVEL 2 SEQUENCING-PEH

VACUUMIZE CONTAINMENT LAB

The computer responded instantaneously.

PEH 006A6TY7488 DENIED—SENTINEL ENERGIZED

Jonomy smiled tightly. "I have just asked PEH—Primary Ecospheric Homeostasis—the Level Two system responsible for maintaining the atmosphere throughout the ship, to withdraw the air from this lab. I used the proper command override and PEH was preparing to carry out my order. PEH *would* have removed the air from this chamber. However, there was no valid reason for me to issue such a command, since drawing the air from this room would kill both of us. SEN recognized my command as a danger to the integrity of the *Alchemon*—a senseless order, which would result in the deaths of two crew members. Therefore, a Sentinel was awakened and injected into PEH's primary circuitry. The Sentinel disallowed my command."

Mars Lea frowned. "How do these Sentinels know what to obey? I mean, where do they get their logic from."

"All Sentinels follow a series of dictates established by the directors' board of the Corporeal. All Sentinels are bound by a common set of ethics, so to speak, whether they function within the private sector, like aboard our Pannis-owned starship, or within the public sphere. All Sentinelized ships are programmed by Corporeal engineers, and in a strictly regulated environment to prevent tampering."

She nodded. "Sentinels obey—does that phrase have any special meaning?"

"Not that I know of."

"I generate superluminal currents, too. Is there any way that the *Alchemon*'s Sentinels could react with my psionic flows?"

Jonomy regarded her silently for a moment. "What you possess and what the *Alchemon* possesses are as different as night and day. Organic and artificial superluminals do not interface with one another."

Mars Lea grinned. "June Courthouse told me something like that a couple of weeks ago. She was talking about Lytics. She said that your kind rarely, if ever, made love. She said that Lytics and humans did not interface with one another."

Jonomy turned away from her. "There are naturally exceptions to every rule."

"Then maybe I'm an exception. Maybe I'm interfacing with the superluminals on the *Alchemon*."

His voice was suddenly cold. "That is not scientifically possible."

"You're angry," she stated.

Jonomy took a deep breath. "I am not angry."

"Yes, you are."

He stood up. "I should return to the bridge. I believe the Homebound will be ending soon. Hardy will probably be returning here."

She swallowed. "I'm sorry. I didn't mean to upset you."

"I'm not upset." He turned off the containment status monitor and walked to the door. "I will speak to you soon." He exited the lab without so much as a backward glance.

She sighed. "Good-bye, Jonomy."

The door blasted shut.

She shook her head. *I'm stupid in more ways than one.*

They had been making love regularly for the past seven months. Only one other person knew about their affair and that discovery had been accidental. Jonomy had insisted on secrecy, though Mars Lea had no idea why; frankly, she was still puzzled as to what had attracted him to her in the first place. But she did know that he hated talking about such things, even when the subject was broached indirectly.

There was no sense in dwelling on her mistake. She would go for a walk through the *Alchemon*'s corridors. Sometimes, a walk of the ship relaxed her.

Jonomy would call her again in a few days, set up another carefully arranged clandestine rendezvous. Things would work out.

9

Remnants of the Homebound littered the east social room. Elke's natal suit lay crumpled at Ericho's feet; crushed and discarded orbs spotted the floor. Someone's shirt hung from a velcro hook jabbed onto one of the pillars. Wine stains streaked the west wall—a Dianaldi extravaganza. Janitorial pups would clean up the mess.

Ericho drew a final sip of brandy and dropped his empty orb. Although the carpeted floor produced natural audio damping, there was a noticeable thud as it hit. The room was deathly quiet.

Hardy lay curled in a fetal position on the cushions in front of the south airseal, sound asleep. A few meters away, Alan was sprawled on his back, the stroke lenses still intact over his eyes. Every few seconds, a muscle in Alan's arm would twitch, as if the young intern were undergoing mild seizures.

Elke Els, also asleep, floated half-naked in the center of the geonic chute. Rigel sat nearby, his back to a pillar. The tech officer gazed vacantly at one of the plastiform portraits on the east wall.

Ericho studied the nameplate beneath the painting. T. Roosevelt. He knew little about that particular emperor other than the fact that the man had lived in an era when humans had still been confined to the Earth.

In front of the west airseal stood Tom Dianaldi. As usual, he was being weird. His arms were crossed and he was up on his toes, delicately pirouetting as if trying to imitate a slow-motion ballerina. Ericho sighed. The celebration was over. It was time to return to the real world of starflight.

They were going home. That was a pleasant fact, but it also meant the most boring portion of the journey was still in front of them. On the voyage out, the anticipation of discovery always produced a certain edge of excitement; going home offered no such relief, although it was always nice to see Earth again from orbit. But even that pleasure became muted after too many expeditions.

Of course, four and a half months from now there would be a break in the monotony; a flurry of activity in preparation for entering the Sycamore terminus of the transpatial Loop. The *Alchemon* would arrive at the ten-kilometer-wide hole in space—a black void surrounded by navigation beacons—and then the ship's spatiotemporal system would be carefully phased into the odd energy patterns of the Loop. The *Alchemon* would accelerate into the transpatial corridor and emerge almost instantly at the other end: the Earth terminus, located at the outer reaches of the solar system. Another five months of standard rocket travel would bring them into Earth orbit.

Dianaldi stopped pirouetting and faced Ericho. The lieutenant's mouth twisted into its familiar grin.

"I am the offspring of excitation, Captain, the skulking metaphor extracted from synergy."

Ericho approached.

Tom clapped his hands softly. "I believe it is time for me to leave this center of undigested disturbance, to seek a final bed unruffled by the shards of night."

"I'll walk you to your room," Ericho offered. He would make sure Dianaldi got safely to bed, and that chore done, he would go to June's cabin. She had departed the Homebound over an hour ago, leaving Ericho an invitation to drop by when he finished baby-sitting the lieutenant. With any luck, June would still be awake and in the mood.

The west airseal opened and they trooped silently out of the social room and into downdeck's transverse corridor. Tom appeared to be lost in thought; Ericho was grateful for the absence of conversation. He was not in the mood for philosophy.

They crossed through the central lock that divided the east and west halves of the ship. As the airseal slid shut behind them, Dianaldi halted and stared up at the ceiling.

Ericho waited a polite moment. "Something wrong?"

Tom squirmed, then released a piercing laugh. He twisted to face Ericho.

"Do you really like me today, Captain?"

The voice was somber, controlled. Ericho smiled. "Of course."

Tom backed away, his face twisting into a grimace. The

lieutenant fell into a half-crouch, arms dangling at his sides, fingers bent inward at the first joint. There was no mistaking a fighting stance and Ericho responded instinctively with a similar posture.

This is crazy. Ericho forced his body to relax, held out his hand. "Come on, Tom. We're both a bit tired. Why don't you taper down."

Dianaldi charged.

Ericho jerked his head back, felt the wind from a vicious karate swipe. *Purgefire!*

Dianaldi retreated slightly, then swung his booted foot toward Ericho's crotch. Ericho made a grab for the foot, missed. Tom pivoted slightly, then rammed the boot home into Ericho's gut.

He doubled over in pain, backpedaled with all his strength. *Jesus, the maniac is fast.* Tom charged again and another wild kick grazed Ericho's elbow. He sidestepped, tried to bring his own foot up into the lieutenant's belly, realized with a sickening sensation that he was an instant too late. Tom's arm descended; the fist smashed into Ericho's neck. He flew backward, gasping for air. Some coherent part of his mind calculated that he was going to come very close to cracking the side of his skull against the corridor's wall.

Luck was with him. He missed the wall, landed flat on his back with a loud crash. Pain jarred his senses. When his head cleared, he looked up to see Tom standing over him. Dianaldi's left eye was grotesquely pinched shut, his face warped by fury. The mouth opened and a hideous wail, a mixture of agony and triumph, echoed through the corridor.

Ericho clutched his neck, struggling to breathe. Tom's wail died away and his face melted back into a semblance of sanity. His voice fell to a sad whisper.

"Not my fault, Captain. Not anyone's fault."

And then he was racing away, toward the airseal junction into downdeck's main west corridor.

Ericho sat up, then immediately collapsed to the deck in a wave of dizziness. He lay there for an interminable moment, breathing deeply, waiting for his strength to return. He tried again.

This time he made it to his knees. He grabbed a support bar on the airseal behind him and struggled to his feet. An intercom lay nestled in the wall a few meters away. He staggered over to it, opened a communication link to the bridge.

"Jonomy, Tom's out of control. He's on the loose, somewhere in downdeck west. Locate him and seal him off."

There was no response. Ericho keyed a query into the terminal. The intercom's tiny screen came to life.

LYTIC JONOMY IN TRANSIT

MESSAGE RELAYED

Christ! Why the hell wasn't Jonomy on the bridge?

Then he remembered. During the Homebound, the Lytic, with Ericho's blessing, planned to visit the containment lab. Jonomy was going to check Hardy's private data banks to make certain that the science rep had not secretly added any items to his adjusted experiment agenda. It was somewhat unethical for them to breach a private system, but Ericho had felt it was a matter of ship safety. He did not trust Hardy Waskov and he was not going to risk the science rep performing unsanctioned, possibly dangerous, experiments.

In Transit meant that the Lytic had probably just left the lab and was on his way back to the bridge. The computer had relayed Ericho's message. Jonomy should be racing toward the nearest terminal. Any second now, the Lytic should be responding.

Come on, damn it! There was no telling what Dianaldi could do in his present state.

The intercom came to life.

"Jonomy here, Captain. I've just returned to the bridge and I'm plugging into the umbilical—"

A heavy vibration shook the corridor and the rest of the Lytic's words were lost in a wail of alarms. It sounded as if a dozen systems had just gone on emergency alert: sirens, low-pitched bells, a shrieking mélange of frequencies, each struggling for attention.

What the hell? Nothing short of a major disaster could trigger so many alerts. Ericho gave up trying to listen for Jonomy and raced toward the nearest geonic chute at the end of the corridor.

The pain in his guts eased momentarily as he entered the freefall shaft and propelled himself to updeck with a strong kick. His head began to clear.

He leaped out of the chute, broke into a run along updeck's main west corridor, toward the bridge. He struggled to differentiate among the multiple alarms. The highest-pitched one was an all-ship Sentinel alert—that meant big trouble. A harsh beeping indicated the problem was internal and a low wail proclaimed a complete airseal shutdown, meaning the ship was being automatically compartmentalized against some danger. Airseals opened well in advance of him—Jonomy must have been tracking his progress, clearing the way for his mad dash.

Ericho listened more closely, distinguished two other warnings: a birdlike chirping, indicating radiation problems, and the sharp whine of a gravity aberration signal. In the background, a rhythmic drumming cautioned that the *Alchemon* had lost a significant portion of its internal telemetry system.

What the hell happened?

The final airseal flashed open and then he was on the bridge and in his command chair. Jonomy sat at the far side of his data circle, eyes tightly closed, the umbilical reconnected to the hole in his forehead and drooping over his shoulder to the floor.

Rigel barreled through another airseal and threw his sweat-covered bulk into a chair on the bridge's perimeter. The tech officer began typing madly into a terminal.

Ericho rubbed his sore neck, forced patience. Jonomy's expression indicated that he was totally interfaced with the computer, and Rigel would be manually questioning the network. Ericho would learn soon enough what had occurred.

Rigel shouted first. "The problem's in downdeck, southwest section!"

The containment and the lab! It had to be. Other than one of the lander holds and the entrance to the west storage pod, there was nothing else down there of any consequence.

And Dianaldi had been heading toward that section.

But what could the lieutenant have done to cause this much pandemonium? No more than a minute could have elapsed between the time Dianaldi knocked him down and the advent of the alarms. An explosion? There had been that heavy vibration in the corridor. And an explosion would account for most of the alarms. His heart pounded. *Purgefire!* The radiation alert! If Dianaldi had somehow set off a nuclear detonation, half the ship could be gone.

Jonomy's eyes opened and began blinking rapidly, a sign that he had released himself from the computer enough to permit conversation.

"Total sensor loss in the containment and the lab, Captain. Low level gamma radiation in the adjacent corridor. Every system down there has been terminated. Status of Lieutenant Dianaldi is unknown. The final transmission from the ID monitor outside the lab indicates that he passed through approximately sixteen seconds prior to the incident."

Jesus! "What could he have done?"

"Unknown at present, Captain. Every piece of hardware down there registered a near-simultaneous overload and then dropped out of the system. About seven seconds later, significant radioactivity was detected by the corridor sensors in and around the lab door. I'm trying to locate surveillance files of those final seconds inside the lab. It appears that several of the Sentinels were awakened prior to the actual incident, which means there's a good chance of getting video."

Ericho nodded. Sentinel alerts usually triggered emergency surveillance systems.

The Lytic began to blink more rapidly. "I'm having problems withdrawing data, however. The mishap has literally given the computer a traumatic shock. The network is currently trying to restructure itself, reroute lost elements into temporary subsystems. And there are Sentinels everywhere, Captain—Level One is almost completely cut off."

Rigel cursed. "What about those air vents into the lab— any radiation leakage there?"

Jonomy activated several bridge monitors. Each showed an identical scene: a ceiling camera's view of the corridor outside the lab. The bulky portal was to the left, about ten meters from the camera. The whole vista appeared innocent.

"The air vents in the lab were sealed by Sentinels seconds before the incident," said Jonomy. "Maintenance pups were dispatched into those tubes to monitor leakage. So far, there's been none."

The multiple alarms still wailed, although they were somewhat muffled by the bridge acoustics. Ericho spun to Rigel. "Has everyone reported in?"

"No. I can't locate Mars Lea. I've sent a call into every private area on the ship. She's not responding. And Dianaldi of course—"

"Everyone else accounted for?" Ericho demanded sharply.

The tech officer nodded. "June's on her way to the medcenter. Alan's at his emergency station in backup control. Hardy and Elke are in there with him."

Ericho turned back to the Lytic. "Override all this noise— just leave the flashers on so everyone knows we're still on alert. Can you get a Sentinel to look inside Mars Lea's cabin?"

"No, Captain, at least not right now. The Sentinels hav
their own priorities and they are very busy."

"Fuck their priorities," growled Rigel. He jumped to his
feet. "I'll go look for her."

Ericho shook his head. "No, I want you here. Jonomy,
tell Hardy and Elke to start searching for her, room by
room. Tell them to check her cabin first." He paused.
"Could she have been in the lab with Dianaldi?"

Jonomy did not answer. He closed his eyes again, mind-
locked himself fully into the computer.

The alarms fizzled out, one by one, until the bridge was
cloaked in silence. Ericho drew a sharp breath, rubbed his
bruised neck. His guts had begun to throb and he suspected
that Dianaldi's kick had, at the very least, bruised his ribs.

Jonomy's eyes popped open. "Two maintenance pups
have updated, Captain. They've discovered minute radiation leakage around the vent seals above the lab. They're
scouring and report that it's presently controllable."

Ericho nodded. "What about the corridor?"

"Higher levels out there, up to four rems in the immediate
vicinity of the door. It's increasing. IBS has declared the corridor
an unsafe zone and is preparing to activate cleanup pups."

Rigel grunted, then said what no one wanted to hear. "If
it's that hot outside the door, then the inside of the lab must
be almost molten. That airseal was made to withstand just
about anything."

Jonomy did not respond. Ericho continued staring at the
monitor. Unless Dianaldi had managed some sort of a mir-
acle down there, he was dead.

Ericho balled his fists. "Could it have been a mininuke?"

"No, Captain. It was not that severe. We would have
registered shock waves all over the ship."

"I felt a vibration down in the corridor."

"It wasn't a mininuke," agreed Rigel. "That kind of
shitstorm would have taken out half the ship—we probably
wouldn't be here talking about it." He paused as a message
came through on his terminal. "Elke and Hardy are searching for Mars Lea. They're on their way to her cabin—"

Jonomy broke in. "Captain, I've located the video seg-
ment from inside the lab. See for yourself."

The view took shape on Ericho's monitor. It was from a
ceiling camera inside the containment lab. Dianaldi was
racing through the room.

Jonomy spoke quietly. "These are the final nine seconds before the incident. Notice what the lieutenant has in his hand."

Dianaldi was clutching a short stubby cylinder.

"A goddamn laser-cutter," Rigel muttered. "Where the fuck did he get that?"

Ericho felt suddenly drained. It did not really matter where Tom had gotten the device. The important thing was that he must have had it with him throughout the Homebound. *I should have searched him.*

I should have been more careful. I should have relieved him of duties weeks ago, safely vegetated him until we returned to Earth. I should have known something like this could happen.

He sighed, realizing that now was not the time for self-recrimination. He forced himself to watch the inevitable unfolding of events on the screen.

Dianaldi raced to a sealed storage cabinet in the center of the lab, turned on the laser-cutter's tiny beam, and used it to cut through the lock. He yanked open the cabinet, exposing a large rectangular fusion battery on the bottom shelf. He directed the incinerating blue beam of the laser-cutter straight into the side plate of the fusion cell. It took less than a second for the laser to burn through the battery's thick shielding.

An instant of frozen time. The viewscreen went white.

No one spoke. On a starship that possessed safeguards against the unimaginable, an insane man had performed a simple act. An active laser source had been applied to the unstable elements of a fusion cell. Precise physics had determined the result: a melt, an expanding ball of intensely hot fire, absorbing all nearby matter in the space of microseconds.

Rigel broke the silence. "We're lucky it was the lab. Most of the other areas on the ship don't have such thick walls."

Ericho nodded solemnly. Had Dianaldi orchestrated his violent death somewhere else, the *Alchemon* could have been severely damaged, perhaps even destroyed.

Elke's taut voice came over the intercom. "We're in Mars Lea's cabin. She's not here."

"Keep searching," ordered Ericho. "I don't think she was in the lab—at least the video doesn't show her in there. She has to be somewhere."

Elke's voice rose in pitch, began to crack. "Is . . . To. . . . is he—"

"He's gone," said Ericho coldly. "Keep searching for Mars Lea. Report as soon as you've located her. Bridge out."

He turned back to Jonomy. "Do you think the containment itself was breached?"

"Absolutely. That glass wall was not powerful enough to withstand a melt. All of our sensors in there are also nonfunctional.

"And that vibration you felt, Captain. I believe it was caused by explosions in the lab, following the melt. Hardy stored a variety of pressurized canisters down there."

Rigel said, "If the containment was breached, then blue blob was probably incinerated as well."

"Possibly," replied Jonomy.

The tech officer continued. "All right. Let's suppose that the creature's been destroyed. That means we essentially have two useless chambers, both hot as hell, filled with radioactive waste. We might be able to clean up the outside corridor and keep the air vents sealed, but that mess in there is going to be hot for a long time, and it's going to keep on leaking. I say we blow the airlock hatches in the containment chute and give the whole mess a vacuum enema—blow it out into space."

Ericho raised his eyebrows to Jonomy. The idea sounded good.

The Lytic spoke slowly. "In theory, your suggestion is sound. Sudden depressurization should work, making the eventual cleanup far easier. However, there are two problems. One—we're not positive the creature has been killed. Remember, Rigel, that this is the same life form that survived for over a half million years in a horrendous environment on Sycamore. For all we know, it might be capable of surviving a melt."

"No way," muttered Rigel.

"Problem two is a bit more fundamental. We can't open the inner containment seal because we can't control it. That airseal was knocked out of the system just like everything else down there. And even if we could reroute the controls, the mechanism itself has probably been fused by the intense heat."

Rigel came to his feet. "Fine. Then we go outside the

, crawl up the chute, and plant a small explosive charge the inner lock. We open the outer lock, set off the charge, and blow it. Same result."

"You're forgetting about the creature," said Jonomy calmly.

"Fuck the creature. It's gone."

"We don't know that."

"We've got a goddamn melt down there! I say blow the mess out—"

"Enough!" snapped Ericho.

Hardy's voice emerged from the intercom. "We've found Mars Lea, Captain. She was asleep in the dreamlounge."

"She's still asleep," said Elke, her voice coming from somewhere in the background. "We can't seem to wake her."

"Take her straight to the medcenter," Ericho ordered.

Hardy spoke calmly. "Captain, I realize we're in an emergency situation and that we've lost a crew member. Nevertheless, I would like to remind you that the life form in the containment may have survived whatever devastation occurred. I urge you to assume that our creature is still alive until proven otherwise."

Rigel opened his mouth to speak but Ericho silenced him with a wave of the arm. Hardy and Jonomy were right. The creature might have survived. They could not risk vacuuming the lab without knowing for certain.

"All right, Hardy. We're going to check out the lab before we take any action."

The science rep sounded relieved. "Thank you, Captain."

Ericho wondered just how reasonable Hardy would be later on. Captains might not be considered the masters of their vessels, but Ericho knew from experience who got blamed when things went wrong.

He sat up. There was no point in dwelling on future trouble; he had enough problems to face right now.

"Rigel, break out a cyberlink. I'm going to take a look inside the lab."

Grumbling, the tech officer moved to obey.

10

Mars Lea floated, engulfed by the blackness. Far away, on the edge of perception, distant stars shone, tiny sparks of life burning through that tapestry of endless night. Fear seemed to be closing in on her like a contracting balloon, crushing her as it collapsed. She tried to ignore the fear, tried to concentrate on the reality beyond it: the starfield; impassioned gems, hope against the omnipotent blackness and the terror that it brought.

But the more she concentrated on the stars, the more distant and lifeless they seemed to become. The contracting balloon of fear touched her and a silent scream emerged from her body. She lunged outward, away from the terror, toward the stars, toward her only possible escape.

The stars betrayed her. They mutated into something other than stars, becoming mere points of cold light. Threads of energy erupted from each one, reaching across the blackness to connect together, forming an icy gridwork of glowing strands.

A vast spiderweb, linking the universe.

From out of the blackness came a voice; some alien presence, a light of consciousness. In desperation, she reached for it.

Fear is the entrance, Mars Lea. The alien words washed over her and she knew that it was the same voice—the same consciousness—that had spoken to her in the pool. It was the voice that had said, "Sentinels obey."

Go where you cannot go, the inner voice continued. *Enter the—*

"No!" Mars Lea screamed, rising. Hands grabbed at her shoulders, tried to push her back down. She opened her eyes and squinted as white light poured into her head.

She was lying on her back. June Courthouse was leaning across the bed, gripping her shoulders. Above the crewdoc's head, the jagged monstrosity of a medical soothe-scanner hung like some multitentacled creature poised to spring.

"Let me go!"

June released her shoulders, allowed her to sit up. Mars Lea looked into the soft black face, saw the lines of worry, the concern.

She felt her mouth quivering as she spoke. "I'm . . . all right. I had . . . a nightmare. I'm fine now." She threw her legs over the edge of the bed. June backed away, gave her room to stand.

They were in one of the tiny private rooms of the med-center—a white cell softly lit; the bed and soothe-scanner, a chair, a table with a small orb of fresh blue roses from one of the ship's gardens. Mars Lea slid her feet to the floor. A rush of dizziness almost knocked her over.

"Take a deep breath," suggested the crewdoc.

She sat on the edge of the bed and gulped air. "What happened to me?"

June hesitated. "You were found . . . sleeping. In the dreamlounge."

The dreamlounge? She hated that place. It was too disturbing, too unreal.

"How did I get there?"

The crewdoc shrugged. "You don't remember?"

"No." She recalled leaving Jonomy, leaving the containment lab. She remembered wanting to take a walk. And then . . .

Her heart raced with the memory of terror: the blackness, the stars imprisoned in a vast spiderweb, the alien voice urging her toward some greater horror . . .

June gripped her hand. "You had a psionic experience, didn't you?"

"I . . . think so."

"Do you want to talk about it?"

"No."

"It might be important. And it might make you feel better if you let it out."

"No."

June sighed.

Mars Lea twisted her wrist until the crewdoc released her hand. "I'm all right," she insisted.

June shook her head sternly. "No, I don't believe that you are. And I can't help you if you won't talk to me."

"I want to go back to my cabin."

June hesitated. "It would be better if you stayed here, for a little while, at any rate."

"Why?"

The crewdoc ran her fingers along one of the soothe-scanner's jointed mechanical arms. She seemed unwilling to answer.

"What happened?" Mars Lea demanded.

"There's been an accident."

11

―――――――――――――

"Move your right foot," Jonomy instructed.

Ericho could see nothing; the Lytic's words came to him from speakers inside his cyberlink headpiece. He lifted his heavy boot and dragged it forward. A soft hum filled the helmet and the weight of the suit decreased as gravity transducers came on. The cyberlink was now correctly positioned within a small outlined circle beside the bridge's north wall.

The inside of his visorless helmet came to life; three-score of evenly spaced control dots, alternating columns of gold and green, glimmered brightly. Above the dots, twin monitor screens dissolved into serrated test patterns. Below, a miniature readout informed him that the cyberlink had achieved full operational status.

Jonomy said, "Captain, you'll be using robot number two. Your location is downdeck northwest, closet twelve."

Ericho nodded, then remembered that the motion could not be seen by the Lytic. It did not matter; Jonomy was a step ahead of him. The monitor test patterns vanished as the robot's twin camera lenses opened. Through the robot's eyes, Ericho saw a dimly lit wall: the interior of the tiny storage closet.

He could not actually see the robot, since for all practical purposes he was inside it, but memory sketched a good image. The robot was man-sized, and covered with an outer layer of rubbery skin to protect it from shocks. The head boasted a pastiche of specialized sensors and, except for the camera-eyes, more closely resembled a small communications satellite than a human pate. Arms and legs were inhumanly thin, yet strong and fully bendable at the joints.

"Captain, I'm opening the closet."

Bright light filled his screens as the airseal parted from the wall. He glanced at the status readout. All green.

"System checks are positive at this end, Captain."

Ericho had not used a cyberlink for some time, but

he quickly readapted to its strange actuality. On the bridge, he moved his right leg forward; in the downdeck closet, the cyberlinked robot responded with an identical stride. He "walked" out into the corridor and turned south. By the time the robot reached the next airseal, the comfortable illusion that he was actually striding through the ship solidified in his mind.

In reality, Ericho would never step beyond the perimeter of the small circular treadmill on the bridge. But through the *Alchemon*'s complex circuitry, his every move would be translated by the cyberlink into an equal action by the robot. A machine, not a man, would enter the contaminated lab.

"Captain, the corridor radiation levels have stabilized. The cleanup pups are holding their own."

He passed an external maintenance lock and, twenty meters farther on, the airseal junction where the transverse shaft intersected this downdeck west corridor. A few meters ahead lay the section of irradiated passageway adjacent to the containment lab.

"I'm at the final airseal."

"Very good. Remember, Captain, you are going to have to move quite fast once I open the door. PEH has created a slight pressure differential to prevent contaminated air from escaping. Even so, the Sentinels will only permit me to open the airseal for five and a half seconds."

Rigel grunted. "Plenty of time. Just keep your arms tight against your body. Those goddamn Sentinels aren't playing games. That airseal might try and shut in five and a half seconds whether you're through it or not."

"I'm ready."

The seal parted. He dashed through, twisting his head sharply to the left. In response to his exaggerated movement, the robot's head did a 180-degree spin, displaying a rear view of the airseal as it slammed shut behind him.

He moved his head back to center position, surveyed the twenty meters of corridor that lay before him. Red lumes flashed at regular intervals along the passageway, warning of the contamination. Five basketball-sized cleanup pups hovered around the lab door, soaking up the invisible radioactive poisons leaking from the edges of the heavy portal. Two of the pups had connected themselves to thin hoses that trailed along the corridor and vanished into an air vent near the south airseal. Contaminated air was being pumped through the *Alchemon* to radiation neutralizers located in the bowels of the ship. PEH was probably cycling fresh air back into the corridor through other vents.

Ericho blinked several times to moisten his eyes, then concentrated on the alternating rows of green and gold control dots on the inside of his helmet. Together, the sixty dots formed a sight-typer, similar in principle to one of the *Alchemon*'s computer terminals. But instead of fingers touching keys, microscopic lasers tracked his eyeball movements as he focused on particular sets of dots, then relayed his "typed" orders directly into the robot's circuitry.

Sight-typers were very effective in certain applications, but they were also tricky to use. A random blink in the middle of a sequence could negate or alter an entire command. Long ago, as a Pannis intern, Ericho had gotten a speck of dirt in his eye during a sight-typing exercise and had watched with horror as his robot tried to punch its way through a wall. The incident had been doubly embarrassing since he had completely forgotten about overriding his misguided robot with the cyberlink's thumb switch.

No such trouble plagued him now. He completed sight-typing his order, then blinked three times to initiate the sequence. His twin screens dissolved into a thermic overlay of the lab door. He approached slowly.

The center of the airseal appeared dark, but toward the edges, blues and violets melted into brighter colors. A white ribbon outlined the actual perimeter of the door—the hottest area, where most of the leakage was occurring.

He moved his eyes back to the typer and keyed another command. A long list of radioactive isotopes flashed across his display monitor.

Jonomy spoke with his usual patience. "Captain, there's no need for you to run any scans. We already have a full breakdown of the corridor contamination."

Ericho nodded absently. "Just checking." He was wasting time and he knew it. Fusion melts left ugly results; he recognized his own unwillingness to enter the lab.

He took a deep breath and sight-typed a third command. A thick rod extended itself from the robot's chest. He gripped the rod firmly with his right arm and guided the flexible device to a spot above the door's control panel. He squeezed. A pencil-thin beam of blue light leaped from the barrel of the laser-cutter. Where the beam touched the door, plasticized metal began to bubble and melt. It took only seconds for the laser to burn a hole through the door's thick outer membrane.

Quickly, he reached his hand through the hot opening and felt around inside until he located the door's emergency activation lever. He shoved the lever sideways and withdrew his arm.

He waited. Five seconds. Ten.

Nothing.

He frowned. The airseal should have opened. "Jonomy, could the Sentinels be interfering? Maybe they're not going to allow us to enter." With the lab door open, the corridor would be flooded with far higher levels of radioactive contamination.

"Captain, both PEH and IBS believe that they can handle any additional contamination, provided you can get the door shut behind you once you're in the lab. Also, the entire network is, for lack of a better word, curious. The *Alchemon* wants to assess the internal damage as much as we do.

"The Sentinels aren't interfering, Captain. All evidence indicates that the inside of the door is fused along the perimeter. Give the emergency system some more time. It is entirely located within the door and it is heavily shielded. It should not have been damaged."

"It's a smart system," Rigel said, "and fully independent. It's probably looking at options, trying to figure the best way to get the door open."

"It has its own lasers," added Jonomy. "It may be attempting to cut through the fused metal."

Ericho thought they were both being too optimistic.

A sharp hiss sounded in the corridor and he took an involuntary step backward.

Groaning, the heavy portal slid back. Thick white smoke poured into the corridor, engulfing him.

"Inside, Captain," the Lytic urged. "Quickly!"

He could see nothing. He stepped through the portal, spun the robot around, and fumbled for the inner control of the door's emergency system. But before he could locate it, the door groaned shut.

"Excellent, Captain."

"I didn't do anything. It closed by itself."

There was no response.

"Jonomy, do you read me?"

"Yes, Captain. I was just considering your statement. The emergency system's sole intelligence applies to finding ways for opening or shutting that airseal in critical situations. But any action *must* be precipitated by a direct manual command."

"A malfunction," answered Rigel.

"That is the highest probability," Jonomy agreed.

Ericho asked, "Could the Sentinels have found a way into the emergency system?"

"I don't believe so, Captain."

"Then it must have been a malfunction." Ericho sight-typed for alterations in his camera frequencies, seeking a way to penetrate the thick layers of white smoke. Infrared proved useless. Ultraviolet and X rays likewise had no effect.

"Ambient radiation is too high," said Jonomy. "The entire spectrum is distorted. You should be able to get some clear imagery with ultrasound."

He sight-typed new instructions, watched computer-enhanced outlines take shape on his screens. Even though he knew roughly what to expect, the images shocked him.

The center of the lab was gone—no consoles, no equipment racks, no floor—nothing. A small molten lake, bubbling wickedly, was all that remained. Only the indomitable force of the *Alchemon*'s simulated gravity plane, sweeping beneath what had once been the deck, had prevented the molten energy from burning straight down through the hull.

Above, the ceiling looked remarkably like a rough slice of cheese, badly warped and sprinkled with holes. The walls had suffered similar damage: Cabinets and canisters—the ones that had not exploded—were melted into the distorted side panels. A floor still remained around the perimeter of the room, although it looked more like the lunar surface than the base of a lab. In the far corner, a stalagmite grew out of the twisted deck. It had once been a chair.

"A goddamn mess," muttered Rigel.

Ericho felt a sense of relief. Even though logic dictated otherwise, some dark fantasy had hinted that he might find Dianaldi's badly charred remains. Tom had obviously perished instantly, his body incinerating within the first microseconds of the melt.

Ericho guided the robot around the outside perimeter of the lab, staying as close to the walls as possible. This part of the floor seemed stable enough, though he suspected that it would not take much for the robot to fall through into the molten mass below.

The wall separating the lab from the containment area had disintegrated. A few slabs of what looked like frosted ice hung from the ceiling; below, a jagged lip was all that remained of the original floor line. Ericho stepped carefully over the debris and entered the containment.

Inside, the damage did not appear quite as severe—the wall had probably absorbed a great deal of the melt's initial energy. Nevertheless, floor and walls were badly distorted. Enclosed racks containing monitoring equipment drooped from the ceiling.

In the far corner, next to the semimelted airseal leading to the containment chute, lay the creature.

"I believe it's dead," said Jonomy. "I'm getting no bio-readouts from your sensors, Captain."

Ericho approached cautiously, even while recognizing the inherent inanity of his prudence. He remained safely encased in the cyberlink control suit on the bridge. But his emotions had "shifted" into the lab.

Something sizzled loudly behind him. He whirled. There was nothing there.

"Sensor burnout," said Jonomy calmly. "In your primary modules, Captain. I've shifted that system over to secondaries."

He chuckled, feeling foolish. The sound had come from the back of the robot's head.

Blue blob lay on its side. The gelatinous skin appeared badly charred. Ericho bent over the organism and sight-typed a command for a more detailed bioscan. A needle probe slid from the robot's arm and punctured the creature's flesh.

"Nothing," said Jonomy. "No signs of internal metabolic activity, Captain. I'm quite certain it's dead."

Ericho sighed. He would probably be known throughout history as the starship captain responsible for destroying the scientific find of the century.

"Any suggestions for preserving the carcass?"

"Captain, our best plan of action would be to free that inner seal, guide an ecocapsule up the containment chute, and then transfer the remains to one of the storage pods."

"Rigel?"

"I still say we blow the seals and dump blue blob along

with the rest of that mess." There was a long pause. "But Jonomy's idea would be my second choice. The storage pods are isolated enough from the rest of the ship so that whatever contamination we put in there shouldn't pose much of a problem."

Ericho nodded. "And after that, we vacuum the lab—dump everything into space."

"Affirmative, Captain."

Ericho examined the airseal next to the creature. "It looks badly melted. And knowing how thick the external locks are—"

"It may take hours to cut through," finished Jonomy.

"Let me do it," urged Rigel. "I'm more experienced with cutting jobs. I can probably laser through in half the time."

"All right. I'm coming out of the cyberlink—"

"Don't shut the robot down completely," the Lytic warned. "We've already lost one of the sensor packages and it could prove difficult to reactivate some of the other systems once they've been deenergized."

"I'll put it on standby."

The robot was being slowly destroyed by the intense radioactive exposure; this foray into the lab was a one-way expedition. Any process of decontamination would be far too complex to be cost-effective.

Jonomy had estimated that the robot would remain at least partially functional for five or six hours before the intense heat and concentration of unstable isotopes finally rendered it totally inoperative. They would dump it into space along with everything else.

"Captain, I'm reading a slight power surge in the robot. Its main batteries are located inside the shoulders. Has any of that circuitry been exposed to the elements?"

Ericho raised his arms and ran his palms across the machine's thick shoulder pads, then across the sensor-studded head. He frowned. "I can't feel anything."

"We had better transfer the cyberlink over to Rigel as quickly as possible. The malfunction rate is proving to be higher than I initially computed. A power surge could be the forerunner of serious system problems."

Ericho nodded absently, then sight-typed a standby command. The robot straightened and froze in position.

"I'm coming out."

12

There were places on the *Alchemon* that felt bad.

Mars Lea disliked the so-called gardens, east and west, with their claustrophobic conglomerations of submerged plants and twisted piping. The four lander holds, full of scarred metal, seemed to shape dreariness into something more tangible, more unpleasant. The containment lab . . .

At least she would never have to enter that place again.

Still, none of those areas upset her as much as the dreamlounge.

The room appeared to be of tremendous size. In front of her, a golden desert, swept by gentle winds, spread out to the horizon. In the distance, a range of mountains rose from the arid floor; dry, molasses-colored ridges slicing through splotches of organic green, each mountain narrowing until it erupted into an icy summit framed against a cloudless blue sky.

The illusion filled the room, extending beyond her peripheral vision. Only by turning completely around could she see past the holographic vista, locate the drab white walls and the dark airseal defining the dreamlounge's true perimeter.

She wanted to run from this place but dared not. The others, standing beside her, would never understand.

A dry breeze touched her face and the aroma of the desert filled her nostrils. She heard the soft rustle of flowing sand, of winds whistling across stunted cactus and over rock faces scarred by centuries of erosion. The room's dehumidifiers sucked moisture from the air, forcing her even to taste the dryness.

This is not real—this is illusion. The thought calmed her. She would endure the ceremony by concentrating on that idea. She would look out upon this fantasy and see only a thirty-foot square room.

It was not the desert vista itself that disturbed her; it was the possibilities inherent in the dreamlounge. By scanning the *Alchemon*'s library, or merely by creating from one's own imagination, the holographic machinery could be programmed to display an almost infinite variety of locales, blessing each with sounds and smells and textures.

This was only the second time in Mars Lea's life that she had willingly entered an activated dreamlounge. The first occasion had occurred during childhood. She remembered being taken to a huge theater by her mother, being seated in a plush chair, waiting excitedly for the lights to go down. And then . . . the front wall of the theater had dissolved into a raging ocean and a massive tidal wave had swept down to engulf the patrons in the front rows.

Mars Lea had screamed.

The terror had been too real; for the first time in her life, she had been hurtled, for an instant, into the psionic netherworld. She had touched the blackness.

When June Courthouse had explained to her that she had been found sleeping in this dreamlounge after the accident, Mars Lea had been aghast, unwilling to believe the crewdoc.

Why would I come here?

It made no sense.

June stood beside Mars Lea, looking very dignified in the formal garb of a Pannis medical officer: a creased blue formsuit with gold medallions laced across the shoulder pads. The crewdoc appeared calm. Next in line was Elke, casually dressed, her body stiff, shoulders thrown back, eyes locked into some unreadable stare.

Hardy and Alan, like June, were formally attired. Both men had assumed identical poses; their chins raised and their hands folded behind their backs, like soldiers prepared for duty. Rigel, dressed in a dirty gray jumpsuit, stood with his arms sprawled leisurely across his massive chest. He looked bored.

The captain faced them all. Age lines rippled his brow and his voice sounded old, tired.

"We're ready, Jonomy."

In the sky, beyond the range of icy peaks, a ball of hazy white light took shape. Music faded in: a synthesized piano melody with some stringed instrument lilting in the background. The piece was by an ancient composer, Pachelbel: the Canon in D Major. The captain had explained that the music had been listed in Dianaldi's file as a personal favorite.

High in the imaginary sky, the ball of light moved toward them. As it approached, it began to coalesce into the face of the lieutenant. The hologram must have been recorded years ago, or else an artist had enhanced it, for the image portrayed did not match the man that Mars Lea had known on the *Alchemon*. The three-dimensional creation showed a relaxed and good-looking Tom Dianaldi: ruddy cheeks, a warm open face, quiet brown eyes; a creature at peace with himself.

The captain began reciting. "We gather to honor the spirit of Thomas Andrew Dianaldi, Class Four officer of the Pannis Consortium, bridge lieutenant of the starship *Alchemon*. Born thirty-four years ago at the Keith Observatory, Earth orbit. Activity trained in the Corporeal schools of Holbrook-Hastings. A graduate, with honors, of the Academy of Primary Sciences . . ."

The eulogy continued; the face in the sky grew larger, moving closer to where they stood. Mars Lea found herself caught up in the vision, absorbed by the emotions it engendered. Yet at the same time, she remained a great distance away. The dreamlounge imagery—the desert, the mountains, Dianaldi—took on a quality of translucence, as if she were trapped within a slab of glass, witness to her emotions, yet held distinct from them.

Tragedy. She knew instinctively that it was the lieutenant's death that had caused her to experience that sensation on Sycamore, when they had first discovered the creature. Mars Lea had psionically touched the future; she had perceived his demise.

But even that explanation did not fully encompass the word/thought. Tragedy was like a great castle, chambering many halls and rooms, a domain of possibilities. And these other places remained just out of reach, ramifications suspended on the event horizon beyond consciousness. She was caught up in *Ta-shad*—the psionic experience that could not be experienced.

She drew a deep breath and clenched her fists.

The captain continued reciting, tracing the lieutenant's history, his past assignments, decorations for meritorious duty, his family, his outside activities. He had been an ocean fisherman, and an amateur historian. He had enjoyed camping in the great woodlands of Canada.

Elke began to cry.

The hologram stopped moving, hung in the sky almost directly above them. Mars Lea wanted to run. But *Ta-shad* was overpowering—she felt as if she were being sucked into a swirling vortex of psionic possibilities. She stared up at the lieutenant's face and the thought came to her that this was how he had always wanted to appear.

Her fists tightened; sharp nails dug into the flesh of her palms. The baroque melody soared to greater heights as more strings entered the fray, fighting a gentle battle for preeminence with the synthesized piano.

" . . . and as captain of the *Alchemon*, I decree that Tom Dianaldi's chosen epitaph be forever bound into the Corporeal flow." The captain paused, read from a small card held at arm's length. "The only evil is that which prevents the individual."

Elke's sobs filled the room; a tear ran down June Courthouse's cheek. Alan's face broke into a series of strange expressions, the flesh expanding and contracting, like some faulty hologram trying to hold itself together. If Hardy and Rigel were affected, they did not show it.

Mars Lea felt her palms growing moist. She looked down, saw tiny rivulets of blood running from between her clenched fingers. Her sharp nails had pierced the flesh. She tried to open her fists and was surprised when she could not. Carefully, so as not to attract attention, she placed her hands behind her back. She hoped none of the others had noticed that she had hurt herself.

Up in the sky, the lieutenant's image began to shrink and drift back out over the desert. Pachelbel's Canon reached its soaring epiphany, with countless stringed instruments now encircling the piano, a dizzying array of satellites orbiting a central melody.

"Does anyone wish to add anything?" asked the captain, solemnly, as if the words were mere ritual and did not require a response. He waited a moment and then said, "All right, Jonomy, we're ready."

The music faded. Dianaldi's face began to break up, forming a mass of discrete digitized fragments. The fragments exploded, becoming a cloud of particles, a symmetry of sand poised above the desert. For one perfect instant, the particles hung together, like a hazy thunderstorm seen from a great distance. And then the cloud dissolved. It rained sand.

"Ashes to ashes, dust to dust," June murmured.

The desert hologram vanished and the seven of them were left standing in an empty chamber with plain white walls. Elke, crying uncontrollably, turned and fled through the airseal.

Silence.

The captain sighed. "All right, we all have our duties to attend to. We're still on emergency status, but that's just precautionary. All major systems are back to normal. We've survived the incident—the ship is in pretty good shape."

Hardy cleared his throat. "Captain, you've had time to consider my request. I would like an answer."

Mars Lea watched the captain's features slowly dissolve into a frown. "I haven't reached a decision yet."

"The longer you wait, Captain, the longer our journey will become. You know yourself that you cannot refuse."

"Refuse what?" asked June.

Rigel strode forward, monster hands planted on his hips. "Hardy wants to return to Sycamore. Those bacterial samples were also lost in the mishap. He wants us to drop back down to the surface and collect some more."

"The Sycom strain," Hardy pointed out, "provided the initial focus for this expediion. The loss of the creature has already turned this expedition into something of a disaster. It would be doubly foolish to return to Earth without samples of the living bacteria."

"We've had a serious accident—" Ericho began.

"Accident?" Hardy bristled. "We have had a tragedy based on command negligence. Please do not compound your error, Captain."

June shook her head. "For our own safety, Hardy, I believe we should return to Earth as soon as possible. With all the maneuvering necessary to turn the ship around, we'd surely lose several days in transit,"

"At least a week, total," said Rigel.

"I don't think we can afford that," added June.

"Why not?" Hardy demanded.

The crewdoc hesitated. "There are medical problems . . . the forces that affected the lieutenant . . . they could affect all of us."

Hardy scowled. "What forces? What are you talking about?"

Mars Lea felt a lump in her throat. She opened her fists

...d held her bloody palms outward for all to see. "She's .alking about me. I killed the lieutenant."

"Jesus Christ," muttered Rigel, staring at her hands.

June grabbed Mars Lea's wrists, wiped away the blood with a handkerchief, examined the wounds. "It's all right, they're just nail punctures, not too deep." The crewdoc gently lifted her chin. "I want you to come to the medcenter with me. We'll get this taken care of."

I killed him. Mars Lea was suddenly sure of it. She had psionically destroyed the lieutenant—not deliberately, perhaps, but the reasons ultimately did not matter. He was dead. She was responsible.

She wanted to cry but the tears would not come.

The captain moved to stand before her. "Mars Lea, Lieutenant Dianaldi committed suicide. He may have been affected by your psionic preence, but even that remains uncertain. At any rate, you can't blame yourself for his actions. He took his own life."

"Listen to Ericho," pleaded June. "It is not your fault, Mars Lea. You meant the lieutenant no harm. We all know that. And none of us blame you for his death."

"This is all nonsense," snapped Hardy.

The captain held his anger in check. "For the safety of this expedition, Hardy, I have to agree with June. The *Alchemon* is faced with . . . special problems. The longer we delay, the more at risk we place ourselves. We won't be going back to Sycamore."

Hardy's voice rose. "Captain Brad, I am ordering you to return to the planet. And as science rep on this ship, I am within my rights to issue such a command!"

"Perhaps," said Ericho calmly. "But I am within my rights to ignore it."

Hardy shook. He raised his finger and wagged it at the captain's face. "You will regret such a decision. I will personally see to it that Pannis has your command when we return! You will never set foot on a starship again!" In fury, the science rep turned and marched from the room.

"Bastard," muttered Rigel.

"He'll calm down," said Ericho, still gazing at Mars Lea.

She could not meet his eyes. She could not look at any of them. She stared at the floor.

"Hardy has his corpse," said Ericho softly. "He has the

remains of blue blob to occupy him for the rest of journey. He'll calm down."

Mars Lea knew that the captain did not believe that.

Jonomy's voice filled the chamber. "Captain, we'll be ready to flush the containment in about an hour."

"Any problems?" Ericho asked.

"No, Captain. Rigel cut through the inner airseal cleanly and deposited the remains of the creature in the ecocapsule. One of the outside maintenance pups just finished rewelding the containment seal. The lock's been repressurized and the ecocapsule is on its way to the west storage pod. As soon as the creature has been safely deposited and the ecocapsule scoured, we'll be ready for a vacuum purge."

Ericho nodded. "All right. Alan?"

The intern eagerly stepped forward. "Yes, sir?"

"I'd like you to go to backup control until we've vacuumed the lab. Just as a precaution."

"Yes, sir."

The captain faced Mars Lea again. She tried to meet his gaze, could not.

"Do not blame yourself," he repeated. "It is not your fault."

"Come," said June. "We'll take care of your hands."

Mars Lea closed her eyes and allowed herself to be led from the dreamlounge.

—From the papers of Thomas Andrew Dianaldi

Five years.

Five years ago, my obsession took root. Five years ago, Renfro Dackaman murdered my cabinmate on the Theodoris.

I've been secretly investigating Dackaman all that time, searching through the complexity of his personal finances, tracking down his vices, interviewing people whom he victimized during his steady climb up the Pannis hierarchy. I've learned a lot. I'm fairly certain that my cabinmate on the Theodoris *was not the first man that Dackaman killed, or had killed. Unfortunately, I can't prove that.*

Renfro Dackaman covers his tracks too well.

Yesterday, I saw Dackaman for the first time since the Theodoris *incident. We were both part of a large inspection tour aboard one of the new starships being constructed in lunar orbit. Pannis engineers and a couple of Lytics were*

ing us the latest technology designed to thwart chro-
muters.

Dackaman stood in the midst of a group of Pannis execs, *calmly* observing, and I could barely contain my fury. What made it almost unbearable was knowing that the bastard had been recently promoted; he was no longer a simple head-hunter, but a genuine Pannis Supervisor—probably his little reward for being such a good lackey all these years. Not bad for a murderer.

I kept my eye on him as we listened to a Lytic discuss chronomuters.

Chronomuters—temporal pirates. The consortiums, understandably, give little publicity to that curiously disturbing theorem of theoretical physics that states what will happen to you if you defeat your starship's safety circuits and ignite the Loop engines before actually entering the boundaries of a Loop.

In terms of movement across space, you go nowhere. But you get blasted forward in time—chronomuted—thrown into the future, and that is about all anyone really knows for certain. Few scientists are willing to predict just how far forward you will be hurtled—the calculations remain ridiculously complex, full of variables. A hundred years, a thousand, thirty-five million . . .

The bottom line is that chronomuting is a growing problem for the consortiums. Other eras had pilgrims and skyjackers, return-to-naturists and defectors. Our century has chronomuters.

"The consortiums naturally dislike having their starships hijacked into an unclaimable future," explained the Lytic. "And so we've introduced a little surprise for any potential chronomuters. If you attempt to temporally pirate one of these newer ships, Sentinels will automatically activate warrior pups—killer robots programmed to regard chronomuters as malfunctioning units."

For our demonstration, a pair of Class Five androids had been programmed to attempt to chronomute the ship. The androids had managed to unlock the Loop engine safety circuits. That was as far as they got. Two warrior pups flashed onto the bridge.

It was over in a matter of seconds. The androids were blown to bits.

But I didn't really pay much attention to the demonstration; I was watching Dackaman the whole time. Face flushed,

eyes watering with excitement, Renfro Dackaman stood there
and passionately absorbed the violence the way a sponge
sucks liquid. After it was over, he withdrew an icicle earring
from his pocket, ignited the microrefrigerator, and carefully
pinned it to his right lobe. And as the ice began to form a
tapered cylinder, Dackaman smiled.

I stood there in a cold rage, my mind full of deadly
fantasies, seeing Dackaman as one of those luckless androids,
his body being shredded by lasers and mag projectiles.

It's too bad I lack the courage to commit outright murder.

But even if I did, Dackaman deserves a worse fate. I've
cultivated my obsession for too long now to allow him to
escape without suffering.

13

The west diner, located between the dreamlounge and the bridge, was a tiny rectangular arena crammed full of cabinets, sinks, thermal/microwave cookers, and suspended minifreezers. Two tables, with attached seats, mushroomed from the floor, side by side, providing just enough clearance for diners to navigate between them without bumping into one another. A pair of skinny pups hung from the ceiling, awaiting verbal commands.

State-of-the-art Corporeal psychology indicated that meals were best digested when diners sat in cramped quarters and allowed pups to serve them. Ericho found the *Alchemon*'s twin dining areas claustrophobic. And he disliked serving pups, usually preferring to cook his own meals on one of the open ranges, using his personal set of antique replasticized Tupperware pans.

Today, though, he was tired; he had permitted the pups to take his order. The stir-fried rice and steamed veggies had tasted as good as if he had prepared them himself.

June sat across from him and Rigel had squeezed his bulk into the slightly smaller seat at the far end of the table. June nibbled on a piece of ship-grown celery. The tech officer sipped peppermint tea and suggested vegetating Mars Lea for the remainder of the voyage.

June sighed. "Rigel, I don't think it would do any good. The intensity of her superluminal powers remains strong whether she's awake or asleep."

"At least we wouldn't have to worry about her slicing her wrists," argued Rigel. "Or worse, going crazy like the lieutenant and trying to blow us up."

"She didn't slice her wrists," June said calmly. "She suffered minor cuts caused by extreme tension."

Ericho rubbed the side of his neck, the spot where Dianaldi's hand had chopped him. June had given him painkillers but it still hurt. His midsection had fared better.

There were no broken ribs, just a large expanse of bruised skin.

He shook his head. "Just the same, Rigel may be right. Mars Lea knows that she's responsible for driving Tom crazy. She might do something drastic."

The crewdoc scowled. "Mars Lea *thinks* that she killed Tom. She obviously affected him. But did she induce him to commit suicide? Did she actually make him enter the containment and destroy himself in a melt?"

Ericho shrugged. "According to Elke, Mars Lea expressed fears about the creature—she believed that it shouldn't be returned to Earth. Subconsciously, she could have psionically induced Tom into destroying blue blob . . . and himself."

"Even granting that she's a powerful Psionic," June argued, "that sounds pretty fantastic. And maybe we have this whole thing backward. Maybe it wasn't Mars Lea who caused Tom to trigger the melt. Blue blob was a strong source of superluminals. This creature was alone and trapped on the surface of an alien world for over half a million years. For all we know it wanted to die. Maybe *it* influenced Tom."

"You're saying this creature committed suicide?" Ericho shook his head. "I don't buy it."

"Why not?" said June. "After all those years alone, death could have been its only goal. Or maybe neither blue blob nor Mars Lea was ultimately responsible. Tom could have simply reached a state of psychosis on his own."

Ericho frowned. "Tom attacked me and entered the containment lab during the same short period that Jonomy was on his way from the lab to the bridge. By any normal means, Tom could not have known that Jonomy was in transit. From a certain perspective, it was perfect timing."

"And," Rigel added, "the son-of-a-bitch had that laser-cutter with him throughout the Homebound."

"Where did he get the laser?" June asked.

Ericho sighed. "Jonomy checked—there's one missing from the west mech repair shop. I saw Tom wandering around in there shortly before the Homebound. I should have suspected something."

"You couldn't have known what his intentions were," said June.

Ericho nodded. "Maybe not. But I should have watched him more closely."

Rigel shook his head, in agreement with June. "Hell, you

couldn't have known that he was planning to incinerate himself. Face it, the bastard put one over on all of us. Even our Lytic screwed up—Jonomy says he wasn't monitoring the mech repair shop when Tom stole the laser."

It doesn't matter, thought Ericho. *I'm responsible.*

"What does EPS say about all this?" June asked.

Rigel smiled grimly. "Jonomy ran the data; the computer attributes a negative probability to the entire event sequence. EPS says no way we're talking coincidence here."

The crewdoc gave a slow nod. "Does EPS have any concrete theories?"

"Improper data for conclusions."

June leaned back in her chair and pointed her finger at one of the ceiling pups. "Water, please."

The small robot filled a beaker from an overhead hose assembly, then descended to the table in front of the crewdoc. June took the beaker from the pup's thin arm and the servant returned to its ceiling slot.

She stared at the water. "Psionically, I suppose just about anything's possible. But I also think it's a waste of time trying to find reasons for Tom's final madness. Superluminal interaction remains outside the realm of our physics, beyond the understanding of our natural senses. We're talking about space/time conceptions that we do not even have mathematical formulas to explain.

"There is one theory . . . a vague idea, really . . . about a psionic universe existing all around us, a faster-than-light universe full of telempathic projectors, receptors, and conveyors, all influencing one another. This theory suggests that the effects of that interaction spill over into our universe, in turn influencing us.

"Most everyone possesses at least some level of psionic prowess, however unconscious. That psionic aspect, in each of us, would have a place within this other universe. But the truly powerful Psionics like Mars Lea . . . they would have an actual embodiment, so to speak, on the other side."

June continued staring into her beaker. She appeared to be transfixed by the water. "There are many facets of the paranormal that have not yet been franchised by the superluminal theorists. Our history is rich with examples—ghosts, ancient demons—"

The crewdoc stopped talking. Her eyes grew distant; she seemed to be hypnotized by the water.

"Ancient Babylonian demons?" suggested Ericho quietly.

June stared at him blankly for a moment, then broke into a wry smile. "Who knows?"

Rigel grunted. "I don't give a shit about ghosts and demons and parallel universes. I want to know what the hell we're going to do about Mars Lea."

Ericho faced the crewdoc. "All right. Let's assume we're all being affected, or are going to be affected, by this psionic storm emanating from her. Then we also have to assume that things are going to get worse. We're out of touch with Earth until we go through the Loop four and a half months from now, so that means we have to rely upon ourselves.

"You said that a more active sex life might cut down on her powers, but short of raping her, I don't think the males aboard this ship are going to have much luck in that regard. And you say that vegetating her won't do any good."

There was a touch of anger in June's reply. "I don't know what we can do. We have to figure out some way of lowering her tension levels, I suppose, force her to relax a bit. But I don't know how to do that. Drugs are useless—they seem to get her more wired, and that increases the psionic turmoil." The crewdoc gave a weary nod. "I'll go back through the library, see if there's any information on superluminals that I haven't already accessed—"

Jonomy's voice erupted from the intercom speaker. "Captain, there's something you should see. Please turn on your monitor."

Rigel gave a verbal order to one of the pups. The robot descended and rolled over to expose its flat bottom, which contained a fourteen-inch screen. The pup positioned itself so that all three of them could observe.

An image of the destroyed lab came into view, obviously originating from the cyberlink robot. It was a wide-angled shot, showing heavily damaged walls and a few of the distorted objects that had not been totally incinerated by the intense heat of the melt. As they watched, the scene changed: The cyberlink panned right and left and slowly began marching around the perimeter of the room. Ericho observed closely, but he could detect nothing out of the ordinary. Things appeared as they had when he had first guided the robot into the containment.

He glanced at June and Rigel, met puzzled stares. "Jonomy, what are we missing?"

"There's no one controlling the cyberlink, captain. It's operating by itself."

Ericho frowned. "A mechanical failure—the radiation buildup must have reached its servo programs."

"Captain, this would appear to be a very unlikely malfunction, involving a series of logic and servo systems that ordinarily do not interact."

"Did you try regaining control?"

"Yes. Neither the cybersuit nor direct programming commands have had any effect."

"Rigel?"

The tech officer spoke slowly, his attention riveted to the screen. "I don't know. That's one hell of a weird malfunction. I've never seen—"

The robot halted. Its head tilted back to display a view of the warped ceiling. Cameras zoomed in on one of the damaged vents.

"Captain, preignition of the robot's laser system has been confirmed. I believe it intends to burn through that air vent."

"Jesus Christ," muttered Rigel. "If that bastard cuts through, we'll have more radiation spillover."

"Jonomy, are we ready to vacuum purge?"

"No, Captain. The ecocapsule containing the creature's remains has not yet completed predocking procedures at the storage pod. A portion of the purge would definitely hit the capsule, possibly damaging it."

"How long?"

"Approximately another fourteen minutes."

"To hell with the creature," snapped Rigel.

"Captain, there's been a Sentinel alert. I believe our problem will be dealt with in another manner."

"How?" June asked.

Rigel abruptly relaxed and his face opened into a grin. "I've got a pretty good idea."

On the screen, the cyberlink's laser-cutter popped out of its chest cavity. The robot's arm was reaching for the trigger handle when the ceiling vent exploded inward. Thick dust and debris fell on the cyberlink's head.

Through the haze, they watched a silver sphere roughly the size of a basketball drop into the containment lab. A mélange of curved white panels, sensor probes, laser mirrors, and projectile launch tubes covered the shell of the small robot.

"Warrior pup," said Rigel, with a trace of excitement in his voice. "Multiple lasers, mag projectiles, defensive screens, and the nastiest attack guidance system ever designed. I wouldn't want to get one of them pissed at me."

The scene on the monitor flip-flopped; point of view changed to the warrior pup's main camera. An overhead panoramic shot of the containment lab came into focus with the cyberlink robot staring upward. The malfunctioning machine continued panning its head slowly back and forth.

"It looks confused," offered June.

Rigel scowled. "It's a goddamn robot with a messed up servo system. It doesn't get confused."

Jonomy remained calm. "Captain, the warrior pup had to blow out the ceiling vent to get in there, but the radiation's been contained in the section of duct immediately above the containment."

Ericho nodded absently. Warrior pup. There were four of them aboard the *Alchemon* and that was four too many. He had never liked the idea of these deadly little machines patrolling the corridors of starships, waiting for a Sentinel to activate them and send them out to destroy malfunctioning robots . . . or, if so ordered, malfunctioning humans.

The cyberlink stopped panning. It seemed to be frozen in place, the head leaning back to stare at the small silver fighter hovering above it. For a moment, the out-of-control machine was perfectly still. Then the cyberlink raised its arm and aimed the laser-cutter at the warrior pup.

The screen became a blur of motion as the warrior pup dropped in on its target. Blue laser light flashed between the two machines and for a moment it was impossible to tell which of the robots had fired.

Ericho breathed relief when a cloud of thick gray smoke poured from the cyberlink. The warrior pup's pencil-thin laser carved through the front spine of the malfunctioning robot, burning into its main servo package. The cyberlink jerked sideways; its left arm whipped through the air as if it were trying to grab hold of something for support. The warrior pup immediately ignited a second laser and neatly sliced off the grasping arm at the elbow.

"Burn that sucker," urged Rigel.

With blinding speed, the warrior pup moved, the scene

again blurred on the monitor, and suddenly the fighter was behind its target. Close-range projectiles blasted into the back of the cyberlink's head. Ericho imagined the miniature magnetic fields igniting around each bullet, distorting what little of the robot's logic circuitry remained active.

The cyberlink's leg servos gave out and it started to fall backward. A coiled arm exploded from a compartment in the warrior pup and a pincerlike hand grabbed the cyberlink's neck, preventing its tumble. The fighter ascended, easily lifting the destroyed robot up off the deck. The warrior pup carried the cyberlink to the center of the containment, where the floor was still molten: a bubbling lake suspended by the *Alchemon*'s simulated gravity plane.

For an instant, the cyberlink robot hung there, gripped firmly by the neck, almost dead, but not quite. Its leg motors remained partially operational and the rubberized limbs kicked wildly back and forth. Ericho was aware of a feeling of revulsion: The scene resembled an ancient hanging—the victim's neck in a noose and the legs flailing in desperation.

It's just a machine.

The warrior pup opened its pincer and the cyberlink fell into the molten mass. A tremendous cloud of thick white smoke rose from the burning lake, enveloping everything.

"End of malfunction," said Rigel.

Ericho sighed. The problem had been solved but he couldn't say he liked the solution. Still, better that the cyberlink be destroyed than risk further damage to the ship.

He had no time to savor the victory, though. Jonomy's voice sliced through the diner.

"Aberration signal coming from the warrior pup, Captain."

What now?

The smoke in the containment cleared; the warrior pup's cameras must have automatically phased themselves to penetrate the latest visual distortion. But the scene on the monitor now resembled a ride on a zero-G rollercoaster: The warrior pup hurtled around the room at high speed, tumbling and rolling madly yet somehow managing to avoid crashing into any of the walls.

"Stabilizer failure," suggested Rigel.

Ericho doubted it.

The warrior pup suddenly froze in the middle of a particularly violent gyration. Turning slowly, its cameras zoomed in on the exploded ceiling vent directly above it. The robot hesitated for just an instant, then rocketed up through the vent and into the tiny access corridor above the lab.

The out-of-control warrior whipped down the dimly lit access shaft with breathtaking velocity. Multicolored lumes, indicating the status of various modules, flew past the camera so quickly that it was impossible to see anything except pinpoints of light.

The tunnel curved sharply and the pup shot around the bend without slowing. But a few meters ahead, the shaft ended; a small airseal had closed, blocking the passageway and preventing further lab wastes from contaminating other parts of the ship.

Either the warrior pup did not register the obstruction or it was unable to stop in time. The fighter smashed into the seal. There was a tremendous flash of light and then the monitor went dead.

"Jesus Christ!" shouted Rigel.

A radiation alarm chirped madly; the airseal had been breached. Contaminated wastes were now pouring into other sections of the access system.

"Sentinel override on all adjacent seals," said Jonomy. "Radiation contained in tubes I-twelve and P-thirty-four."

Rigel shook his head. "This is crazy. There's got to be a major malfunction somewhere in the network, maybe within the Sentinel system itself. Two psycho robots in one day is not possible!"

The Lytic continued. "A maintenance pup is on the scene. The warrior pup was destroyed in the crash. Fragments from the collision have lodged in the tube walls and a pup recharging facility has been rendered inoperative. No primary systems damage, though—that's confirmed by Level One PAQ and the Sentinels."

Ericho found himself gripping the edge of the table. He drew a deep breath, forcing his hands to unclench.

"Jonomy, what does EPS say?"

"Probabilities would indicate that the warrior pup malfunctioned due to the high radiation levels in the containment lab—"

"Like hell!" snapped Rigel. "I don't give a shit what EPS says, that was no goddamn malfunction. We're talking about warrior pups—those little bastards have enough radiation shielding to fuck the sun!"

Jonomy did not reply.

Ericho stood up. "Jonomy, Rigel and I are on our way to the bridge." He turned to the crewdoc. "June, get to Mars Lea. I want you to stay with her until you hear from me."

June frowned. "I hope you don't believe that Mars Lea could have had anything to do with this."

"Right now I don't know what to believe."

14

Reluctantly, Mars Lea followed June into the odd little subshaft that branched off downdeck's main east corridor. The subshaft curved up and out of sight, yet as they walked along it, there was no sensation of encountering a hill; the ship's artificial geonic mechanisms maintained a level deck, making the perception of climbing strictly visual. Their bodies remained perpendicular to the floor.

The problem was, it felt wrong. Mars Lea found herself slowing down, taking each step carefully.

The crewdoc smiled. "Still having that sight/balance dichotomy?"

"If you mean, do I feel as if I'm going to fall over backward, the answer is yes."

"Try not looking straight ahead. Keep your eyes on the floor."

Looking at her feet helped somewhat. But they were approaching the worst part of the climbing corridor, where the gravity plane twisted most severely. Her stomach danced. She imagined that at any moment she would fall over backward and roll out of control down the length of this impossible tunnel. She knew that such a fall could not occur, but that fact brought no relief.

Talk—don't think about it.

"I saw Alan a few minutes ago," she blurted out. "He said we were having a lot of malfunctions. Have they been fixed?"

"Yes, I believe that they have."

"What happened?" She swallowed hard, repressing a sudden urge to vomit.

"Some robotic problems. Nothing to worry about. They've been taken care of."

Mars Lea could tell by June's casual tone that the crewdoc was not being completely candid. The malfunctions must have been serious.

"Was anyone hurt?"

"Oh, no—nothing like that. It was just some robots that became contaminated by the high radiation levels in the containment . . . they went crazy. That sort of thing happens sometimes."

"Uh-huh." They reached the end of the curving corridor, where it tunneled at a weird angle through the floor of updeck. Mars Lea's guts pinched together; she grabbed June's arm and closed her eyes tightly, allowing the crewdoc to lead her the last few steps. There was one final odd sensation of stepping onto a surface that curved away from her body; now it felt as if she would fall forward.

"You can open your eyes."

They were standing on a level floor in a tiny dead-ended corridor leading to an airseal. Gravity was normal again: up was up, down was down. Mars Lea twisted her neck and glanced behind her at the subshaft they had come through. It plunged downward from the floor like a descending escalator tunnel without steptreads.

She shook her head. "There should be an easier way to come up here."

"Look at the bright side. There is an easier way to go down."

Mars Lea grimaced. The other way was easier, but not necessarily preferable.

The crewdoc smiled. The disciplined bubble of white hair stood in sharp contrast to the creased black flesh, yet the age lines served to pleasantly accent her face, giving it character. Her red jogging suit fit like skin.

Mars Lea found herself suddenly staring at June. Insights exploded into awareness.

She is a strong woman, her femininity cloaked behind a shield of efficiency. She is an entity permanently attached to earth—grounded, like a Lytic with an umbilical link to a starship. June Courthouse might explore the universe, yet she would remain forever bound to a past and to a place. And in that moment of insight, Mars Lea knew that June would never truly understand the turbulence of psionic torment.

Elke had hinted that Captain Brad often slept with June. Mars Lea reflected upon her own relationship with Jonomy.

Jonomy is my ground. He helps me remain attached to the world.

Without Jonomy, she would have fallen off a long time ago.

"What are you thinking about?" June asked.

"Nothing."

"Your face just went blank. Where do you go when that happens?"

"Nowhere." How could she even begin to explain such things to one who had never known the terrifying intimacy of the superluminal universe?

June stared at her for what seemed like a long time. Then she asked: "Do you know anything about mythology?"

Mars Lea shook her head.

"Have you ever heard of Humbaba . . . or the *Gilgamesh Epic?*"

"No. Why?"

June sighed. "I guess it's not important. Come on."

They passed through the airseal into a small circular chamber, softly lit by golden lumes embedded in the hemispheric ceiling. The deck was soft—spongefloor—and had six openings in the center. Each two-foot-diameter hole was capped by a plastic lid.

June stripped off her jogging suit and kicked her boots to the other side of the chamber, where they clattered against the wall. Mars Lea slipped out of her pants and vest . . . slowly.

"I still don't see why I have to do this," she complained.

Naked, June stepped onto one of the plastic lids. "It's good for you. You know that."

"But it's not my time yet. You said we only have to take these baths once every two months. I just had a plunge three weeks ago."

"Yes, but you just returned from a planetary excursion a few days ago—"

"I went through decontamination," Mars Lea argued. "You're lying to me."

"All right. I brought you up here for a bath because I'm hoping it will help you relax. I'm hoping that it will subdue that part of you that causes you such misery."

Mars Lea sensed real concern in the crewdoc's words. In a purely emotional way, June did understand her turmoil. But understanding made no difference.

"That part of me that makes me feel bad . . . that's the same part of me that killed Tom."

June scowled. "We don't know what killed Tom. And I don't believe you do either."

"I killed him," she stated simply.

Anger distorted June's face. "Get on the plate."

Slowly, defiantly, Mars Lea stepped onto the closest lid.

"Drop us!" June ordered.

Somewhere in the chamber, an automatic system responded to the crewdoc's command. The lids they were standing on seemed simply to disappear. With a gasp, Mars Lea plunged downward into the nutriment bath.

For a moment, she dropped out of control. Then geonic counterforces broke her fall, suspending her in a warm and humid freefall zone near the center of the bath. June floated upside down, a few meters away. Shafts of light, diffused and refracted from above and below, painted rainbows all around them, a spectral wonderland inhabited by two humans and a zoo of multicolored gelatinous bubbles.

The floating orbs—living globules of artificially created nutriments—ranged in size and shape from marbles to human torsos. Each had its own intense color, or set of colors: deep aquamarine blues and vivid Irish greens, teals, cool violets, shrieking mauves. Some orbs were gold with bands of scarlet around their midsections, and some were completely transparent, visible only when they moved through the thick murky air of the bath.

The colors were beautiful but the smell was even more pleasing. Mars Lea closed her eyes and inhaled deeply, luxuriating in the stinging aroma of sharp spices: thyme and asaweed, a mélange of mints, the odors of many worlds, mixed together specifically for the *Alchemon*'s crew by the Pannis psychoarts department.

"Let's break one of each today," urged June, her voice muffled by the acoustically deadened chamber.

Mars Lea opened her eyes and the nutriment bath abruptly lost some of its attractiveness. It remained pleasing to look at and wonderful to smell, but those facets were designed to make its true purpose less distasteful.

June kicked at one of the large golden orbs with the scarlet bands. As her foot rammed its midsection, the bubble exploded into a dozen smaller globules, each of them tumbling away at high velocity. Some of the flying fragments crashed into other orbs, and more of the delicate nutriments shattered, with pieces flying in all directions.

The crewdoc flailed wildly, splattering anything within reach. Her hand smashed through a fist-sized amber bubble, creating a thousand miniature shooting stars.

"Not so fast," Mars Lea urged, already knowing that her complaint was too late. The chamber had been agitated; a reaction had begun and there was no way to stop or control the expanding storm.

An exploding fragment shot into Mars Lea's partially open mouth. She spit, appalled by its bitter taste. But only a portion of the globule came out. The rest of it remained lodged in the back of her throat.

June, spinning head over heels, laughed merrily. "One in the mouth, huh?"

"It's stuck!"

"Swallow it."

She dared not. What if the bubble clogged her windpipe?

June punched an elongated pink orb, splitting it perfectly in two. The halves spiraled away in opposite directions.

"I can't swallow," Mars Lea whispered.

"Open your mouth wide and throw your head back. It'll come out—gravity plays no favorites."

Mars Lea did as she was instructed and the yellow chunk drifted lazily out of her mouth. She smacked it away from her face.

June chuckled. "Relax; it can't hurt you. Nothing in here can hurt you. This place is safe—a haven. Relax."

"I have an awful taste in the back of my throat."

The crewdoc pointed to a couple of slender white strands floating near Mars Lea's legs. "Grab one of those and swallow it."

She reached down and caught the strand and popped it into her mouth. Hesitantly, she bit down. The strand exploded into droplets.

Wintergreen! The taste delighted her, bringing to mind a vague recollection from childhood: walking through some sort of bright indoor orchard with her mother—a huge terrarium with giant orange trees and wonderful smells.

She hugged her arms to her body, thrilled by the warm memory.

"Keep moving," June urged. "You won't get a good bath just by floating."

The crewdoc became a literal vortex—an epicenter for the turbulence. Her legs and arms thrashed wildly, splattering globules into dazzling patterns. The chamber darkened as it filled with visible gases released by the agitated nutriments. In the dimming light, June appeared as a hazy figure with pulsating rainbows hurtling away from her body.

Mars Lea coaxed her legs into a smooth kicking pattern. Globules were hitting her from all sides now; it felt as if she were undergoing a slap massage. A small violet orb floated lazily past. She reached out and mashed it gently between her hands.

"More effort!" yelled the crewdoc. "Don't just play with the bubbles—smash them to pieces!"

It was no use; she could not do it. There were pleasant aspects to a nutriment bath, but in a very fundamental way, there remained something inherently repulsive about floating in this mad sea of genetically modified protein clusters, bacterial cleansers, megavitamins, and whatever else the Pannis medical people had dreamed up.

The contents of nutriment baths were designed to be convulsed into action by vigorous motion. Once agitated to a certain level, the globules released a variety of gases. The vapors either osmotically penetrated the skin pores or found their way into the bloodstream via regular breathing. To Mars Lea, it still seemed like madness to go to such extremes. But Jonomy had assured her that regular nutriment bathing was one of the best methods known for staying healthy on long star flights.

Still, she could not bring herself to take an active part in the process. She would let the bath just happen, as on the other occasions when June had forced her to come here.

"Let yourself go!" shouted June.

Mars Lea shook her head, inadvertently swallowing one of the wintergreen strands that had stuck to the roof of her mouth. Again, the pleasant childhood memory returned—the huge terrarium with the orange trees and the wonderful smells . . .

This time, though, something felt wrong about the memory. Something was out of place.

The smells—she could make no sense out of the odors. They were pleasing, but no matter how hard she tried to bring them into her conscious mind, assign names to them, relate them to similar smells—no matter how hard she thought about them, they remained beyond assimilation, foreign to experience.

The childhood memory of the terrarium began to lose its grip on her, mutating into a mere intellectual recall of an ancient event. That process seemed normal; deep memories always seemed to decay rapidly into pure mental abstracts. But as the memory lost its sharp edge, the smells grew stronger. She began to make sense out of them, began to relate them to other more familiar odors.

Wet flowers on a muggy riverbank.

"No!" Twisting desperately, she gasped for breath. Her violent movement sent her spinning out of control.

The spectral agitation of the bath vanished and a vast universe took shape in its place—the blackness—filled with distant stars. Fear began to close in on her.

Fragments of bizarre thought/image pulsated through consciousness, indescribable. *The eternity of the soul . . . the event horizon beyond consciousness . . . an entrance . . . a doorway outlined with terror . . .*

"Get away from me!" she cried, grabbing hold of her head, squeezing, trying to force the blackness away.

The strange thought/images continued to plummet through her, each wrapped in the smell of wet flowers . . .

Entropy junctions . . . focal points in the process of matter/energy degradation . . .

"Let me alone!"

Ta-shad—the crossing over . . .

"Go away!"

Sentinels obey . . .

She screamed, then raked her fingernails across her thighs. The pain brought her back—the blackness and the alien thought/images disappeared and she was in the nutriment bath again. June floated beside her, the crewdoc enshrouded in a fog of tiny globules.

"Get me out of here!"

"Easy, easy." Strong hands closed on her shoulders, embraced her. "Be still," June whispered. "It's all right."

She started to cry. "It's not all right!" Warm tears dripped onto her cheeks. A small white globule attached itself to her wet face and she batted it away.

The crewdoc held her, gently patted the back of her head. Soothing words: "It's all right, Mars Lea. It's going to be all right."

"You don't understand!" she sobbed. "Everything is part of the whole—everything all around us is a part of the whole! Look at it!" She pulled away from June and waved her arms wildly. "Look at this place—it's a part of the ship's biosystem. This bath is connected to the rest of the *Alchemon*, and it's connected to the natatorium and to the diners and to the dreamlounge and to my cabin and to the labs . . . it's all *connected!*

"Don't you see!" she cried. "It's all a part of the whole!"

June nodded. "Of course I see that." The crewdoc grabbed Mars Lea's hand and began swimming toward the bottom of the chamber, toward the bath's exit and the entrance to the showers.

Mars Lea did not understand why June could not see it. So obvious. "We're all a part of everything! It's all connected!" She pulled sideways to get June's attention, then pointed to the walls of the chamber.

"Even the gravity! Don't you understand! Even the gravity is a part of it! It bends and twists just so a subshaft can pass beside this chamber! Because there's no gravity in here, then that means there must be warped gravity right outside, and then on the other side of the warped gravity, it can be normal again—real directions, real up and down! Don't you see? It's all just a part of the whole! It's all *connected!*"

June kept leading her toward the exit, saying: "Yes, I see . . . uh-huh . . . yes, now I understand—"

Mars Lea hugged herself and wept. "You don't believe me! No one believes me!"

"Hush—it'll be all right. We'll shower and then I'm going to give you something to help you rest."

Abruptly, Mars Lea stopped crying. She stared down at the scratch marks on her thighs, where her fingernails had slashed through the skin. Blood lines. The wounds were not deep, but they stung worse than the cuts she had inflicted on her hands in the dreamlounge.

I'll become like the lieutenant. The attacks will grow so bad that only the ultimate pain of death will put an end to them.

And she suddenly knew, with terrifying certainty, that even death would not grant her permanent rest.

15

The *Alchemon* had been the first manned vessel to pass through the Earth/Sycamore transpatial corridor—at least according to the data contained in the ship's library. Aside from some Loop test probes and the unmanned explorer that had originally mapped Sycamore and discovered the bacteria, no other vessels had ever made the jump. And when Pannis had launched the *Alchemon* from the solar system less than ten months ago, no expeditions were slated to follow.

Then who in the hell is out there? Ericho wondered.

He stood behind Jonomy at the perimeter of the data circle, impatiently waiting for the umbilically attached Lytic to establish an image on the main screen. Rigel sat a few meters away in Dianaldi's chair, accessing information from the armrest keyboard. The bridge was silent.

A rescue ship? But that made no sense. Rescue efforts were generally not undertaken until years after the primary voyagers failed to return. That was standard Corporeal policy, harsh but essentially sensible. The reality was that if a starship did not appear at the Earth terminus of the Loop when it was supposed to, chances were it wasn't coming back.

A parade of images flashed across the Lytic's monitor, too quick for Ericho to assimilate; jumbles of texture and color, the computer's best efforts to display what its long-range sensors indicated was tracking them.

He and Rigel had been on the bridge with the Lytic for the past hour. The containment and the lab had been successfully vacuum-purged and the ecocapsule with the remains of blue blob had been safely brought into the west storage pod. Jonomy had assigned the *Alchemon*'s major backup systems to a high-speed trouble search—a thus far futile attempt to locate any major malfunctions in the network. Something other than overdoses of radiation had to have caused the cyberlink and the warrior pup to go crazy. A major glitch in the system would explain their problems, but thus far, no distortions had been uncovered.

And then, five minutes ago, during a minor routine course correction, the *Alchemon*'s sensors had picked up the other starship.

Jonomy sighed. "No use, Captain. They're too far away. Presently in the neighborhood of three hundred twenty-five thousand kilometers, still maintaining a parallel course. Our sensors can pick up nothing but electromagnetic anomalies at this range."

Ericho leaned over the Lytic's shoulder. "But you say that they definitely changed direction right after we did."

"Yes, and I suspect that is why we discovered them. Our course correction brought us closer to their position, but the instant our remote sensors located them, they moved out of range again. I would guess that they've been out there for some time, tracking us. Our course alteration must have caught them by surprise—they didn't move in time, and we spotted them."

Rigel scowled at the Lytic. "What I want to know is, why in the hell doesn't EPS have any theories about what's going on here?"

Ericho, leaning over Jonomy's shoulder, felt the Lytic tense. "Rigel, I explained earlier: EPS can only calculate probabilities based on a certain statistical ratio of clear data to indigenous quirks. In this situation, and in the situation relating to the malfunctioning robots, a positive information base does not exist. EPS cannot, and will not, formulate theories based on a multiplicity of unknown factors."

"Fuck," muttered the tech officer.

"All right," said Ericho. "We have to look at the data we have." He faced Jonomy. "EPS is certain that the ship is a Corporeal vessel?"

"Absolutely, Captain, unless we assume an alien culture with almost identical starship development. PAQ has done a shape analysis based on our meager data input at the time of the contact. They appear to be smaller than us—a hundred twenty-five to a hundred fifty meters in length, standard slab configuration, with at least one storage pod hanging from the stern. Electromagnetic leakage patterns match Corporeal standards."

"But no caste-code."

"Correct. And they are ignoring the *Alchemon*'s attempts to initiate communications."

All Corporeal computers, whether space- or planet-based, broadcast long-range telemetry beacons or caste-codes—ID signals allowing for high-speed computer interfacing. Without caste-codes, two starships could not "talk" to one another.

Jonomy added the obvious. "The lack of a caste-code places them in violation of Corporeal law."

"Bastards," muttered Rigel.

Ericho ran his gaze up the spindly leg that supported the HOD. The holographic orb currently displayed a starfield which, according to their instruments, contained the other vessel. At this range, of course, there was nothing to be seen but distant suns: tiny pinpoints of light floating in a three-dimensional sea of darkness.

He rubbed a hand across his face, tried to wipe away drowsiness. He had been awake for the past thirty hours; snorts of caf and natural adrenaline boosts had kept him going so far, but at some point, very soon, he was going to have to get some sleep. Right now, he envied the Lytic's ability to stay awake and alert for days on end.

"Three hundred twenty-five thousand kilometers," grumbled Rigel. "A real interesting figure, wouldn't you say?"

Jonomy nodded. "Yes. Just beyond the range where we might be able to pick up any primary data leakage."

"Can we try closing in on them again?" asked Ericho.

"Waste of fuel," said the tech officer.

"Agreed, Captain. They are probably aware that we came close enough to spot them. If we move, they'll move, and unless their engines are notably substandard, we could chase them for weeks and not gain enough real distance to enhance our data base."

"Suggestions?"

Rigel stood up and planted his massive hands on his hips. "If we had a couple of intercept torpedoes, I'd tell you what we could do."

"This other vessel has initiated no hostile action," Jonomy pointed out.

"Well, they sure as hell aren't acting too friendly, either."

"It's a moot point," said Ericho. "We have no torpedoes." The four landers bore short-range attack missiles, but that was the extent of the *Alchemon*'s external armaments.

Another idea occurred to him. "Could this vessel be a chronomute?"

"An interesting speculation, Captain, but I've already checked. There are no records of any starships that chronomuted anywhere near this sector. It would, however, explain why they were broadcasting no caste-code. A chronomuted starship from some past era would naturally remain wary of contact until they had ascertained whether enough time had passed to make their arrest and prosecution under Corporeal law—"

"Jesus!" growled Rigel. "Enough of this! I want to know just one thing—what in the fuck is going on here? And I don't want to hear any crap about EPS not having enough data to work with! I mean, just look at this whole mess. We find an incredible life form on a planet that can't support life, our lieutenant goes insane, kills the life form, and almost burns us to a cinder. Mars Lea, who's bizarre enough to begin with, is about to go over the edge, we've got robot malfunctions that are just not possible, and now we have a goddamn starship out here in the middle of nowhere, tracking us! Jesus Christ—add it up. Something's going on!"

"What?" asked Jonomy calmly.

Rigel reddened. "How the hell should I know! You and EPS are supposed to figure it out."

Jonomy stared at the tech officer. "Rigel, I am in the dark about these events as much as you are. I do not perceive the parameters of these actions, nor do I understand how they relate to one another. I agree with you, however, that we are no longer within the realm of coincidence. In some way, there is purpose behind these events."

Rigel wagged his finger. "Yeah? And I'll give you one guess who's fuckin' us over!"

"Pannis," said Ericho quietly. "Some sort of bizarre experiment." He shook his head. "But that makes no sense, Rigel. We all know the consortiums can be ruthless, but I can't believe they would risk our lives."

Rigel cracked a laugh. "Hell, for enough profit, they'd blow us out the fuckin' airlocks without shieldsuits!" The tech officer suddenly hunched forward and leaned against the data circle. His eyes narrowed. "What if that unmanned probe that mapped Sycamore and discovered the bacteria— what if that probe also discovered blue blob. Pannis might have been correlating data about the creature for a long time. Remember how Mars Lea got added to this expedition at the last minute? Maybe the Pannis scientists discovered something about blue blob, about it being telempathic. Maybe they were worried about it being too dangerous—a no-shit, one-of-a-kind, hostile alien organism.

"So they put a real state-of-the-art Psionic aboard the *Alchemon*—Mars Lea. And they set things up so that they could monitor us from a distance—another starship, outfitted with long-range tracking gear, probably jammed full of scientists. They probably followed us through the Loop. And if things go badly for the *Alchemon*, no doubt this other ship has a couple of intercept missiles waiting to blow us to pieces. End of *Alchemon*, end of hostile alien."

Jonomy spoke very quietly. "Rigel, there are numerous aspects to your theory that do not interface with our current troubles. The malfunctioning robots, for one. And the fact that Lieutenant Dianaldi, a known telempathic receptor, was put into a closed environment with an extremely powerful Psionic. Plus the actual discovery of the creature, which occurred in a far more complex manner than a simple exploratory probe would have been capable of achieving. And if this other starship is seriously monitoring what is going on aboard the *Alchemon*, a secret network of communications hardware would have had to have been installed aboard our vessel."

The Lytic met Rigel's gaze. "If such a network existed, it is not feasible that it would remain completely undetected by me. I have access to the entire ship and I have come across no such network."

Rigel locked eyes with Jonomy. "I guess if there were such a network, the Lytic would have to know about it, huh?"

"Yes," said Jonomy firmly. "And I do not."

The tech officer turned away. "All right, fine. But maybe there wouldn't have to be a whole network of monitoring gear. Maybe just one crew member and a hidden transmitter."

"Who?" asked Ericho.

"Hardy."

Jonomy frowned. "Agreed—the science rep would be the most likely member of the crew to be engaged in such a conspiracy. And one small transmitter could be hidden. Coded broadcasts could be modulated into our normal data leakage, shielded from our scanners. But that does not explain the malfunctioning robots—"

"Some kind of goddamned psychological testing, maybe. Pannis wants to find out how we handle extraordinary stress—

Ericho held up his hand. "Rigel, that makes no sense. Listen to what you're saying. It's crazy."

Rigel sat down and glared at his keyboard. "I watched those robots the same way you did. Don't tell me about crazy. Robots do not lose control like that. No way, no how."

I've got to get some sleep, Ericho thought. *We all do. We're not looking at things rationally.*

He walked to his command chair and plopped down in the soft cushions. "All right—enough speculation. There's got to be a way to get more data on this starship. I want ideas."

Rigel shrugged. "Put one of the landers on automatic and launch it toward them. Under full acceleration on a short run, a lander should be able to close on a starship. We'd probably lose the lander, but we might get some hard data transmitted back to us."

"No good," said Jonomy. "If this other ship does carry long-range tracking gear, then prelaunch preparations would give us away. They would know we were going to launch and that would give them time to move their ship farther out of range."

"You have a better idea?"

Jonomy turned to Ericho. "The *Alchemon*'s Level Six ETI system utilizes standard Phase Fourteen external telemetry trackers. The Phase Fifteen models became available shortly before we left lunar orbit. There was no time to retrofit us for this expedition, but the construction specs and workprints were filed in our library, in preparation for upgrading the ship upon our return.

"Obviously, we can't rebuild our external telemetry trackers—even upgrading a Level Six system like ETI would require substantial drydock time."

Rigel came alert. "But we could modify one tracker and attach it to the outside of the hull, bypassing ETI."

"Precisely. One tracker will not give us full Phase Fifteen capabilities, but according to the specs, it should substantially increase our sensor range."

Rigel came to his feet. "Enough to scan their data leak-age profile?"

"Yes."

Rigel grinned. "One good look at that profile and we'll be able to ID them for sure."

Ericho should have become excited by the plan; it was a positive step toward solving the problem, and that was better than sitting here bandying theories back and forth. But an uneasy feeling remained in the pit of his stomach.

The captain needs to master that the master's not the captain.

Maybe that was it—for the first time in his career, he was being placed in a situation where he had to function like a real commander of his vessel, making decisions and issuing orders that were not covered by standard regulations or routinely dealt with by Lytics.

Am I afraid of such responsibilities?

He knew the answer without thinking. *No, I can handle the pressures. Something else is bothering me.*

He became conscious of his bruised ribs. They were beginning to ache again and he rubbed a hand across his stomach.

What disturbs me is what Rigel tried to express earlier. There are too many things going wrong—there are too many unnatural events occurring aboard this ship.

He drew a deep breath and tried to ignore his discomfort. "How long to build this tracker?"

Rigel was already accessing data from his terminal. "Two hours to modify a unit, maybe another hour for the install."

"Captain, this is Alan." The intern's voice blared from the intercom.

"Yes?"

"Sir, I'm in the natatorium. I just came out of backup control, following the completion of my active duty period. Rigel said it was all right for me to begin a four-hour sleep session. But I guess I was too tense to fall asleep so I came down to the pool for a quick swim—"

"Alan, get to the point."

"Sorry, sir. You probably have this on your monitors already, but the pool is really messed up. I've never seen this much backup from the biosystem. The water's really weird-looking too, full of algae and other stuff that looks like it came from the nutriment bath."

Ericho raised his eyebrows toward the Lytic. Jonomy

shook his head. "Nothing here, Captain. No abnormal indicators in any of the systems feeding the pool."

What now? "Jonomy, get us some visuals."

"Captain, that's a designated privacy area."

"Sorry, I forgot. Alan, break out a camera and feed the output to the bridge."

"Yes, sir."

"Rigel—any ideas?"

The tech officer licked his lips. "If we pretend that nothing else is going wrong—if, in other words, we're dealing with an isolated incident down there—it sounds like it could be a simple fluid leak. Some pollutant is getting into one of the feedwater pipes, and if the leaking pipe is nonpressurized, it's possible we wouldn't get any immediate malfunction indicators."

Jonomy nodded slowly. "Yes. That's possible."

Ericho wanted to believe it too.

Alan did not sound so certain. "Sir, I don't think this is a fluid leak. Wait till you take a look—it's very strange." They could hear a storage locker opening in the background; Ericho imagined the intern snapping a power module into one of the tiny handheld cameras.

"Okay," said Alan. "You should be getting an image now."

"Jesus," said Rigel.

The water was almost black, like oil, only lacking any sheen. Long strands of algaelike material floated on the surface and only a soft bubbling in the center of the pool gave away the fact that the water was indeed aqueous—it looked more like dark mercury. Various sized gelatinous globules floated along the perimeter and a hazy white mist seemed to hang in the air directly overhead.

"That is not a fluid leak," said Jonomy.

"Damn right," muttered Rigel.

Ericho frowned. "And we have no malfunction indicators? Nothing at all?"

"Captain, Level Six LSN oversees the natatorium functions, and that system is all green. Level Two PEH has registered the presence of that white mist in the air, but no alerts were sounded—the mist was analyzed and deemed harmless. The only other anomaly I record comes from Level Four—Internal Bio Scanning. IBS has closed off all feeder pipes into and out of the pool. The natatorium has been isolated from the rest of the biosystem."

Rigel shook his head. "How come you didn't notice that before?"

"IBS routinely quarantines portions of the biosystem. Until now, I had no reason to pay any particular attention to this incident."

Ericho nodded. At least the contamination was being contained in the pool. "Jonomy, get us an analysis of the liquid."

"Captain, associated problems make that action difficult. Since there are no actual malfunctions registering, the normal trouble systems will not respond—they simply do not see any problem. I can order a pup to run a bioanalysis of that liquid, but pups are normally not assigned to such tasks and it will take some time to outfit such a robot."

Ericho accepted the news calmly. "All right, get me Hardy."

A moment later, the science rep's deep bass filled the bridge. He sounded annoyed. "What is it, Captain?"

Ericho explained the problem. "We need an analysis of that liquid."

"I'm very busy down here. This storage pod is not ideal for experimentation and it is vital that I transfer the remains of the creature from the ecocapsule to a more permanent facility. I do not have the time to analyze polluted water."

"This is important. We need your expertise."

Hardy's tone became shrill. "Don't patronize me, Captain. If you think you're going to get back in my good graces before we return to Earth, you are deeply mistaken. Your incompetence has destroyed a valuable scientific discovery and your stubborn unwillingness to return to Sycamore for bacterial samples can only be ascribed to the actions of a fool!"

Ericho kept his anger in check. "We need the pool water analyzed immediately. A major biosystem problem could be serious and I'm afraid I have to make this an order."

"Fine, Captain. I'll send Elke. When I'm testifying at your court-martial, I wouldn't want it said that I failed to cooperate. Hardy out."

Rigel laughed grimly. "We ought to detach the storage pod and leave the son-of-a-bitch and his precious corpse out here."

Ericho entertained a more direct fantasy: He suddenly imagined ramming his fist into Hardy's fat mouth.

He shook his head, shook away the anger. Now, more than ever, he need clarity, calm rationality in the face of their expanding troubles. He could not afford the luxury of becoming furious.

He closed his eyes and rubbed his temples, trying to ward off the beginnings of a headache. In the darkness, he saw a lander, flying down though Earth's atmosphere, surrounded by lightninglike blades of energy.

His eyes snapped open. *I've got to get some sleep.*

16

I've fallen out of bed.

Mars Lea opened her eyes, stared groggily at the white ceiling, at the soothe-scanner hanging above the medical cot like some kind of tenacious mechanical demon.

I've fallen out of bed. The fact hit home, seeped into the deeper reaches of consciousness, wiped away the last traces of sleep. She lay on her side on the floor in one of the private medcenter rooms. Her left leg had been bent back and twisted beneath her hip. She was uncomfortable. And alone.

On the wall above the door, two perpendicular lines of a time/date clock indicated that she had been asleep for less than an hour.

An hour? She remembered June bringing her here from the nutriment bath, giving her a tranquilizer shot, helping her into bed, promising that the drug would produce a deep sleep lasting at least a day.

You need rest, June had murmured. You will feel better when you awake. Sleep.

Kind words, but Mars Lea had slept for less than an hour. Kind words . . . lies.

She twisted her leg out from under her and used the edge of the bed to rise. Her foot ached. She opened the door and hobbled out into the small corridor separating the private rooms from the main expanse of the medcenter. Meter-high windows provided an open view into the tiny labs and June's office.

Empty.

She staggered out of the medcenter and into downdeck's main west corridor. A hundred meters away, at the south end of the ship, lay the containment lab. Behind her, just around a bend, was the west mech shop.

Important places. Strange impressions sailed through her,

fragments of thought; fleeting icons, endowed with the great power of lost knowledge.

The west mech shop. A memory took shape.

Tom Dianaldi was standing in the small repair facility, his fingers caressing the cylindrical barrel of a laser-cutter. In the background, a time/date clock marked the event as occurring two months ago. Mars Lea perceived Tom's thoughts, saw them as clearly as if they were her own.

He's thinking about destroying blue blob!

Two months ago! Impossible!

But there was a truth inherent in the vision that she could not deny. The lieutenant had begun making preparations for his final journey into the containment well in advance, planning his demise before the *Alchemon* had even reached Sycamore's orbit.

She reeled in confusion. *How could he know what we would find on Sycamore?* The answer was obvious: The creature on the surface had been in psionic contact with him.

And with utter certainty, Mars Lea knew that it was she who had acted as the superluminal conveyor, transferring the creature's desires to the lieutenant. It was she who had served as the telempathic bridge, unconsciously allowing Dianaldi to be overcome and destroyed by the will of an alien mind.

Other visions of Tom in the west mech shop came to her—other times when he had gone there to touch the laser-cutter, fondle it, allow his flesh to caress the tool that would bring about his own death, knowing that he was helpless to prevent his fate, that he was being manipulated by a power that could not be deterred. Worse yet, Mars Lea sensed that Dianaldi knew just when it was safe to enter the west mech shop: He only went there when Jonomy was not on the bridge, when the Lytic was far away from his umbilical.

Dianaldi only went to the west mech shop when Jonomy was with me—when we were together . . .

Mars Lea clutched herself, reeling. The angles of the corridor, where walls met ceiling, seemed to change, distort. Her stomach contracted and she fell against the wall, gagging violently.

She understood, horribly, the deeper meaning of the lieutenant's journeys to the mech shop. *He went there only when I was making love to Jonomy. When I was lost in passion, Tom was granted respites: brief moments of near-freedom. He spent those precious times clutching the laser-cutter, seeking ways to overcome his fate, to turn away from the path that led inexorably to his death.*

But why? Why did blue blob want to kill itself?

Maybe it was bored.

A loud giggle suddenly escaped her. She threw a hand over her mouth but she could not stop. She laughed wildly. There was nothing funny but she could not stop. Her howls of laughter filled the deserted corridor.

She dropped to her knees and leaned against the wall and forced herself to think of Jonomy, imagining his soft oval eyes, the fine curves of his chin, the granular funnel in the center of his forehead where the skin twisted inward, toward a dark place.

A dark place, but warm. The image helped her to regain control. Her laughter died away.

Make love to me, Jonomy. Help me to hold on. I'm falling.

She sensed someone behind her. She wanted it to be Jonomy, knew it was not. Slowly, she turned around.

Hardy.

The science rep's tiny eyes peered at her from behind his shaggy eyebrows. The face moved closer and the cheeks bubbled into a leering smile. But the deep voice sounded pleasant.

"Mars Lea—I've been looking for you. I need your help with some experiments."

Experiments. Hardy was still interested in doing experiments. That was funny too, but in a more fundamental human way. She did not laugh.

"What do you want me to do?"

He gripped her shoulders and helped her to rise. "Come with me to the west storage pod. The remains of the creature are there. I have a new agenda, plenty of work to keep you busy."

"What will we do?" she asked, her voice trailing off as she became fascinated by a tiny birthmark beneath his right ear.

"Telempathic enhancement. You'll wear an isolator hood."

"What will I be isolated from?"

He looked at her strangely for a moment and then his voice grew stern. "I'm very serious about this, Mars Lea.

The scientific impetus of this mission has been seriously jeopardized by the captain's actions. I do not intend for our research efforts to be crippled any further. We must all pull together and create a genesis of new understanding from the ashes of our failures. Only in this way—in the careful creation and application of a new experiment roster—can we hope to overcome our defeats and return to Earth as a successful expedition."

She looked him in the eye and knew that he was crazy. But perhaps an experiment would keep her occupied, keep her from falling. She decided to go with him.

17

Ericho was in the pilot's seat but he had no control.

The lander plunged through the upper atmosphere, spiraling toward the surface of the planet at dizzying velocity. Ericho felt no fear, no awareness that they were in trouble. He knew that the outside temperature had climbed well past the danger level and that the heat shields should be incinerating. But those things did not matter. He stared out the window at the energy display surrounding the lander: thick strokes of rainbow lightning, a spectral wonderland guiding the craft and protecting it from the effects of rapid reentry.

He started to turn around to tell the others that everything was going to be fine, and then suddenly the lander was through a final patch of white cumulus and they were leveling off, ripping across the sky above a vast desert ripening into early dusk. The horizon appeared; a flaming sun outlining puffs of white—distant clouds tinged with amber and mauve.

Such beauty, he thought. *Sunset over the desert . . .*

He awakened, bolting upright in bed. A glance at the antique digital timepiece on his dresser showed that he had been asleep for two hours.

The dream.

He remembered coming to his cabin from the bridge, flopping across the bed in total exhaustion, and then he was in the lander, soaring down through the atmosphere of a planet that he sensed had to be Earth. His black formsuit felt soggy, pasted to his skin by a layer of sweat. He had neglected to key an autobiotic temperature cycle; his cabin's regulatory system had not responded to his increased perspiration.

The dream took me further this time.

The beautiful sunset above the desert—that was something new. Always before, he had awakened with the lander still spiraling through the outer atmosphere, flanked by the odd streaks of lightning. But now, after having experienced the identical dream more than fifty times, a change had come.

Fresh beads of sweat suddenly broke out on his forehead. He rolled from the bed, his chest heaving, sucking air in huge gulps, desperate to breathe, his lungs out of control, as if there were not enough oxygen in the room.

Steady . . . relax . . . slow your breathing . . .

He followed his own instructions and his breathing returned to normal. With some astonishment, he realized that he had just saved himself from hyperventilating.

My dream . . .the changes . . .

Quickly, he stripped off his soggy garments and hopped into the shower, turning his thoughts away from the dream, trying to forget. Air/water jets scoured his body; preset dehydrators blew him dry. In less than a minute, he emerged from the shower feeling physically refreshed. But his thoughts kept returning to the dream.

Am I afaid of the change in my dream? Is that what sent me into a panic, made me hyperventilate?

He sat down on the edge of the bed and wormed his legs into a fresh formsuit.

Is there meaning to the fact that my dream progressed further this time? Does the dream directly relate to Mars Lea's telempathic output, as June suspects? Could my extended dream somehow indicate that Mars Lea is becoming more powerful?

His breathing quickened again, but this time he averted the attack, forcing himself to inhale and exhale slowly. And suddenly he knew the real source of his fear.

There's an end to my dream and I'm getting closer to it. And I don't know if I'll survive.

He leaned over, velcroed his shoes, then opened an intercom line to the bridge. There were more important things to worry about.

The dream is just a series of images in my mind—it's not important. I'll not allow myself to think about it anymore.

Jonomy's voice came on line. "Captain, I'm glad you're awake."

Ericho found himself breathing hard again. *Am I really awake? Or is the* Alchemon *and everything that's happening to us really just another sort of dream?*

"Captain?"

My dream feels more real than the Alchemon. The idea was terrifying. He shook his head, shook away the mad thoughts, forced himself to speak.

"Any new problems?"

"No, Captain. As a matter of fact, things have been remarkably quiet. Rigel and Alan have completed the tracker modifications and have taken the Phase Fifteen unit to the northwest airlock. They are preparing a cyberlink for outside work."

"The other ship?"

"The electromagnetic anomalies we're still receiving indicate that the vessel has initiated no further course changes. They are still paralleling us, three hundred and twenty-five thousand kilometers out."

"What about the problem in the pool?"

"Elke retrieved samples of the water. She has, as yet, been unable to isolate the source of the pollution, but it appears that a very esoteric mixture of biochemical ingredients has been somehow introduced into the LSN feed-water system. Elke has gone to the medcenter and is using one of June's microscanners to run a more sophisticated series of tests."

Ericho nodded. "Is the computer aware of the pollution yet?"

Jonomy hesitated. "Yes and no. The natatorium malfunction has some very confusing parameters. Most of the network is now cognizant of the trouble down there. The problem, is we had to indoctrinate the computer with the concept that there was a serious malfunction. In essence, we had to create a feedback loop within the system so that the data from the pool was routed back into the network. Once that was accomplished, the ecospheric system with overall responsibility for the natatorium—PEH—was able to respond. PEH now recognizes the existence of a major pollution problem. Yet, at the same time, the computer maintains that there is nothing wrong with LSN. Overall, this situation would seem to indicate that we still have a major glitch somewhere in the network—possibly the same glitch that created the trouble with the robots."

Ericho sighed. "Is the pollution still contained—limited to the pool?"

"Yes. And just to be on the safe side, I had Elke set up a contamination monitor and had Alan mount the handheld camera, giving us a wide shot of the pool. The signals from both these devices have been routed directly up to the bridge on a backup Level Two data circuit, which completely bypasses Level Six LSN."

Ericho felt his body untensing. It was reassuring talking to Jonomy; the Lytic always seemed to have things under control. "I'll see you in a few minutes. I'm on my way to the bridge."

He left his cabin, thinking about hydropollutants and crazed robots and a mysterious starship. But in the back of his mind remained the image of a desert sunset.

The bridge seemed crowded when Ericho arrived. Alan stood near the circular treadmill, garbed in the heavy cyberlink control suit. Rigel stood beside the intern, helping him to wrestle the clam-shelled helmet over his head. Jonomy sat on the far side of the data circle, umbilically linked, his face a blank stare. June Courthouse paced nervously between the graviform chairs suspended in the center of the room. Her arms were crossed tightly over her chest and she looked to Ericho like a scared child about to face parental wrath.

"What's wrong?" Ericho asked. "Where's Mars Lea?"

June swallowed nervously. "She's all right . . . I guess."

Ericho gently gripped June's shoulders. "What is it?"

"Mars Lea started to have a breakdown," the crewdoc whispered, "in the nutriment bath. I took her to the medcenter and . . . I decided to vegetate her. It seemed like the only thing to do."

Ericho felt June shudder, as if a chill had just raced up her spine.

"I didn't tell Mars Lea what I was doing to her. I lied, told her that I was giving her a tranquilizer to help her rest—" June's voice cracked. "Very unethical of me."

"You did what was necessary," Ericho soothed.

"Necessary?" June laughed bitterly. "Yes, it was probably necessary, but unfortunately it didn't work.

"I gave her a dose of prevegetative formula that should have knocked her out for at least twenty hours. I put her to bed and left the medcenter. When I returned to check on her an hour later, she was gone."

"Where is she?"

"It's all right; we found her. I came right up here and Jonomy scanned. She's in the storage pod. Hardy says that he ran into her in he corridor and that she volunteered to help him with his experiments."

"Did you talk to her?"

"No. Hardy's put her into an isolator hood."

He shrugged. "Well, maybe that will keep her occupied for a while."

June clutched his arm. "Ericho, you don't understand. The drug I gave her should have put her into a deep sleep. It didn't."

"What does that mean?"

"How should I know what it means?" the crewdoc snapped. Her face abruptly softened. "I'm sorry . . . I didn't mean to yell. It's just that I'm getting very tense. I haven't had much sleep. I shut my eyes and I see"—her voice fell to a whisper—"I see that image of Dianaldi's, the demon Humbaba." She gripped him tightly. "I don't know what's happening to me."

Ericho thought of the desert sunset and his hyperventilation attack. *Whatever it is, it's happening to all of us.*

"Sit down," he urged, motioning her to his chair. "Try and take it easy." He knew that his words sounded totally inadequate, but he did not know what else to say.

Stiffly, Junc took the seat. Her hands wrapped around the armrests as if she were terrified of floating away.

Rigel completed fastening the two bulky sections of the clam-shelled cyberlink helmet over Alan's head. "We're ready," the tech officer said, backing away from the intern.

Alan was now completely encased: from the neck down, smooth, steel-reinforced plastic, gray and featureless, ending in heavy, sensor-studded boots. At the shoulder blades, the front and back pieces of the helmet hinged to the rest of the unit.

Jonomy seemed to come to life; his full attention returned to the bridge. "Alan, did you run a systems check?"

"Yes, sir. I'm at full status, lock modules positive. I'm linked."

Ericho masked new concerns. He did not like the fact that Rigel was having Alan do the actual tracker installation. Working out on the hull was difficult enough in a shieldsuit and it became more challenging when using a cyberlinked robot. Many of the normal sensory channels that gave you a feel for the robot—sensations that keyed off air density and audio waves, for instance—were useless in a vacuum, and

Alan had little experience with hull work. But Rigel obviously had confidence in the intern and as captain, Ericho loathed interfering with engineering assignments.

It also bothered Ericho that they were using another cyberlink. He would rather have had a live crew member—preferably Rigel—perform the installation in a shieldsuit. He voiced his anxiety.

"Jonomy, did you run a complete check of Level Five CYB?"

"Of course, Captain. The cyberlink network checks out perfectly. And just to be on the safe side, Rigel has done some special modifications to the robot."

The tech officer grinned and pulled a tiny white keypad from his pocket. "This is an emergency cutoff control. I put a direct receiver and a detonator in the head circuitry of that cyberlink. If it goes crazy, I'll transmit a command that'll blow its brains out."

Jonomy narrowed his eyes. "Not a particularly elegant solution, but it should put the robot out of commission in the event of a serious problem."

"Damn right," said Rigel.

Ericho glanced at June. The crewdoc's face had gone blank. He suppressed his worries and turned to the Lytic. "All right, let's do it."

Jonomy energized the control suit. Alan walked carefully forward onto the treadmill. "One more step," urged the Lytic. "Good. You're in position."

"Here I go," said Alan.

Ericho heard the excitement in the young voice, and he recalled his own first voyage as an intern, the thrill of each fresh experience, the newness of it all. But that was long ago. And right now it was vitally important that they identified this other starship. There could be no foul-ups.

"Alan, I want you to take your time and be extremely careful. Don't try any fancy tricks."

"Yeah," added Rigel, throwing a grin at Ericho. "Don't do anything dumb, like weld yourself to the hull."

"Yes, sir," came the dutiful reply.

The intern lifted his right foot and stepped forward. As his boot sensors touched the new spot on the metal grating, the two discrete sections where his feet presently rested automatically slithered back to the middle of the circular plate. The treadmill boasted a sophisticated tracking system, able to compensate for any motion. Even if Alan broke into a brisk run, the devise would keep returning his feet to the most central position.

Ericho gazed at the main screen above Jonomy, which displayed the view from the cyberlink's camera-eyes. Signals were being transmitted properly: As Alan "walked" on the treadmill, the robot marched in perfect rhythm with his movements. At the bottom of the screen, Ericho could see the upper part of the sealed tracker assembly, attached to the robot's chest for transport.

Alan halted the cyberlink in front of the northwest airlock.

"When you exit the lock," Jonomy instructed, "you are to walk seventy-three standard paces along the lower edge of the main sensor channel. Stop there and I'll give you further instructions."

"Affirmative."

The cyberlinked robot entered the airlock and waited for depressurization. A moment later the outer seal parted. Alan walked the robot out of the ship.

"What an incredible starfield!" the intern exclaimed.

Rigel grumbled. "Don't worry about the goddamned stars. Pay attention to what you're doing."

"Affirmative."

In the zero-G environment, frictionized material on the heels of the robot kept the cyberlink attached to the hull. Alan walked the robot effortlessly down the side of the *Alchemon*, making sure that one foot remained in contact at all times.

"I'm at the main sensor channel," he said calmly.

The channel was a two-meter-wide depression running across the bow of the *Alchemon* and down the east and west sides of the ship, almost to the stern. Alan halted at the edge of the channel, then raised his right foot and stepped across the deep gash.

"I feel like I've just crossed a miniature canyon," he said triumphantly.

"CYB malfunction," warned Jonomy.

Ericho felt his whole body go tense. "Alan, stop moving."

"Yes, sir."

In the control suit, Alan turned sideways and began marching in a new direction. Out on the hull, the robot obeyed, and started walking away from the sensor channel, away from where they wanted it to go.

"Alan, didn't you hear?" growled Rigel. "Stop moving."
The intern's reply chilled them. "I can't."

"What the hell do you mean you can't!" yelled Rigel.

"CYB malfunction is in the suit," said Jonomy, "not in the robot."

Alan's voice remained composed. "This is weird . . . I can't stop moving. The suit's taking the steps for me."

The intern kept walking on the treadmill, his arms swinging freely at his sides. He looked like some kind of antique windup toy, marching in position. Ericho glanced at the main screen. Out on the hull, the robot perfectly mimicked his actions.

"Alan," said Jonomy calmly, "use your sight-typer and try and shut down the suit's main power modules."

"I'm doing it now."

Ericho slowly counted to five. That should have been enough time to sight-type a simple command. Alan—and the robot—continued to march.

"Emergency abort," ordered Jonomy. "Use your manual thumb switch."

Alan's voice rose in pitch. "I already tried that—it's not working."

Rigel stepped closer to the treadmill. Ericho turned to the Lytic.

"Do something—cut power to the whole CYB system."

"I can't," said Jonomy. "The network is not responding. This CYB malfunction is exhibiting the same parameters as the trouble in the natatorium. I'm attempting another feedback loop, rerouting the data so that the rest of the network becomes aware that we have a problem."

"Fuckin' wonderful!" snapped Rigel. "The whole goddamn system's going blind!" The tech officer leaped up on the treadmill behind Alan and reached into the back of the intern's helmet, where the main power modules were located.

The cybersuit jerked forward before Rigel could touch it. Alan shuffled off the treadmill and staggered toward the center of the bridge. Rigel stood on the empty treadmill, dumbfounded.

Ericho knew his own face betrayed identical emotions. *It can't leave the treadmill. That's its energy source—that's where the modules receive their power from!*

Alan yelled. "The typer's going crazy! All sorts of commands! I can't make it stop! I'm fighting it, but I can't make it stop!"

Rigel ran up behind the cybersuit and tore open the rear neck panel. He jammed his hand into the tiny compartment and began ripping out power module connections.

Alan whipped around. A cybersuit glove fastened on Rigel's neck and lifted the tech officer up on his toes. Rigel's face reddened; legs kicked as he struggled for air. His hands encircled the thick plastic arm and tried to tear it away from his throat.

Ericho hurtled forward, grabbed the choking arm, and bent it downward. His strength, combined with Rigel's weight, proved too much for the cyberlink. With a loud crack, the plastic arm split at the elbow. Alan let out a piercing scream.

"It's not me!" the intern cried. "It's not me!"

The cyberlink released Rigel. The tech officer stumbled away, holding his throat, chest heaving as he gulped for air.

The intern sobbed desperately. "It's not me! I'm not doing it!"

Ericho dove for Alan's legs. With blinding speed, the cyberlink moved. Ericho's arms encircled emptiness and he crashed to the deck. Quickly, he jumped to his feet and spun around just in time to see a plastic boot flashing upward at a ninety-degree angle. The cyberlink's toe rammed him in the groin.

He doubled over, collapsing to the floor, all thoughts lost in a fog of pain. His body curled into a fetal position and his hands locked around his crotch. He knew that he was helpless until the pulsing agony subsided. In the distance, he could hear Alan yelling.

"I didn't do it! I can't make it stop! It's not me!"

The cyberlink spun around and approached June. The crewdoc tried to move from the chair, but she was an instant too late. The broken plastic arm reached out and shoved her back into the cushions. The other arm grabbed her by the throat and squeezed.

Ericho struggled to his knees, began crawling toward them, trying to ignore the awful pain in his groin.

"Not me!" cried Alan. "Not me!"

The cyberlink yanked the crewdoc out of her chair. June's face turned a shade darker. Her feet kicked futilely at the cyberlink's legs.

With superhuman effort, Ericho made it to his feet. But

the pain was still too intense and he collapsed back to his knees.

The cyberlink lifted June up off the deck.

He watched helplessly—witness to a nightmare—a cyberlink with a screaming man trapped inside. A cyberlink trying to kill them.

Impossible!

And behind the bizarre tableau, on the main viewscreen, the robot outside the ship in the vacuum of space, hunched over, its arm extended as if it were holding onto something, perfectly synchronous with the actions of the control suit.

And on the far side of his data circle—Jonomy, looking perfectly calm.

"Do something!" Ericho shouted.

Jonomy blinked several times, then his eyes snapped shut— signs of a concentrating Lytic, signs of deep interfacing.

"Goddamn it!" Ericho raged.

June battered her fists helplessly against the clam-shelled helmet.

"Stop me!" pleaded Alan. "Stop me!"

Ignoring the pain, Ericho struggled to his feet and lunged forward.

The cyberlink, apparently sensing Ericho's charge, dropped June and whirled to face him. The unbroken arm snapped back, preparing to strike, and with sickening certainty, Ericho knew that his forward movement would carry him straight into its fist.

"No!" cried Alan.

Something smashed into the cyberlink's midsection. Alan stumbled sideways and his voice ascended into a wail of agony. June, gasping, crawled out of his path.

Rigel, with a spare shieldsuit work arm clutched tightly in his fists like a giant ballbat, approached Alan for a second strike.

The cyberlink regained its balance and charged the tech officer. Rigel drew back the heavy work arm and swung. The arm's shoulderpiece, where it normally attached to a shieldsuit, caught the cyberlink directly in the chest. Alan released a muffled cry as the force of the blow lifted him off his feet and sent him flipping backward through the air. He somersaulted over the chair and crashed to the deck.

On the monitor, the robot performed an identical backflip

and tumbled away from the hull, hurtling end over end into the void.

Grimly, Rigel raised the weapon again, ready to inflict a third blow. But it was unnecessary. Alan lay on his back, unmoving. Dark pressure fluid, mixed with blood, trickled out of his smashed chestplate.

"Oh, Jesus," whispered Rigel, abruptly aware of what he had done. "Oh, Jesus."

Ericho staggered to the cyberlink, reached behind the neck, and tore away the remainder of the power module connections.

"Help me get his helmet off."

Rigel stood like a statue, the shieldsuit arm drooping to the floor. "Oh, Jesus—oh, Christ, don't be dead. Oh, Jesus."

June helped Ericho; they unfastened the front section of the helmet. Alan's eyes were closed, his face drenched in sweat. Twin rivulets of blood trickled from the edges of his mouth. The crewdoc laid her palm against his neck.

"He's still alive—let's get him to the medcenter."

They removed the back half of Alan's helmet. Rigel dropped the shieldsuit arm and rushed over to help. Together, the three of them lifted the intern.

Ericho winced in pain as he stood up.

"Rigel and I can handle this," insisted June. "You'd better sit down."

"I'll be fine," he said grimly. "Are you all right?"

The crewdoc nodded.

Jonomy opened his eyes. "Captain, I hesitate to report this, but CYB still registers no malfunctions."

Rigel muttered something under his breath.

"Keep at it," urged Ericho, trying to keep his voice even. He was angry, angry with the Lytic, angry with the *Alchemon*. Nothing made any sense.

They carried Alan to the southwest exit. Jonomy opened the airseal.

"Captain, please don't think that I'm being insensitive to this incident, but I must tell you why I was unable to initiate a feedback loop to Level Five CYB."

Ericho gritted his teeth. "We'll be in the medcenter. Call us."

The Lytic's voice rose. "Captain, please. I was not able to initiate a feedback loop because the network insists that there was no malfunction."

"Like hell," growled Rigel.

Jonomy continued. "The network maintains that this incident could not have been caused by electronic or mechanical error. All evidence points to Alan as the source of the trouble. EPS concludes that our intern has suffered a mental breakdown."

"Fuck the computer," hissed Rigel.

They eased Alan through the airseal opening and into updeck's main west corridor.

"If Alan should awaken," Jonomy called, "please be careful."

The airseal snapped shut.

18

Hardy had converted the huge middle level of the west storage pod into a makeshift lab. The dirty metallic floor now supported a small ecocabinet containing the radioactive remains of blue blob and, nestled beside it, a shoddily arranged compact research station. A patchy gridwork of ceiling lumes, suspended from cables, augmented the pod's dim lighting, illuminating the ecocabinet and research station but throwing a web of shadows into the surrounding darkness. The lab was cold; storage pods had less than adequate heating systems. Mars Lea sat beneath a circle of light, fighting chills.

She stared through the window of the ecocabinet at the dead creature sealed inside. Hardy, at his control panel, smiled faintly and gave her the thumbs-up signal.

"I'm ready, Mars Lea."

The science rep's voice sounded muffled; the heavy isolator hood Mars Lea wore distorted audio waves, an unpleasant side effect to its main function of shielding the wearer from the primary bands of the electromagnetic spectrum. Worse yet, she was not supposed to move her head more than a few inches in either direction; the hood's bizarre covering of minidishes, antennas, and cables required the operator to remain relatively still for optimum efficiency.

All her senses warned her not to do this thing.

"I'm ready," repeated Hardy. His voice was louder this time, and bore a trace of annoyance.

Mars Lea nodded ever so slightly, so as not to disturb the positioning of the helmet, and inserted her hand into the sphincter opening of the thick glove. A warm tingle radiated through her arm as the glove's sensor field ignited. She leaned forward and carefully pushed her fist through the rubber membrane until her entire shielded arm protruded into the contaminated ecocabinet.

"Good," said Hardy. "Now open your hand and touch the carcass."

She obeyed before she could think of more reasons not to.

An earpiece attached to the isolator hood beeped gently, warning her that her glove was now in contact with the dead organism. She squeezed. The blue gelatinous skin compressed in her palm.

She felt relieved when nothing else happened.

The isolator hood theoretically blotted out all extraneous radiation; supposedly, only superluminal impulses now remained for her mind to register, making her perception of them stronger. But Mars Lea knew that such extraneous impulses were negligible in the first place. The isolator hood was a useless device; no energies existed that could interrupt her own powerful telempathic flows. She wore the bulky helmet only because it was easier than arguing with Hardy.

But another aspect of the experiment carried real meaning: The closer she came to a psionic source, the more intense the potential contact. And it made little difference whether the source of those superluminals was dead or alive.

Why am I doing this? she wondered.

The familiar odor—wet flowers on a muggy riverbank—hit her with almost sickening intensity. It was as if her body were literally awash in the strange scent.

And suddenly, with her gloved palm squeezing the carcass, she knew.

The strange thought/images, the pungent odor; these were aspects, characteristics of the dead creature. Blue blob was psionically projecting these things at Mars Lea. The smell had been important to the creature, had once carried deep meaning. And now, from beyond death, from some other place and time, the creature was still projecting itself.

But why?

She sensed the alien consciousness straining, reaching out, trying to communicate. Fleeting thought/images, seeking solidity, raced through her awareness.

Entropy junctions . . . focal points in the process of matter/energy degradation . . . the event horizon beyond consciousness . . .

Mars Lea found herself standing on the shallow bank of a great river, bare toes touching warm brown sand. The river stretched at least a kilometer across, and on the farshore, a jungle of twisted vines and massive trees intertwined, thrusting high into a pale green sky laced with gentle puffs of gray cloud. The smell of wet flowers enveloped her; this place literally reeked of the odor, but in a natural way—the scent belonged here. And she knew that she was experiencing another world—blue blob's world—through alien senses.

Abruptly, the vision changed. The river bubbled violently, began to overflow its banks. Trees and vines disappeared beneath swirling waters. Green skies darkened; gray clouds were sucked under the surface, becoming a part of the encompassing liquid.

Time seemed to accelerate: The river grew into a huge lake, and land masses shrank to islands. The lake became an ocean and the ocean enveloped the entire world, obliterating land and sky. Everything connected, everything lost identity, everything became a part of the whole. . . .

Tragedy. She knew that this sensory vision represented the decimation of an entire world, of an entire species. Overpowered by the odor, Mars Lea felt an incredible sense of sadness.

And then, suddenly, as if some heightened communication channel had been opened, the thought/images coalesced into a string of words.

All was lost on our world. But we found a way to save others.

An intense chill swept through Mars Lea. There was something inherently dreadful in that statement. Every sense warned her to withdraw her arm from the ecocabinet, get as far away from this storage pod as possible. But at the same time, she knew that there was truly nowhere to run.

The alien consciousness began to fall away from her. But she could feel it straining, trying to keep open the telempathic bridge, trying to communicate.

You . . . are . . . part . . . of . . . the . . . psionic universe. . . . Enter the blackness . . .

"No," she whispered.

A hand touched her shoulder. She jerked around in panic. It was Hardy.

"Now, Mars Lea, everything's going to be all right. Don't be afraid. I am beginning to receive a pattern of interesting readings from the isolator hood. With a little more data, I believe I can formulate a theory that will prove—conclusively prove—that this alien creature was, and is, a strong source of superluminals."

She sobbed with laughter.

Hardy patted her arm reassuringly, then returned to his instrument panels. "Just a little while longer, Mars Lea. Just a little more effort."

She closed her eyes and whispered a thought into the darkness: *What am I?*

Enter the blackness, said the alien consciousness.

She opened her eyes and there was no dead organism, no Hardy, no storage pod—just an endless night full of burning stars, loci of a vast spiderweb that glimmered hazily in the distance, like a nebula seen from afar.

And out of the blackness came . . . a thing . . . encircling her, omnipotently powerful, a juggernaut seeking to crush her spirit as a fist crushes a delicate flower to extract the fragrance.

Terror.

"I can't do it!" she screamed, and then she was back in the storage pod, with Hardy, with her fisted glove poised against the surface of the dead alien flesh.

She yanked her hand from the ecocabinet and tried to rake her fingernails across her arm. But suddenly she stopped, aware of what she was doing.

I cause myself pain to escape the psionic universe.

The clarity of that thought tore through consciousness and for the first time she realized—truly realized—the madness inherent in her self-inflicted pain.

By hurting my own body, I ground myself to the here and now. Feeling physical pain wards off the psionic universe.

From far away, she could sense the alien urging her: *Enter the blackness . . .*

She projected her thoughts back at the creature. *No. I won't do it.*

Her body went tense: Rigid strips of plastic abruptly seemed to surround each muscle. Her hands clenched into fists; a band of steel girdled her stomach, slowly tightening, crushing her. At the top of her spine, a pulsing sensation metabolized into a deep headache.

And she knew where the tensions and aches came from.

She had refused to face her fear; she had turned away from the blackness. And her body was reacting to that refusal.

Until now, she had always been able to handle the burden of the psionic universe by causing herself pain. But a change had come. She could no longer ward off its assaults in that way. By becoming fully cognizant of that process—by becoming conscious of why she was causing herself pain—she had effectively neutralized that method's usefulness as an escape mechanism. Her mind had been forced to find another way to retreat from the blackness.

Her fear had been internalized. Muscles and tissues now assumed the burden of repression.

Her legs felt so stiff, so locked with tension, that she feared she would not be able to stand up.

"Incredible readings, Mars Lea!"

Hardy's excitement brought her thoughts back to the storage pod.

"Astounding parameters! I've never registered such field strengths before! This lab was literally awash in superluminal impulses!"

She twisted her head and removed the isolator hood. Her skull was pounding. Her arms felt as if they had been removed and replaced with mechanical limbs.

I'm losing touch with my body.

The thought terrified her. But not as much as facing that fear, entering the blackness. She was accustomed to physical discomfort; pain could be endured. She would not surrender.

Hardy's eyes pinched into slits of unguarded excitement.

"Mars Lea, I must have an oral record to complement these readings. What was it like? What did you experience?"

Terror.

She tried to keep her voice calm. "I don't remember," she lied. "It was like . . . falling into a deep sleep."

"But you must recall something?"

"Nothing."

Hardy's cheeks twisted into an ugly grin. He wagged his finger at her.

"Mars Lea, I have been most lenient with you these past months and I have, for the most part, graciously accepted your denials of describable psionic events. But my patience is wearing thin. I urge you to recall the reason that you were selected for this expedition."

She remembered the Assignor's office, and the Supervisor with the icicle earring, and she remembered a voice—her own voice, full of arrogance—demanding to be assigned to a starship expedition.

I told them I liked storms. What madness!

Hardy smashed his fist down on the table. "Mars Lea, I demand a response!"

For the first time, Mars Lea saw Hardy as a man totally unaware of the great depths that surrounded him. He was perched on the edge of an abyss, secured by ropes of his own making. Safety lines—facts and figures, discrete digital data—all these prevented Hardy from perceiving the deeper truths. He was a lost soul. She pitied him.

"I can't help you," she said simply.

Hardy raged. "You are a stupid ignorant Psionic! If you cannot be of assistance to me, then leave my lab! Go! At once!"

By the time the power elevator swept her back up to the main corridors of downdeck, her body had grown so stiff, so burdened by tension, that it became a chore just walking. She was glad none of the others were there to see her.

I must look like a robot covered with flesh.

19

From the doorway of the medroom, Ericho watched the crewdoc make final preparations for turning Alan over to the soothe-scanner. June attached a transparent breathing mask to the intern's face and carefully injected a trio of monitoring tubes into his bloody, caved-in chest. She snapped the other ends of the tubes into a receptacle pocket behind the bed.

A moment later, the robot medic awakened, purred softly as it descended from the ceiling, its six mechanical arms unfolding like those of some giant insect. The belly of the machine halted a foot above Alan; four surgical claws immediately attacked his chest injury.

"Please step back three paces," ordered the soothe-scanner, in a polite female voice. "X rays must be taken."

June moved to the doorway and nestled close to Ericho. He put his arm around her. "What do you think?" he asked.

Gently, she rubbed his neck. "I don't know. He's in pretty bad shape. At least five broken ribs and a host of internal injuries, including a punctured lung. The right arm's badly fractured."

"X rays have been taken," said the soothe-scanner. "Distancing is no longer necessary."

The crewdoc sighed. "I've done what I can. The S-S can handle intricate surgery faster and more efficiently."

Ericho nodded. "If he makes it, how long will his recovery take?"

"Months, probably."

A weary-looking Elke strolled into the room. She had been working in one of the small biolabs across the hall, using medcenter equipment to analyze the pool contamination.

Ericho pulled his arm away from June.

The scientist's formsuit was rumpled and her long blond

hair hung in disarray at her shoulders. She collapsed into the room's only chair.

"You need sleep," ordered June.

"Is he going to make it?"

"We don't know."

Elke raised her head and stared at them. "What's happening to us?"

"We don't know that, either," replied Ericho, keeping his voice low, trying to act like a captain, trying to enforce calm. A dull pain still pulsed through his neck—the spot where Dianaldi had chopped him—and his crotch ached from the cyberlink's kick. Compared to Alan, though, he had been lucky.

"How about that mess in the pool?" he asked. "Any luck with your analysis?"

Elke sighed. "Not really. At first I thought it was some sort of algae infestation, but the more I study it, the less sense it makes. There are transformations occurring in the water that simply do not correlate with anything we know of."

"You must have some idea?" Ericho prodded.

The scientist shrugged. "Overall, it would appear that the pool is turning into one gigantic growth culture. Before IBS sealed off the natatorium, LSN must have sucked in organisms from all over the ship—protein clusters from the nutriment bath, floral root systems and seeds from hydroponics, even waste products from FWP. Who knows what else? About the only thing I'm certain of is that the mess is growing, and at a rather spectacular rate.

"Part of the problem is that organic transformations, in general, are not my specialty. Hardy has way more expertise than I do, but I can't get him to leave his precious creature. He won't even take a minute to look at my data. I think he's becoming obsessed."

Like the rest of us, thought Ericho.

Elke faced June. "I want to know what my psionic parameters are. Years ago I looked them up, but I don't remember. Not exactly. I think I'm supposed to have some minor ability as a receptor."

"Why do you ask?"

Elke smiled faintly. "Dear, don't play games with me. I just want to know if I might be the next one to go crazy, all right?"

"Are you feeling anything . . . out of the ordinary?" asked June.

"Well, I've done more crying in the past day than I've done since I was about seven. Other than that, nothing out of the ordinary."

The crewdoc folded her arms. "Aside from Mars Lea, Tom was the most powerful psionic receptor on the *Alchemon.* According to Pannis files, the rest of the crew—yourself included—have low to negligible ratings."

Elke sighed. "I was hoping that would make me feel better. It doesn't."

June shook her head. "I'm not sure our psionic parameters mean anything at this point. Alan is below the curve—he simply has no measurable telempathic abilities, which makes him just about as rare a human as Mars Lea. Yet he went crazy, too."

Ericho interrupted. "You're assuming Alan caused the problem—"

"How else could it have happened?" June argued. "You saw it, Ericho. He left the treadmill up there; his suit power modules were not electrically connected to anything. And the way he . . . came at us. He was trying to kill us." She shuddered. "What kind of malfunctioning robot does that?"

She hugged her chest. "No, Alan went crazy up there— that's the only explanation that makes any sense. Tom went crazy and Alan went crazy and there's no psionic pattern to it. And in one way or another, the rest of us are also being . . . affected."

"Patient status improving," intoned the soothe-scanner. "Classification changed from subcritical to critical."

Ericho grimaced and turned away as a mechanical arm injected a long needle into the intern's stomach. "I don't believe Alan went crazy. The way he kept hollering . . . that suggests he wasn't responsible for his actions. Somehow, that cybersuit was the cause of the problem."

"Damn it, Ericho! He tried to strangle me!"

Elke crossed her legs, Indian fashion, on the chair. "I can't believe Alan would do something like that."

"Did you ever have sex with Alan?" the crewdoc challenged.

"Sure," replied the scientist.

"When was the last time?"

"It's been a while. Maybe three weeks."

One of the soothe-scanner's arms swung out over the side

of the bed and deposited a piece of blood-soaked skin in a disposal chute.

"I never had sex with him," June said. "And Mars Lea turned him down. Alan could have been experiencing a natural sexual frustration, and that frustration could have formed the basis for his actions. This superluminal storm that is affecting all of us might have had no influence on Alan mentally, because he is not tuned into the psionic world. But maybe it got to him on another level. It's possible that he suffered a telempathic assault to his limbic system—a purely emotional assault—and that his conscious mind never even knew what was happening to him. Repressed sexual desire helped trigger his rage."

Ericho did not believe it. "I suppose things could have occurred that way. But there's still a starship out there, tracking us, and if Alan's craziness had not intervened, our improved sensors would have identified them by now. As things stand, it'll take hours to build and install another modified tracker."

Elke frowned. "You think this other ship is somehow responsible?"

Ericho shrugged. "Maybe we're part of some insane Pannis experiment. The *Alchemon* could have been secretly hardwired so that this other ship can control portions of our network, including the cybersuit system."

June unfolded her arms. "You don't really believe that?"

"No. But right now, I'm willing to consider any possibility, however remote."

"Personally," said the crewdoc, "I find it easier to make the case that Alan was driven telempathically crazy. Our whole situation is outlandish enough, but I can't accept the idea that we're all Pannis test subjects."

The corridor airseal flashed open. Rigel marched sternly up the short hallway and entered the room.

"How's the kid doing?"

June glanced at a readout on the side of the soothe-scanner. "Surgery is proceeding smoothly. I'd say he has a fair chance of making it."

"Great," said Rigel, without emotion. He turned to Elke. "You still got that microscanner set up to look at the pool contamination?"

She nodded.

"Then all of you come with me. I think I've got an idea about that mess."

They followed the tech officer into the biolab.

The microscanner, a two-meter-high cylinder with a black base, dominated the small room. Beside the scanner, on the table next to Elke's portable terminal, lay a rack of sealed vials.

When the four of them were inside the lab, Rigel closed the door and withdrew a flat, three-inch-diameter disk from his pocket. A faint, low-pitched hum filled the room. Rigel walked to the biolab's computer terminal and flicked off the intercom.

Elke raised her eyebrows. "A safepad?"

"You got it." Rigel laid the energized device on the table. "June, where's the surveillance camera in here?"

Frowning, she pointed to a corner near the ceiling.

"That the only one? No recent additions? No special analog cameras, for instance? No special installs that wouldn't be listed in the regular ship schematics?"

Bewildered, she shook her head.

Rigel exhaled sharply. "All right, I think we're safe from any prying eyes and ears. The entire spectrum should be distorted in here—Jonomy should be receiving fake audiovisuals. I think we can talk."

Ericho stared grimly. "What's going on?"

"I'll tell you what I *think* is going on. I think our Lytic has flipped over the edge. I think Jonomy has gone crazy. And I think he's going to try to kill us all unless we do something about it real quick."

Elke broke into a hesitant grin. "You've got to be kidding."

Rigel bared his teeth. "Do I look like I'm fuckin' *kidding?*

"I just finished ripping apart that goddamn cybersuit and one thing's for certain. Alan didn't go crazy up there. Somebody electronically altered the suit's power modules—opened up a batch of new circuits so that the suit could operate off the treadmill. Modulated wattage—a direct transmission from Level Five CYB."

Ericho accepted the news calmly. He felt as if he had gone beyond the point where anything could shock him.

"How does that prove Jonomy did it?"

An icy smile came to the tech officer's lips. "Who else? He's been connected to the computer since this whole mess started. He has direct access to CYB. He could have done the power circuit alterations at any time. And he could have overridden the automatics and taken control of the cybersuit just as easily."

"Just by thinking about it," June murmured.

Ericho's thoughts returned to the notion of a secret Pannis experiment. He spoke slowly. "I still don't see . . . how that proves Jonomy is responsible."

Rigel pounded his fist on the table. "If you figure Jonomy as the cause of our problems, this whole mess fits together tighter than a shieldsuit! We start with one simple assumption: Jonomy is crazy, a totally out of control maniac. This psionic whirlpool probably got to him the same way it got to the lieutenant, maybe at the same time. Who knows?

"But just think about it. A goddamn Lytic, umbilically connected, directly linked to every system on the *Alchemon*. The first malfunction was the cyberlink robot in the containment. Jonomy could have done that, right?"

Ericho gave an uneasy nod. "I suppose so."

"And then SEN reacts. The warrior pup is dispatched into the containment to deal with our whacked-out robot. End of robot. So Jonomy gets pissed and tries to take over the warrior pup. Only there he runs into a problem. He's dealing with a Sentinel-activated system now, and it's not so easy. While he and the Sentinel struggle for control, the warrior pup—getting conflicting orders from two sources—goes crazy and crashes itself to pieces. End of warrior pup.

"Then we come to that mess in the pool. Something's growing down there, but what? Maybe Jonomy doesn't even know? But if he's sending weird signals into the network, anything's possible. He could have mixed bacterial waste from FWP into some orbs from the nutriment bath. Who the hell knows? Maybe he's doing it totally unconsciously?"

June frowned. "But this other ship—"

"What other ship?" Rigel snarled. "In Jonomy's warped mind, he figures that sooner or later, we're going to suspect that he's the cause of the malfunctions. So he injects data into the network and creates our mysterious enemy, three hundred and twenty-five thousand kilometers away—just far enough so that we can't get any really solid telemetry. But with the presence of another starship where none is supposed to be, we're suddenly looking away from the *Alchemon*, away from the source of the problems."

"Externalizing our fears," mused June.

"You got it. He's a Lytic and that makes him a clever bastard. With another ship to worry about, we're not going to be looking so close to home anymore. He's safe again for a while, at least until we discover that this other starship doesn't really exist."

"But Jonomy suggested building the modified tracker," Ericho argued.

"Sure he did. Hell, I'm no psychologist. Who knows what's going on in his head. Maybe some part of him is still sane and really wants to help us. But when we started actually building the tracker, he realized that we might soon catch on to him."

Ericho held up his hand. "Wait a minute. Why wouldn't he simply alter the data coming from the modified tracker?"

"'Cause the tracker's not a part of the *Alchemon*. It's an add-on. It would have bypassed the network, fed data directly. All our bridge monitors would have displayed the output of the tracker and Jonomy wouldn't have been able to do a damn thing about it.

"We would have known, or at least begun to suspect, that we had a crazy Lytic running the ship. So Jonomy alters the power receiver to the cybersuit and takes control, making it appear like Alan's trying to kill us, so we all end up thinking that Alan's the one who's gone crazy. And the modified tracker—along with a cyberlink robot—goes tumbling into space."

"Jesus," whispered Elke.

June ran a finger across her lower lip. "An insane Lytic, possessing an absolute understanding of computer dynamics, interfaced with the entire ship. It . . . seems to fit the facts."

Ericho shook his head. "I don't buy it. Rigel, you know Lytic history; there hasn't been a case of insanity in a Lytic since the very early years of their development."

"Yeah, but no goddamned Lytic's ever been put into a superluminal shitstorm like this, either. Look what happened to the lieutenant. With Mars Lea pounding away at our heads, who knows what's possible?"

Elke suddenly threw her hands across her mouth. "Oh my God! Jonomy and Mars Lea!" Looking stunned, she leaned against the table. "Oh, Jesus! I never even thought about it till now. I wasn't supposed to tell anyone!"

"What are you talking about?" demanded Rigel.

"I saw them together about a month before we arrived on Sycamore. Jonomy and Mars Lea. Everyone else was supposed to be on duty, but Hardy left a portable terminal in the natatorium and he asked me to run over and get it for him. I . . . walked in on them. They were making love."

June's mouth fell open. "Jonomy? Are you sure?"

"Uh-huh. The airseal opened and there they were. Jonomy was trying to get his pants on. He must have sensed me coming up the corridor through that relay gadget built into his brain. But he said he hadn't been paying close enough attention and he didn't think I was coming into the pool.

"Anyway, they both got dressed and Mars Lea took off. Jonomy fed me this complicated story about how his Lytic functions might be impaired if the crew learned he was having regular sex with Mars Lea. He asked me not to tell anyone. I figured he was just embarrassed about the whole thing, and I felt glad for Mars Lea, so I said I'd keep things quiet."

June stared intently at Ericho. "This means that Jonomy has been in regular close physical proximity to Mars Lea for months."

"Can't get much closer," muttered Rigel.

June went on. "Jonomy would have been under intense superluminal bombardment each time he was with her. Even though his psionic rating is low, at that distance Mars Lea could have had a strong effect on him. She could have driven him crazy."

Elke shrugged. "So what do we do?"

"I'm still not convinced," said Ericho. "There's no proof that Jonomy is responsible for any of this."

"You're right," said Rigel. "But you have to admit that there's a hell of a lot of circumstantial evidence. And if he is responsible, we sure as hell better not sit around waiting for more trouble."

June nodded. "We have to get him disconnected, get him away from the umbilical. At least until we know for certain."

"You got it," said Rigel.

"If he's crazy," Elke pointed out, "that might not be so easy. I mean, he can manipulate practically any system on the ship."

"Including life support," added June.

Rigel shook his head. "Life support's mostly run by PEH, and that's a critical system. He's going to awaken a Sentinel if he tries anything too extreme, like turning the heaters off or vacuuming part of the ship. And when he fucked with that warrior pup, he ended up in a no-win circuitry war. I think he'll try to avoid provoking the Sentinels, 'cause if he has to handle a bunch of them at the same time, they might kick his butt—disconnect him from the network."

"Can they do that?" inquired Elke.

"Damn right . . . at least in theory."

"Let's say we get to the bridge," June began. "How do we get him to unlink?"

"If we ask him," Elke reasoned, "and he says no—if he becomes unreasonable—then at least we know that we're right, that he *is* crazy."

Rigel shook his head. "But by then, it might be too late. If he knows we're on to him, he might panic and get nasty and say to hell with the Sentinels and start messing around with life support. We gotta be real fuckin' careful about this."

Ericho continued listening to the discussion, trying to understand, trying to make sense out of it—but it sounded so bizarre that for a moment he wondered if they didn't have things backward. Maybe Jonomy was normal and the four of them were completely insane.

I'm losing it. We're all losing it. Nothing is making sense anymore.

He thought of his dream again, and the way it made him feel, the realness of that desert sunset. The dream remained an engima, but the passion contained in it bore the intensity of a true experience.

But maybe that's why I'm having the dream, over and over. Maybe it serves as a temporary escape—a fantasy—something to counterbalance the fact that my real world is coming apart at the seams.

But he had been having the dream for months. It had begun well before their plague of current troubles.

He took a deep breath. *I must force myself to deal with what is happening now. Any other path will lead me straight into insanity.* He thought of Tom. Resolve hardened.

I'm the captain of this ship. And perhaps for the first time in my career, I have no one to fall back on, not even a Lytic. Just me—Ericho Brad. And if I don't handle this situation, handle whatever occurs from now on, none of us are going to make it back to Earth.

And he knew with absolute certainty that there was truth in that final thought.

From deep within, he could sense his dream: dry images of the desert, whispering sands on the periphery of awareness. *If I don't take charge, I might never find out how my dream ends. I'll never know whether or not we touch down safely.*

The notion was silly, yet at the same time, liberating. *I am the captain of this vessel.* For the first time in his career, he truly felt a sense of command. He turned to his tech officer.

"Rigel, I want you to go to a storage closet as inconspicuously as possible and get into one of the combat shieldsuits."

Rigel exhibited rare surprise. "Are we going hunting?"

"If necessary. I'm heading straight for the bridge and I'm going to order Jonomy to disconnect from the umbilical. Whatever his mental state might be—crazy or sane—he's not going to be willing to do that. And with all the malfunctions we've been experiencing, he would have legitimate reasons for wanting to stay linked. But if he is sane—if we're wrong—I know I'll be able to convince him to disconnect."

"And if he's crazy?" quizzed Rigel.

"As soon as you're in that shieldsuit, head for the bridge. If all goes well, I figure I'll get there about five minutes ahead of you. If I haven't convinced Jonomy to disconnect by the time you arrive, give him one warning and then shoot him. Wound him if you can, but if it comes down to him or us, put a laser through his brain."

Rigel's eyes widened. "I start physically threatening our Lytic and we're liable to provoke a Sentinel. And that means warrior pups."

"Maybe not," said Ericho. "Remember, as captain I'll be giving Jonomy a direct order. According to SEN logic, the Lytic must obey such an order. Also, the Sentinels didn't react when Alan's cybersuit malfunctioned. It's possible that SEN is as confused as we are and will remain uninvolved until the nature of our problems is made clear."

June gripped his arm. "Ericho—" She hesitated, then released him.

He smiled grimly. "I hope we're all wrong about this. I want to believe that Jonomy is fine, that something else is responsible for these malfunctions. But Rigel is right: The evidence points to Jonomy. And if he is crazy, then we're playing for keeps. While he's umbilically linked, there's a couple hundred ways he can destroy us. Or worse yet, strand us out here—wreck the spatiotemporal coagulators, or sabotage NAV, or blow the main engines. There's almost no limit to what an insane Lytic could do to the network."

"Look!" Elke pointed a shaking finger at the intercom console. The light was blinking.

"Shit," muttered Rigel. "He's trying to call us. He's going to suspect something's wrong if we don't respond."

"All right," said Ericho. "June, I want you to stay here, keep an eye on Alan. And watch that soothe-scanner! Jonomy might try to mess with the MED system. Be ready to go manual, handle the surgery yourself."

The crewdoc drew a sharp breath, nodded.

"Elke, get down to the west storage pod and stay with Hardy and Mars Lea. If you don't hear from us in ten minutes, get everyone into shieldsuits and head back up here. Next to the bridge, the medcenter is about the safest place on the ship."

"Are you sure you want to go to the bridge alone?" June asked nervously.

Ericho reached for the intercom switch. "I'd rather not, but if Jonomy sees everyone heading up there at once, he might panic."

Rigel picked up the safepad and put it back in his pocket. "Ready?"

The tech officer nodded.

"On the count of three. One . . . two . . . three."

Rigel switched off the safepad as Ericho flicked on the intercom. With luck, Jonomy would have registered the changeover from altered, time-delayed audiovisuals to normal surveillance as nothing more than a minor glitch in that system.

The Lytic's urgent voice filled the biolab.

"Can you hear me? Captain—Rigel—this is Jonomy—"

"We hear you," said Ericho. "Sorry. We didn't realize the intercom was turned off."

There was a long pause, as if Jonomy was considering their words. Then . . . "Captain, the other ship. It's disappeared."

"When?"

"Only moments ago. And I detected no engine ignite readings. Even at this distance, we should have picked up exhaust radiation."

"What does that mean?" Ericho asked calmly.

"There are two possibilities. One is that the vessel fired its spatiotemporal coagulators—chronomuted. And two—"

Ericho finished the Lytic's thought. "The ship was never there to begin with." He met Rigel's gaze.

"Affirmative, Captain. And EPS has given highest probability to that scenario."

"You mean this whole mess has been a malfunction of our remote sensor system?" inquired Rigel, with just the right touch of innocent anger in his tone.

"That appears to be correct."

"Son-of-a-bitch!"

Ericho looked at the others, met worried frowns on the faces of the two women and a grim stare from the tech officer. "All right, Jonomy. I'm on my way to the bridge."

20

With growing physical discomfort, Mars Lea marched through the corridor adjacent to the containment, past the huge door with its flashing red lumes warning of the still-lethal contamination levels inside the lab. The *Alchemon*'s cleanup pups had finished their radiation scouring and had opened the hallway to human transit. But the lab itself remained too hot to enter.

As she passed the huge door, she thought of Dianaldi and the madness that had driven the lieutenant to destroy himself. It was an infectious madness, a virus with a name: Mars Lea Frock.

But now there was no feeling of guilt, no misery at being a telempathic murderer. The blackness, that terrible place the dead creature wanted her to enter, still hung at the edge of awareness, a vortex of possibilities, yet lacking the accompanying sensation of riveting terror.

She gazed at the door and thought of Jonomy, and the last time she had been with him, in the lab making love. But even that passion had congealed; her flesh could recall no memory of his warmth.

Each step now brought tiny lesions of pain—in her calves, in her ankles, in the soles of her feet. Her arms felt as if they had been turned into steel beams, hinged at the shoulders, well lubricated and swinging freely, but becoming stiffer by the minute. Her fingertips had grown numb. The top of her spine prickled. A full-fledged migraine pounded her skull.

She understood precisely what was happening. Her body and her emotions were providing a final line of defense against the ravages of the superluminal universe. She no longer had to create pain for herself in order to ward off psionic horrors; her physical/emotional being had assumed that duty. But automatic repression demanded a steep price: Mars Lea was literally losing touch with herself.

She came to a slight bend in the corridor and there was Elke, approaching at a brisk pace. Eyes downward, the scientist did not see her until the two of them were less than five meters apart.

Elke jerked her head up, startled. Mars Lea caught a flash of intense fear.

"What are you doing here?" the scientist demanded. "I mean . . . I thought you were supposed to be with Hardy?"

"I'm finished with him."

Elke edged a few steps closer. Mars Lea noted that her eyes darted nervously back and forth, as if she expected someone to appear suddenly behind her.

"Mars Lea, listen. I'm on my way down to the storage pod to talk to Hardy. I thought you would be staying there with him."

"No."

Elke licked her lips and began to speak very fast. "Why don't you come back down to the storage pod? It sounds like maybe you're mad at Hardy. Did you have another argument with him? I know he's difficult. Most science reps tend to be like that and believe me, I've worked with a lot of them, and it's something you just have to learn to put up with.

"You have to say to yourself: 'This is my job, my duty, and I have to adjust to their reality and make the best of an unpleasant situation.' And I know you might think that it's just Pannis that has difficult science reps, but let me tell you, I've talked to a lot of other science assistants and most of them say the same thing."

Mars Lea just stared. She had never heard the scientist babble like this before.

"I'm tired, Elke. I don't want to go to the storage pod. My body . . . hurts."

Her legs ached even more intensely while standing still. *I have to keep moving.* With grim determination, she raised her right foot and took a step forward, then another, trying to ignore the pain and the growing realization that her muscles would soon become too stiff for any locomotion.

Elke's eyes widend. Mars Lea imagined how she must appear to the scientist: like a baby first learning to walk, concentrating on each step, gamely trying to remain upright.

"Maybe you should visit June?"

Mars Lea permitted herself a bitter smile. Visit June?

Another shot, perhaps? Some pleasant assurances that everything was going to be all right?

She knew she was being unfair. June Courthouse meant well. But the crewdoc simply had no cure for the superluminal universe.

"I won't go to the medcenter."

"But, dear! You have to get some help."

There is no help. She continued hobbling forward, hoping Elke would let her pass without further argument. But as one agonizing step followed another and Mars Lea approached the scientist, she noticed a curious thing. Elke began slowly retreating, inching toward the opposite side of the corridor, trying to keep as much distance between them as possible.

The reason for Elke's action was suddenly obvious. Mars Lea halted and faced the scientist. "You're afraid of me."

Elke swallowed hard. Pale cheeks reddened. "Don't be ridiculous."

"You're afraid of me," she repeated, turning the words over in her mind, wondering if the rest of the crew would be behaving this way from now on. Would Jonomy also be repulsed by her presence?

It did not seem to matter.

I have no feelings left.

She sighed and began walking again. "Go, Elke. Go to Hardy. He's still down there, working on his experiments. Go to him and let me alone."

The scientist nodded and mumbled, "Everything's going to be all right, Mars Lea. Everything's going to be fine." But even as Elke spoke, she kept backing toward the far side of the corridor.

They passed. With effort, Mars Lea kept her legs moving, kept the twin steel beams engaged in machine rhythm, one step following another, a pair of remotely controlled units with a deteriorating guidance system. She knew she could not go on like this for much longer.

Elke's voice now came from behind her. "Please, Mars Lea, one favor. Go to your cabin. Just stay there—please!"

Mars Lea should not have answered, but she did.

"I'm not going to my cabin."

"Mars Lea, please! Consider this an order from the captain. He wants us all to be safe. We're having . . . a lot of problems. I'm sure that Captain Brad would want to feel that you're safely in your cabin until the crisis is over."

"I don't care what he wants."

"Mars Lea," the scientist pleaded, "we are not the enemy. We're trying to help you!"

She ignored the words and kept marching, hoping she could make it to her destination. It had suddenly become clear where she had to go.

The pool. I'll go for a swim. The water will relax me, soothe my muscles.

The natatorium lay about a hundred meters ahead, near the north end of the ship. She concentrated on each step. *I can make it. If I get to the pool, everything will be all right.*

Mars Lea knew she was deceiving herself. But if she surrendered all hope, then the blackness would take her.

Elke's words sounded even more distant. "All right, Mars Lea. You win. Go wherever you wish." There was a pause. "But stay away from the pool. It's contaminated."

Something snapped inside Mars Lea. A band of tension broke and an intense anger overwhelmed her. She turned around and screamed: "You go to hell, bitch! Don't tell me where I can go and what I can do! I don't give a damn what you or Hardy or the captain want!"

She turned and ran toward the pool, ignoring the sharp pain in her ankles, the awful pounding within her skull. From the periphery of awareness came the hint of wet flowers . . . the echo of alien thoughts.

The pool . . . danger . . .

"Go to hell!" she screamed. The two steel beams, her legs, began to unstiffen; feeling returned to her fingertips; the agony throughout her body began to dissolve. Her inner dam—her final line of defense against the ravages of the superluminal universe—was being washed away by a flood of anger. And the blackness was once again closing in on her.

She ran.

Elke's voice followed, coming closer. "You can't go to the pool! It's contaminated."

Mars Lea rounded the bend in the corridor and there was the natatorium entrance, only meters away. The airseal was closed.

She glanced over her shoulder, saw that Elke was right behind her, running hard.

Faster.

The airseal flashed open and Mars Lea hurtled through

the portal. Elke tumbled in after her. The seal snapped shut behind them.

"My God!" exclaimed the scientist. "What's he done?"

The room was choked in thick white mists; they could barely see more than a few meters. The floor was wet and slippery, and mottled with brown and amber splotches. It was intensely hot, like a greenhouse.

Mars Lea squinted, trying to pierce the fog. She could not even make out the pool from where they stood.

"This can't be," Elke whispered, hesitantly moving forward into the mists.

There was a loud splash. Elke froze.

Mars Lea shuddered. The odor of wet flowers grew stronger. She could feel the blackness closing in on her. Alien thoughts stabbed effortlessly through consciousness, like needles pricking a soft-sponge. *Danger . . . the pool . . .devoured.*

Elke, moving swiftly, grabbed her arm. "Let's get out of here."

The scientist turned to the airseal. It did not open. She smacked the manual release switch. The door remained in place.

Elke pounded on the seal. "Jonomy, goddamn you! Let us out, you bastard!"

Mars Lea felt her chest pounding. Each heartbeat seemed to sweep her closer to that terrible dark universe. The sickly sweet odor grew even more pungent, and she sensed the alien straining, desperately trying to communicate.

Elke dropped to her knees and tore open a small panel beside the airseal. Her fingers reached inside, fumbled with a tiny lume-lit circuit module.

"C'mon!" she muttered. "Open, you bastard!"

For one infinitesimal moment, the smell of wet flowers completely overwhelmed Mars Lea, blocking out all other thoughts, shielding her psyche from the omnipotent blackness. For that brief eternity, a psionic bridge opened. The full consciousness of blue blob, the dead creature, poured into her.

You cannot escape the blackness. But you must not enter it here, not in this place. You will be devoured.

Another splash, louder this time. A sound of dripping water. Mars Lea sensed that something had emerged from the pool and was now leaking water onto the deck.

The powerful smell retreated and the telempathic bridge between her mind and the alien's collapsed.

"C'mon!" cried Elke, her fingers pressing tiny reset buttons, searching for the combination that would spring the door.

The sound of dripping water became louder. Something was approaching, coming at them through the heavy white mists.

Devoured, echoed the alien mind.

The seal flashed open. Elke shouted in triumph. "Let's go!"

The scientist rose, grabbed Mars Lea by the arm, and shoved her through the portal.

Mars Lea stumbled into the corridor, tripped over her own foot, and slammed to the deck. She twisted around, expecting to see Elke right behind her. But the scientist remained at the portal, a baffled expression on her face. Heavy white mists poured out of the natatorium, fouling the hallway.

Elke tried to take a step forward. Her foot moved, but her body did not. Something was holding her from behind.

Confusion turned to horror. Elke struggled desperately, trying to free herself. Beyond the scientist, Mars Lea glimpsed some pale shape, choked in mists. Elke began to scream; her agonized wail was chopped off as the airseal blasted shut.

"No!" shouted Mars Lea. She hurtled to her feet and ran to the airseal and pounded on the unyielding metal.

Turn around, urged the alien.

She spun, half expecting some other monstrosity. But it was worse. The *Alchemon* corridor had disappeared. Nothing remained but cold distant stars linked by shimmering threads.

The blackness enveloped her.

21

Ericho stood in the corridor directly outside the southwest entrance to the bridge. Until now, his trek from medcenter had been uneventful: no life support failures, no glitches, a perfectly functioning geonic chute, downdeck to updeck in one easy float, transit unhindered, starship *Alchemon* as it was supposed to be.

But the final airseal leading to the bridge would not open.

Carefully masking his frustration, he flicked on the intercom.

"Jonomy, I'm having a problem." *And you must know I'm out here; the corridors are under regular surveillance.* "There seems to be a glitch with this airseal."

"Yes, Captain, I see. Unfortunately, IAC registers no problem with this nor any of the other airseals."

Ericho kept his tone subdued. "That may be so, but since you're directly on the other side of this door, it must be obvious to you that a malfunction is in progress."

"Correct."

"Is it possible for you to make Internal Airseal Control aware of this trouble?"

The Lytic hesitated. "Captain, I have tried to do that. But IAC simply does not acknowledge this malfunction. I have attempted going through other systems and I have also initiated feedback loops, all to no avail. It is a very puzzling error."

"Can you open the door manually?"

This time, there was a longer pause. Finally: "Captain, I cannot physically reach the airseal without disconnecting myself from the umbilical. And due to the extraordinary problems we've been experiencing, I believe it would be unwise for me to do that, even for a few seconds."

Ericho restrained an urge to start pounding on the door. He took a deep breath, steadied himself. "All right. I'm

187

going to remove the panel plate and attempt a manual override."

"That is the recommended procedure, Captain. However, please recall that the bridge airseals possess special security features designed to prevent illegal entry. Be extremely methodical when you program the resets. You could awaken a Sentinel, which might result in the bridge being completely sealed off."

"I'll work slowly."

He reached down and flipped open the small compartment. The Lytic's voice rose sharply.

"Captain! I have just picked up Rigel on my monitors, heading this way via the main east corridor. He is wearing a combat shieldsuit and he is not responding to any of my queries."

Ericho had expected more lead time on the tech officer. Unless Rigel ran into unexpected difficulties, he would probably arrive on the bridge before Ericho could override this damned door.

"Is Rigel experiencing any airseal malfunctions?" Ericho asked innocently.

"No, Captain. He is presently two seals away from the bridge. Captain, is something going on here that I don't know about?"

"What do you mean?"

"Rigel looks very angry. And his shieldsuit weapon systems appear to be fully armed."

Ericho kept talking while reprogramming the resets. "Do you think he has the capability of blasting through any unresponsive airseals?"

There was a long pause. "Captain, Rigel is about fifteen seconds away from the bridge and there are no airseal malfunctions. Please tell me—am I in some sort of danger?"

Ericho gave up on the airseal; Rigel could open it from the inside well before he could initiate an override sequence. "Jonomy, listen to me. When Rigel arrives on the bridge, I want you to cooperate fully with him. For your own safety, I want you to unlink from the umbilical."

"You have decided that I am the cause of these malfunctions," Jonomy concluded calmly.

Ericho kept his tone soothing. "Jonomy, it's best that we solve this problem together, in an intelligent manner. Don't do anything rash."

"Captain, you have arrived at an erroneous understanding of our troubles. I am not responsible."

"Open the door, Jonomy."

"I'm sorry, Captain, but I cannot. I have no control over this malfunction."

The airseal sprang back. Ericho did not wait for an explanation; he leaped through the portal.

Jonomy sat on the far side of his data circle—connected—the flesh-colored umbilical curling over his right ear and trailing down his side to the base of the HOD spindle. His eyes were pinched shut; he was fully interfaced with the *Alchemon*. Even so, a hint of worry played across the edges of his mouth.

Ericho moved cautiously toward his command seat. The southeast airseal flashed open before he got there. Rigel charged onto the bridge.

Shieldsuit motors hummed loudly, intruding into the relative silence of the chamber. Heavy mechanical boots stomped a path toward the Lytic.

Four arms jutted from the tech officer's shoulders, his real ones, protected by the thick shieldsuit armor, and below, a pair of fighting arms—thick curving cylinders, hinged at the elbows, and ending in a studded array of projectile launchers and lasers.

The fighting arms were high-speed, direct-drive weapons, totally isolated from the suit's sight-typer and control mechanisms, and linked to the real arms via body sensors. Fighting arms moved automatically, synchronized with upper body muscle groups, dancing in weird out-of-phase tandem to whatever motions the combatant made with his shoulders and elbows. Thumb triggers controlled rate and density of firepower.

There was a look of grim rage behind the transparent faceplate and Ericho hoped the tech officer would not get carried away. An experienced fighter in a combat shieldsuit could wreak terrible havoc.

Jonomy opened his eyes. Rigel spun sideways, placing his body in profile to his target, the barrel of the left fighting arm aligning itself to Jonomy's chest.

With a twist of his opposite elbow, the second fighting arm pivoted violently, flying up and over Rigel's head, and snapping into a new position with the barrel directed behind him. It was a basic combat stance, weapons one hundred and eighty degrees out of phase, set to lay down a storm of fire to the front and rear.

Both airseals snapped shut.

"Get that umbilical off," Rigel commanded. "Right now."

Ericho hoped that Jonomy had also been impressed by the tech officer's demonstration.

The Lytic hesitated. "I am not the cause of these malfunctions."

"Unlink," said Ericho quietly. "Then we'll talk."

"If I disconnect, Captain, even for a few seconds, I fear that it will be too late to talk. It is vital for our safety that I remain umbilically attached."

Rigel responded in a deep whisper. "Look into my eyes, Lytic. Read my intentions."

"You'll kill me," said Jonomy.

"Count on it."

"If I'm correct, Rigel, we could all be dead . . . or worse . . . within the next few days, perhaps hours. End my life now and you stand no chance of countering this threat."

Rigel's eyes became thin slits. "You made me almost kill Alan. Now unlink, or I'm going to blow you through the fuckin' wall!"

Calmly, the Lytic turned to Ericho. "Captain, I am now convinced that the *Alchemon* has been invaded, and is being rapidly infected, by an intelligent alien life form. We are being attacked, primarily via the computer. This umbilical link—my presence in the network—enables me to monitor and circumvent aspects of this assault."

"You're a crazy goddamned Lytic! Now get that fuckin' tube out of your head!"

Ericho held his temper. "Disconnect, Jonomy. Just disconnect and then we'll sit down and discuss your hypothesis rationally. If you can convince either one of us that some sort of an invasion is taking place, then we'll permit you to relink—"

"It will be too late. The invader *wants* me out of the network, Captain. It has engineered a clever series of malfunctions designed to cast doubt on my sanity."

"Last chance," warned Rigel.

Jonomy hunched forward, his voice growing desperate. "It wants me dead, or at least removed from the umbilical. Kill me and you further its plans!

"This invader caused Alan's cybersuit to go berserk in a

way that would focus the blame upon the ship's Lytic. created the presence of the other starship, not merely to lead our uncertainties away from the *Alchemon*, but also to discredit me, by making this phantom vessel simply disappear at an opportunistic moment."

Rigel fired. A blue beam of laser light burned through Jonomy's headrest a few centimeters away from his neck. The Lytic jerked his head sideways.

The tech officer spoke grimly. "The next shot's through your brain."

Jonomy stood up, his face flushed with anger, the umbilical cable flopping through the air. He pointed a shaking finger at Rigel.

"Kill me, then! But first, tell me what we found on Sycamore? What was it, Rigel? You were there! Tell me what it was!"

Rigel did not reply.

Jonomy's voice rose to a shriek. "Tell me! What kind of life form did you discover down there? How can you possibly account for a half-million-year-old organism existing on an inherently lifeless world, a planet racked by ferocious storms and exotic energy transformations, and circling a dying star near the edge of the galaxy?

"Tell me what it was. Tell me what you brought back to the *Alchemon*. Does anything that's happened to us thus far make any real sense? Do you have answers, Rigel? Or would you rather forget answers—ignore your intelligence— and instead discharge your weapons, be emotionally manipulated by a deadly alien that knows you better than you know yourself!"

In fury, Rigel twisted his right elbow. The second fighting arm whipped over his head and locked into position beside the first. Two barrels faced the Lytic now, enough firepower to destroy half the bridge.

And Ericho felt doubts beginning to gnaw at him. Things were not going as he had envisioned.

"Go ahead," Jonomy taunted, "Shoot! After all, it's easier to kill me than to answer my questions."

For a moment, Ericho thought it was all over. He knew Rigel. You could not push the man this way.

But the tech officer surprised him. Rigel spoke with agonizing slowness, the effort at restraint audible between his words.

"All right, Lytic. You tell *me* what we found."

Jonomy released a deep breath. His hands were shaking. "I believe that Sycamore was far more than a mere storm-ravaged world, far more than a random home to some lost alien, marooned there ages ago. I believe that for the past half-million or so years, Sycamore has served as a hightech, maximum security prison planet. I believe that this dead creature—blue blob—was, for lack of a better analogy, an organic confinement cell.

"Something was being kept down there, kept within the physical body of blue blob, presumably because it was too dangerous to be kept anywhere else. Some monstrous undying superluminal creature had been placed in captivity, ages ago, by an intelligent species. And I suspect that its captivity was meant to be permanent.

"But we found it and we let it out. We gave it an opportunity to escape from its prison on Sycamore. And once it was freed from the inhibiting array of that planet's energy patterns, it became stronger. I believe it grew to the point where it was able to influence Mars Lea psionically. And she, in turn, caused Lieutenant Dianaldi to enter the containment, not to kill himself but to destroy blue blob, destroy the last cage holding this superluminal organism. The lieutenant did not commit suicide. He was psionically murdered so that this thing could be released from its jail."

Ericho sank slowly into his command chair. *Nothing is real anymore.* Everything the Lytic was saying made a terrible kind of sense: All the pieces of the puzzle seemed to fit. But it was just as likely that Jonomy was insane, that he had invented this incredible theory.

He glanced at the tech officer, saw by Rigel's puzzled expression that he too was experiencing confusion. Rigel lowered the fighting arms, but only so the barrels were now aimed at the floor in front of the data circle.

"If what you say is true," Ericho challenged, "then why didn't you tell us all this before?"

"Because the opportunity never presented itself. I have been playing a cat-and-mouse game with this creature, within the computer, and I have kept my knowledge of this invader to myself, kept my growing suspicions discrete from the digital information that I actually project into the network through the umbilical. Until this moment—until I revealed my awareness of the creature to you—I had a tactical advantage. I do not believe that this thing knew I was aware of existence."

With a sigh, Jonomy sat down. "I have just sacrificed that advantage. Now the invader may become more subtle, more devious in its methodology of attack. Now I may not be able to stop it . . . if ever I could."

"Let's say we believe you," offered Ericho. "What proof is there?"

"Unfortunately, very little, although I suspect that shortly your desire for hard data will become a redundant matter. This alien is steadily taking control of the *Alchemon*.

"Following the melt, Captain, when you first guided the cyberlink robot into the containment, you will recall that I registered a power surge within the robot."

Ericho nodded.

"I believe that when the lieutenant caused the nuclear mishap, incinerating himself and killing blue blob—freeing this invader—it deliberately attached itself to the robot and began to take control of the cyberlink."

"The first malfunction," mused Ericho. "That power surge was actually this invader entering the robot?"

"Yes. This thing somehow physically connected itself to the cyberlink's circuitry. And although we can't be certain, I suspect that the creature exists as a sort of energy web, which would explain how it actually penetrated the body of the robot. Also, that would probably explain why it was invisible to the cyberlink's sensors within the supercontaminated lab."

Inside the shieldsuit helmet, Rigel's head wagged slowly back and forth. "Maybe I'm starting to believe you. But you're still a Lytic and for all we know, you invented this whole goddamned story."

"Rigel, I grant you that I could have done that. And I am also aware that there is no way for me to prove to you that I am telling the truth. Only another Lytic, with full access to the network, could substantiate my story."

"Then I guess we'll have to trust you," said Ericho. He turned to Rigel. "Safety-lock your weapons."

A grimace distorted Rigel's face. "And what if you're wrong?"

"Then we're in trouble. But I believe him."

Rigel glared at the Lytic. "All right. But I'm not coming out of this shieldsuit until I'm certain."

onomy nodded. "Understandable."

"That containment lab door," began Ericho, "the way it snapped shut when I first guided the robot inside. Did this . . . creature . . . do that?"

The Lytic folded his arms. "I believe so. It probably penetrated the door in an attempt to get out of the containment lab. But while it was figuring out the door's emergency activation system, you opened the airseal from the outside."

"Then why it didn't it simply jump—or whatever—through the open portal?"

"Its actions at that point provide a clue to its psychological makeup. I believe the creature is capable of attacking all circuitry systems. But when given the choice between two or more systems, it will always attempt to control the more sophisticated one.

"At the containment door, the creature had a choice between the cleanup pups in the corridor and the cyberlink robot. Somehow it sensed that the robot possessed more highly developed logic functions."

"So it chose to stay in the lab with the robot," said Ericho. "It shut the door."

The Lytic nodded. "Then, most likely, it studied the cyberlink's movements for a short time, prior to attacking."

"This makes no sense," argued Rigel. "How the hell does it take over electronic circuitry?"

"To begin with, I believe the creature has total freedom of movement, independent of real or simulated gravity. The earlier mystifying behavior of blue blob within the containment—the way it floated—that geonic ability was a function of this organism, not of the gelatinous life form, its prison cell. And on Sycamore, when the creature tumbled into the ecocapsule, that too was a demonstration of its geonic power."

"It *wanted* to go with us," recalled Rigel. "I knew that son-of-a-bitch was being too cooperative!"

"Yes," said Jonomy. "It knew we could offer it a way out of its cell.

"As for taking over circuitry, I believe this creature—this energy web—utilizes its geonic nullification abilities to physically move about and attach itself to the nexus points of electronic systems. And with its superluminal powers, it is able to enter a circuit and attack the same way our Sentinels do, by simply racing through a system faster than normal electrical currents."

"Like some sort of organic Sentinel," mused Ericho.

"Exactly, Captain. But what makes this creature truly dangerous is that it uses those same superluminals to attack human beings. At some point, Mars Lea must have become this creature's pawn. It used her as a psionic conveyor—a sort of superluminal amplifier, if you will. Through Mars Lea, the creature was able to spread its influence to others, most notably the lieutenant."

Ericho spoke grimly. "And in the containment, after it took over the cyberlink robot, it went after the warrior pup?"

"Yes, Captain. But that confrontation ended in the destruction of the warrior pup, although the creature did manage to crash through the ceiling vent and gain access to the rest of our network. But from the outcome of that battle, I believe it also became wary of our Sentinels.

"Since it escaped from the lab and gained access to the network, the creature has been attacking the *Alchemon* very systematically by levels, starting with the outermost, least critical systems of Level Six. ETI—external telemetry—went first."

"The phantom starship," muttered Rigel.

"Precisely. Also the strange problem in the pool: LSN is the Level Six luxury system responsible for maintaining the natatorium. Fortunately, PEH is Level Two and not yet under the creature's control, so the contamination has been confined to the pool."

Ericho frowned. "You mean this thing is making a run at the whole network?"

"Yes, Captain. I have been hindering it, slowing it down, but I have not yet been able to actually stop it from gaining control of a particular system."

"And the problem with Alan? This creature—modified—sabotaged—the cybersuit?"

"Yes. By electronically overriding the suit's power modules."

Rigel pivoted in a slow circle, fighting arms elevated, as if he expected an attack from anywhere.

Ericho understood. "The cyberlink system is Level Five."

Jonomy nodded. "And recall a few minutes ago, Captain, when you were not able to enter the bridge. IAC also is Level Five."

Ericho nodded. "It hindered me at the airseal until Rigel arrived."

A faint smle brewed on the Lytic's face. "It has been monitoring our internal communications, learning about us. The creature must have believed that the two of you arriving simultaneously on the bridge would stand the best chance of removing me from the umbilical. A miscalculation. If Rigel had arrived first—" Jonomy shrugged.

"Maybe it doesn't want you dead," said Rigel quietly.

Ericho agreed. "Maybe it only wants you disconnected from the network."

"I suspect that the creature would settle for either alternative. I am in its way. And now that I have revealed my awareness of it, the creature is probably quite anxious to get rid of me. Fortunately, for a time, I believe I am fairly safe. The bridge is the most secure area of the ship. The creature cannot, for instance, send a Level Four maintenance pup in here with a bomb. The Sentinels would react. I believe the creature will have to penetrate Level Two before it can get at us."

"PEH," said Rigel.

"Yes. Life support could become a most deadly weapon. And if the alien reaches Level One, we're finished. The main engines, Loop navigation, POP, SCO, PAQ—"

"And the Sentinels," said Ericho grimly.

"Most particularly the Sentinels, Captain. But SEN also offers us hope. The existence of the Sentinels is what forces this creature to attack the ship level by level. From its earlier struggle for control of the Sentinelized warrior pup, it must have concluded that an open battle with a network full of Sentinels is a no-win situation."

Rigel stopped panning his weapons and faced the Lytic. "No-win? Christ, Jonomy—we'd all be dead!"

"Correct. But as you pointed out, maybe it doesn't necessarily want us dead. I don't know what its ultimate goals are, but its actions so far seem to indicate a desire for control, not devastation. And to take control without awakening the Sentinels, the alien must infiltrate the network from the outer perimeter—Level Six—and work its way down to the more powerful Level One command circuits. Any other means of attack—a direct assault on PEH, for example—would make the *Alchemon* instantly aware that it was being invaded. The Sentinels would respond."

Ericho turned to Rigel. "Does that make sense to you?"

"Yeah," grumbled Rigel, "it fits. If a hostile computer tried to take over the *Alchemon,* it couldn't just sneak in the back door and butt-fuck us. It would have to come in face forward, take things one level at a time. Try any other method and you start goosing Sentinels."

Jonomy nodded vigorously.

"But can't the ship see that it's being attacked?" wondered Ericho.

"I remind you, Captain, that the *Alchemon* is not conscious per se, and that it possesses the inherent weakness of all computers: It cannot feel an invasion, it can only calculate one. Multiple feedback systems and the Sentinels compensate somewhat for this weakness, but they do not eliminate it entirely."

"The network must know that something is happening to it," Ericho insisted.

Jonomy allowed a bitter smile. "True enough. But the network sees no other potential threats—no other active computer sources in the vicinity. The brief presence of the phantom starship led the *Alchemon* to speculate along those lines for a while; it was fooled just as we were. But now the network knows that there is no other starship and it knows that it has not been invaded by a hostile system. And since it cannot perceive—feel—what is actually occurring, it has reacted to the entire situation according to its basic programming commands. It has run the available data through EPS. And the probabilities now indicate that all troubles are originating with the unstable human crew members aboard the ship."

"Fuckin' wonderful," growled Rigel.

Ericho restrained an urge to laugh. "The computer thinks *we're* crazy."

The Lytic smiled. "You must admit that the behavior of this crew has been, to put it mildly, blatantly abnormal. After all, you were both ready to kill me a short time ago."

"Yes," said Ericho, "we were. But you've been acting pretty abnormal yourself. For one thing, Lytics usually don't carry on secret sexual liaisons with crew members."

Jonomy narrowed his gaze. He answered slowly, "Important factors led to my relationship with Mars Lea."

Ericho waited for the Lytic to expand upon his explanation. But Jonomy remained silent.

"So what the hell do we do," growled the tech officer. "How do we stop this thing?"

The Lytic shrugged. "I don't know."

And if you do have a way of stopping it, thought Ericho, *you can't tell us, at least not openly.* It chilled him to realize that the creature must be eavesdropping on this very conversation.

"Perhaps, Captain, the Sentinels will succeed. But we must consider the possibility that when the creature does reach Level One, it will be able to somehow nullify the Sentinels using some method of control that we know nothing about."

"How long?" Ericho demanded.

"Till it reaches Level One? Impossible to predict exactly. A day or two at most, although it could be merely a matter of hours."

Ericho reached a decision. "I want everyone up here on the bridge. Right now."

The Lytic closed his eyes, interfaced.

"You'd better get into a shieldsuit," suggested Rigel.

Ericho nodded. "Break one out of the closet for me. And check it thoroughly." He did not want to find himself trapped in armor that had been modified, like Alan's cybersuit.

Jonomy opened his eyes, blinked rapidly. "More trouble, Captain. Internal Communications and Internal Bio Scanning both reside in Level Four. The alien has been hindering my use of those systems for the past hour, but now it is no longer permitting me to utilize them at all. I cannot talk to anyone over the intercom and I can no longer monitor anyone's location within the ship."

Rigel snapped his fighting arms into an upright, standby position. Leg motors whined as he walked toward the bridge closet housing the shieldsuit. "Then I guess we go get everybody and haul 'em up here."

Ericho nodded. "I sent Elke to the west storage pod. If she followed orders, then she, Mars Lea, and Hardy should be on their way to the medcenter by now, to join June and Alan. We'll head there first."

Rigel dragged a shieldsuit out of the closet and began examining it.

Jonomy watched the tech officer solemnly for a moment, then faced Ericho. "Captain, you came straight up here from the medcenter, correct?"

"Yes."

"Which route did you take?"

"Center chute to updeck, then north to the bridge."

The Lytic hesitated. "Then you did not pass by the natatorium."

"No. What's wrong?"

"I'm not sure, Captain. About a half hour ago, I lost touch with the special monitoring system that Elke set up down there to measure the contamination."

Rigel, checking the functions of the other shieldsuit with a set of miniature data probes, jerked his head up. His voice bristled with accusation.

"That was a Level Two data circuit—a direct link from the pool to the bridge."

"Correct, Rigel. And the circuit itself remains intact. However, Elke's monitoring gear is no longer functioning. Only the camera remains operational. See for yourself."

The main screen came to life. For a moment Ericho just stared, unable to make any sense out of the scene. The panoramic camera view was being blocked by thick white mists. Near the camera, he could just make out a section of the deck. The floor appeared to be wet, and covered with brown and amber splotches.

"Great," muttered Rigel. "Now what the hell is that?"

"Unknown," said the Lytic. "Based on visual data, GEL could find no pictorial matchups. EPS suggests that the splotches are some sort of fungus or mold, which possesses an astonishing growth rate. The entire natatorium is probably infested by now."

"What about that white mist?" asked Ericho.

"Probably the fog is being created as a side effect of the chemical reactions in the pool. Apparently the pool was used as a giant growth culture. These molds or whatever they are were bred from the original infestation of organisms in the water."

"Assuming our alien created all this, why?"

"I don't know, Captain. But the actions of the creature, thus far, have proven to be very calculating and deliberate. This germination suggests purpose."

Ericho had a feeling that they would know, soon enough, just what that purpose was.

"Your shieldsuit's clean," said Rigel.

The tech officer helped him into the heavy garment. A

moment later, the suit pressurized with a gentle hiss. Helmet readouts came to life.

"All green," said Ericho, wishing the words filled him with more confidence.

The southwest airseal, functioning properly, opened for them.

"Not a very good sign," remarked Rigel, as he walked through the portal. "This airseal's being real obedient." A malicious grin spread across his face. "I guess this alien wants us off the bridge."

The Tech Officer halted suddenly and turned to the Lytic.

"You gotta understand, Jonomy, that I'm only about eighty percent convinced that this alien of yours is for real. That means there's still a twenty percent probability that you're insane, and the cause of all our problems."

Rigel snapped his fighting arms down into a frontal combat stance. "And if you're lying to us, you'd better be sure I don't make it back up here alive."

"Understood."

"Let's go," said Ericho.

22

─────────────────────────

Out of control, she entered the blackness.

It surrounded Mars Lea now, a storm of nonexistence, invisible winds sucking her into its void, as if she were a leaf caught in the turbulence of a powerful jetstream. The stars, jewels of white light, alive with purpose, blazed all around her. She sensed the vast web that bound the stars together and she saw that each strand of the web was like a river of lava, with a dark pulsating core braided by streams of golden fire.

She perceived everything with heightened awareness. Each strand seemed actually to drill a hole through the blackness, creating a miniature tunnel, a void within a void: hot magma coursing in both directions through each tube, connecting pairs of stars, binding them all together.

She tore her awareness away from the fiery strands, away from the web, knowing that it was wrong and dangerous but not understanding why. Unnatural. The web should not exist here. The blackness should contain only stars.

And the blackness was death.

The blackness was the cessation of life, a nonplace where human conceptions carried no meaning. It was death—an emptiness, a distance separating organic creations, shaping and defining their individuality; a vast sea of nothingness permitting each star to exist as a discrete entity.

And each star was the psionic representation of a living creature.

One particular grouping of stars appeared closer to Mars Lea than the others. She focused her awareness on that cluster and concentration brought understanding. They were her fellow crew members aboard the *Alchemon*.

The stars and the blackness formed a natural dialectic relationship—life and death—each defining the other and making the other possible. It was the web, the endless pathways between the stars, that did not belong.

And now I am a part of the blackness.

Strangely enough, Mars Lea no longer felt that sense of numbing dread. *Am I dead? Is that why I'm no longer afraid?*

You are not dead, responded the alien consciousness. The thoughts pulsed through her with razor-sharp clarity, far more intense and powerful than she had ever before experienced them. And the pungent smell of wet flowers was gone. Mars Lea sensed that the odor was no longer necessary to maintain a telempathic bridge between herself and blue blob. They now existed together in the blackness. Communication was direct.

You have crossed the threshold and have entered what your race calls the psionic universe. It was your human awareness—your human conception of death—that brought on your fear. It is the crossing that shapes terror, not the blackness itself.

Can I go back? she wondered.

You are now a true entropy junction, existing in both worlds. You remain a living creature within the Alchemon *but you are also a concentration of energies within this event horizon beyond consciousness.*

Ta-shad, echoed her mind. *I am alive and I am dead.*

You are a focal point in the process of matter/energy degradation.

I am a freak.

A wave of self-pity overwhelmed Mars Lea, an utter loathing of herself that she had repressed since childhood. She was a Psionic, unable to fit into the human world, unable to belong. She hated herself.

I belong nowhere.

You belong everywhere.

Abruptly, she sensed one of the stars from the nearby cluster pulling away from the binding web, trying to break free, the web stretching to accommodate its motion. Strands expanded, permitting the star to move, but only in a certain direction, along a specific pathway.

The web was allowing this particular star—this particular crew member—to come toward Mars Lea.

She stared into the star and knew its name. It was the psionic representation of the *Alchemon*'s tech officer. It was Rigel Keller.

The blackness began to retreat from Mars Lea's consciousness. She sensed blue blob struggling to maintain the powerful communication bridge open between their minds, but it was a doomed attempt. The alien consciousness vanished. The blackness faded . . .

. . . and she was back in the ship's corridor, a few meters away from the entrance to the pool. The airseal was still closed and there was no sign of Elke.

And Rigel Keller was coming toward her, with violence in his soul. She could sense the parameters of his psyche, a boiling mass of hatred and fury. She did not know exactly when the tech officer was coming for her. There was no true temporal flow within the blackness; events within it did not necessarily correspond to the passage of time in the physical universe.

She knew only that at some point in the future, Rigel would attempt to kill her.

She ran.

23

They marched side by side into downdeck west, into the first of the S-curves. Rigel kept the fighting arms in constant motion, panning to the front and rear, searching for movement. His eyes flashed up and down, his attention alternating between the actual view through the faceplate and the combat shieldsuit's tracking sensor readout along his inner visor. Ericho noted the lines of tension on the tech officer's face, the controlled rage.

"Ease up."

A weird grin spread across Rigel's cheeks. "Ever wear one of these suits?"

"A few times."

"In combat?"

"No. Just basic simulations."

The face abruptly darkened. "This is about as relaxed as it gets."

Ericho did not reply. "Jonomy, are you still reading us?"

"Affirmative, Captain. Shieldsuit intercoms *should* remain functional. The dedicated com system is discrete from the network."

"Status changes?"

"Glitches along the outer perimeter of GEL, Captain. I believe our invader is attempting to circumvent the defensive systems protecting the main library."

"Then Level Three has been breached," said Ericho.

"Correct."

Rigel stopped, pointed with his left fighting arm. "The pool."

The entrance lay a few meters ahead. The airseal was closed. "Jonomy?"

"Nothing new, Captain. The camera view inside the natatorium is still being blocked by the mists."

"Do we check it?" asked Rigel.

"No. First we get everybody to the bridge."

The Lytic's voice rose. "Captain—Level Two MED reports that the soothe-scanner working on Alan has been shut down."

"What the hell does that mean?"

Ericho grimaced.

"June may have disconnected him," Jonomy offered. "I have no way of knowing. In terms of surveillance, I'm almost blind—IBS and ICO are no longer responding to any of my queries."

"Maybe Alan's dead," said Rigel quietly.

"Status unknown."

They marched past the pool entrance. From the outside, everything looked normal, but Rigel kept one of the fighting arms trained on the door until they passed around the next bend.

"Any other breaches in Level Three?"

"Nothing yet, Captain."

"To hell with Level Three," muttered Rigel. "GEL is the most critical system there, and we can survive without a goddamned library."

"Don't forget Food/Waste Processing and Hydroponics," said Ericho.

The Lytic added, "EPS is also Level Three. We may shortly lose our ability to predict this creature's actions."

"Well, now," growled the tech officer, "EPS hasn't exactly been doing a great job along those lines, has it?"

Jonomy did not respond.

"Movement!" barked Rigel.

They halted.

"Coming at us," he whispered, his eyes turned upward to scan his sensor panel.

Ericho glanced uneasily at his own status display. It showed nothing. Regular shieldsuits offered fewer features than combat models.

He suddenly wished that he had donned the *Alchemon*'s other combat suit. But in the same thought, he realized that it would have been a wasted effort. Mastering fighting arms took an inordinate amount of time and practice. Such training had never seemed important.

"Jonomy . . . anything at all?"

"Still blind, Captain."

"Eleven meters," hissed Rigel, training both fighting arms to the front. "Right around the next bend."

Ericho sight-typed a command; a laser-cutter slid out of his padded right glove and nestled securely into his fist. The cutter had an effective range of only a few meters, but holding something in his hand made him feel a bit less helpless.

He drew a deep breath. "Maybe it's June or Elke."

"No. Not enough mass. Smaller."

A pair of maintenance pups floated around the bend. Suspended between them was a meter-long planter tray, gripped at each end by the robots' tiny pincer arms. The planter contained a colorful assortment of vegetables and flowers: blue roses, tomatoes, daffodils, stringbeans, and carrots.

Ericho whispered, "Jonomy, are you monitoring this?"

"Yes, Captain, clean imagery from your suits. Those are specialty pups, straight from hydroponics."

The basketball-sized robots continued drifting forward with their cargo, seemingly oblivious to the human presence in the corridor.

"Any reason for them to be in this section of the ship?" asked Rigel. The tech officer kept his fighting arms trained on the robots.

"No. I'm afraid we have to assume that the invader has gained control of Level Three HYP."

"Let them pass," Ericho said evenly.

Rigel nodded. Pups, flowers, and vegetables slowly floated by, continuing northward into the section of corridor that Ericho and Rigel had just come through.

"Captain, perhaps you can follow them, see where they're—"

"More movement," snapped Rigel. "In front of us again." He flipped one fighting arm over his head so that the weapons were trained fore and aft.

Ericho drew a deep breath as a long flat object drifted into view. For a moment he had no idea what it was.

A sigh of relief. "June!"

The crewdoc, wearing a shieldsuit, rounded the bend, pushing the flat object in front of her. It was a floating medbed, vacuum-sealed and containing its own life-support system. Alan, heavily bandaged and still unconscious, lay beneath the transparent cover.

"Where're Elke and the others?"

June's face betrayed her anxiety. "I waited in the medcenter as you asked, but Elke never came back. I started to become worried about something happening to Alan while he was under the soothe-scanner. I removed him—"

"Captain, that explains the earlier Level Two MED readings."

Behind her shieldsuit faceplate, June's eyes opened wide. She stared sharply at Ericho.

He forced a smile. "It's all right—we were mistaken. Jonomy's not the problem. We believe that some sort of telempathic alien is taking over the ship."

He explained quickly, aware from her range of startled expressions that she had a thousand questions. But she remained silent.

Rigel pointed one of his real arms at the medbed. "How's Alan?"

"The soothe-scanner did a pretty good job on him. I expect a full recovery. But he's going to be unconscious for a while."

"You were headed for the bridge?" Ericho asked.

"Yes. I thought maybe I could be of some assistance . . . perhaps . . . talk to Jonomy."

She suddenly broke into a deep frown, as if to say: How do you know Jonomy isn't tricking you, making all of this up?

Ericho forced another smile. "Right now, we're just going to have to trust one another."

June looked about to respond, but something behind them caught her attention.

They whipped around. Dense white smoke or mists drifted lazily down the corridor. Quickly, Rigel moved into the haze, searching for its source. They followed him around the bend.

The pollution emanated from the open natatorium air-seal. The hydroponic pups, with their cargo of flora, were floating through the doorway, allowing the thick white clouds to escape into the corridor.

"Captain, I just spotted Elke inside the natatorium! She appeared in the fog for a moment, then vanished again. I caught only a brief glimpse of a face, but I'm certain it was her."

Rigel scowled. "What the hell would she be doing in there?"

The pups and their cargo disappeared into the natatorium. The airseal closed. PEH aspirators hummed to life, quickly clearing the corridor of polluting mists.

As Ericho stared at the closed airseal, his head began to pound; it felt as if bands of leather had suddenly encircled his midsection, winding tighter, crushing him.

Fear. His body was reacting to something; a telempathic contact, perhaps, translating itself into a gut sensation. The feeling urged him to run, to get away from this place.

He clenched his fists. *I am the captain. I am responsible for my crew.*

"June, get Alan up to the bridge. No matter what happens, stay there. Understood?"

She gripped his shoulder, squeezed. He felt nothing through the thick shieldsuit armor.

"Be careful," she said, and then she was dashing past the airseal, pushing the geonic medbed before her. They waited until she vanished around the bend.

Rigel moved to the front of the door. Airseal sensors detected his presence and it slid open again, refouling the corridor with the dense white fog.

Ericho stared into the mists, heart pounding. "Jonomy, are you sure Elke's actually in here? Maybe you were fed a false video image."

"Captain, I wish I could reassure you, but at this point anything's possible. I have no idea whether I saw the real Elke or not."

"Let's do it," growled Rigel.

Ericho followed the tech officer through the portal. In normal fashion, it slid shut behind them. The ache in his guts grew almost unbearable. He could not recall ever being so scared, at least not as an adult.

Rigel muttered, "Can't see shit."

"Try ultrasound," suggested Jonomy.

"Nothing. I can't even see the outlines of the fuckin' room."

"Ultrasound should function," urged the Lytic.

"Then you come down here and make it work!"

Ericho tried to remain calm, but it was almost impossible. He felt as if he had walked into the middle of a bad dream.

It was not just the visual madness of the room—the swirling white mists, the brown and amber splotches of mold covering the floor. It was not merely that the natatorium had been transformed into an alien place, full of alien or-

ganisms. There was something totally wrong about the ro
unhealthy. Normal biological functions had been altere
perverted.

He took a deep breath and forced himself to concentrate
on the task at hand.

Rigel ignited his external suit speakers. "Elke—you in
here?"

The words echoed through the mists, amplified into Ericho's
helmet by his own microphones. There was no response.

Ericho heard his own voice emerge as a dry whisper.

"Jonomy, we're open to ideas."

"Captain, the contamination-monitoring gear that Elke
set up is located about seven meters from the airseal, along
the south wall. Perhaps she went there . . . to check things
. . ." The Lytic's voice trailed off.

Rigel finished the thought. "Not fuckin' likely. One glance
in here and she would have been out the door real quick!"

The tech officer began moving toward the south wall.
Ericho followed, stepping carefully. The floor was slippery,
even with the special traction pads on their shieldsuit boots.
Warm mists began to condense on his faceplate and external
helmet sprayers came to life, automatically cleansing the
transparent plastic.

"Hate to have to clean this place," the tech officer
mumbled.

Ericho nodded.

They reached the south wall and halted in front of a small
overturned equipment cart.

"This it?" asked Rigel.

"Yes," said the Lytic.

Next to the equipment cart, a rectangular package of
sensor probes lay on the floor. Wires trailed away from the
probes, linking the sensors to a tiny junction box at the base
of the wall. The junction box had connected Elke's contamination-monitoring gear to a Level 2 data circuit, one of a
series of color-coded jacks built into the wall at chest height.
The entire jack assembly hung at a lopsided angle, dangling
from one unbroken pair of wires. The assembly looked as if
it had been ripped violently apart.

"Somebody got pissed."

Ericho stared at the wrecked gear. "Jonomy, could a
human being have done this?"

Doubtful, Captain. It would have taken tremendous strength just to tear that assembly from the wall."

From somewhere near the center of the room came a loud splash.

"Care for a swim?" muttered Rigel.

Ericho called out quietly. "Elke? Elke, can you hear us?"

"Captain, I suggest that you make a quick sweep of the room and then exit as soon as possible." Worry tinted the Lytic's words.

"What about Elke?" demanded Rigel.

"Perhaps I was indeed fed a false video image of her, superimposed over the pool's camera output."

"And maybe you weren't," growled Rigel. The tech officer kept the fighting arms pointed in front of him as he slowly moved toward the center of the room, toward the pool.

Ericho followed.

"Captain, I'm beginning to register severe aberrations throughout Level Three. The invader is obviously gaining control at a far greater rate than anticipated. And I believe the creature has initiated a massive probability scan of the entire library. There is hyperenhanced data flow between EPS and GEL."

"What does that mean?"

"Unknown. EPS is no longer responding to any of my queries."

"Understood," said Ericho, realizing that he no longer understood much of anything.

The small laser-cutter remained tightly clutched in his palm. He kept his head panning from side to side, searching the mists for movement.

At the edge of the pool, they halted.

The water looked almost black. Long strands of algae floated on the surface and scores of various-sized gelatinous globules—refugees from the nutriment bath—clung to the edges.

Rigel kept his fighting arms in constant motion. "Elke, damn it! Answer us!"

The center of the pool began to bubble. Tiny streams of liquid leaped into the air; delicate glistening waterspouts, miniature rainbows of color. For a moment, Ericho found himself transfixed by the beauty of the strange display.

To their left, something moved.

Rigel whirled, training the fighting arms on the two droponic pups that floated out of the mist. The robots clutched the planter tray, with its odd assortment of flo. As they watched, the little pups drifted to the center of the pool, stopping poised about two meters above the disturbance. They released their cargo. Blue roses, daffodils, tomatoes, stringbeans, and carrots splattered onto the surface of the oily liquid.

The water erupted, bubbling furiously, sending fresh clouds of steaming mist into the already overwhelmed atmosphere of the natatorium.

Ericho shook his head. The scene was too bizarre. "Jonomy?"

"I don't know what you're witnessing, Captain—not exactly. But I would speculate that our invader, utilizing the pool as a gigantic growth culture, is experimenting with varied organic forms, perhaps seeking specific cellular patterns in order to create some predetermined end product."

"This is end product, all right," muttered Rigel. "Looks like a goddamned unflushed toilet."

The liquid settled and the mists thinned enough for them to see that the flowers and vegetables had disappeared.

"Over there!" yelled Rigel, pointing one of his real arms toward a grisly object that floated between two large nutriment globules on the opposite edge of the pool.

A human hand.

Ericho bounded after Rigel, almost falling as his shieldsuit footpads lost their grip on the slippery surface. The tech officer arrived at the spot, leaned over, and grabbed the hand. Elke's dripping body emerged from the water.

"Goddamn it!" screamed Rigel as he gently laid the scientist's corpse on the deck. Elke's skin was pale and shriveled, and the long blond hair was streaked across her face. Her arms were covered with the same brown and amber splotches that marred the floor.

Rigel knelt beside her. "Jesus, Elke," he whispered. "Goddamn you—why'd you have to come down here?"

Jonomy spoke quietly. "It must have wanted to experiment with the human form . . . to absorb human cells into—"

"Shut up!" screamed Rigel, leg motors whining as he sprang to his feet.

Ericho felt pain and anger too, but a disturbing thought kept intruding on his emotions. *How did she get into the pool?*

"...osorb this," Rigel yelled. His fighting arms came to in a roar of thunder. The twin barrels spouted fire— ...gh-velocity mag-projectiles with short-range decelerators ...lew gaping holes in the surface of the liquid.

"Rigel—no!"

The tech officer either did not hear Ericho or chose to ignore him. Rigel's weapons panned across the surface of the foul water, creating immense geysers as the mag projectiles exploded beneath the surface. Fragments of nutriment globules, mixed with strands of algae and other unidentifiable forms, were blown high into the air. Steaming chunks of debris rained down all around them. The white mists swirled madly, like clouds surrounding the eye of a hurricane.

Behind the tech officer, a metallic shape charged out of the fog.

A cyberlink robot.

A second robot burst from the water.

Before Ericho could utter a warning, something hit his own shieldsuit from the side. The force of the blow knocked him away from the pool. His footpads lost their grip and he crashed to the deck.

Get up—quickly! He rolled over, felt the gentle vibration of the motors straining to raise him to an upright position.

His attacker, a third cyberlink robot, slammed into him again. Its thin rubbery arms encircled his shieldsuit, driving him backward toward the edge of the pool. He had the mechanical strength to resist, but his footpads had lost all tension with the floor. He was literally skating backward across the deck, being forced slowly toward the water.

He had no idea what the mass of organic chemicals could do to a shieldsuit, but he knew that this was why he and Rigel had been tricked into entering the natatorium. Like Elke, they were to be thrust into this huge growth culture.

His laser-cutter ignited, but the robot batted his arm out of the way. In another few seconds, the creature would force him over the edge.

The sight-typer!

With practiced dexterity, his eyes darted across the control dots. The microlasers tracked his optic movements, instantaneously translating them into machine commands.

ENVIRONMENTAL PURGE ALERT, appeared on his viewscreen. MANUAL INITIATIVE.

His thumb depressed the suit's inner switch and a lo...
hiss blasted his eardrums. For an instant, nothing seemed t...
happen. And then, just as he felt himself sliding over the lip
of the pool, the shieldsuit's pressurized air cylinders purged
their contents.

He rocketed off the deck, away from the pool and the
cyberlink robot. He jabbed the thumb switch a second time,
canceling the command, reclosing the air cylinders. The
shieldsuit began to drop. Another toggle of the thumb switch
decelerated his fall and his cushioned boots touched down
gently on the mottled deck.

Three meters away, the cyberlink robot spun around and
came at him again. But it managed to take only one step
before its head exploded under a torrent of mag projectiles.

Rigel stormed out of the mists, the barrels of his fighting
arms incandescent orange. "I got the other two. Let's get
the fuck out of here!"

They raced to the closed airseal, slipping and sliding on
the mold-covered deck. Ericho got there first. He was just
reaching for the override switch when, to his surprise, the
door slid open.

"Go!" urged Rigel.

They stumbled out into the corridor. The airseal snapped
shut. Corridor aspirators whirred, began clearing away the
mists.

And then Jonomy was yelling in their ears.

"Captain! The outer perimeter systems of Level Two
have been breached. The secondary data quantizers are
exhibiting major problems—"

"Fuck the computer!" shouted Rigel, his face burning
red, the eyes wild, unfocused.

Ericho spoke with all the calm he could muster. "Jonomy,
did June and Alan make it up there?"

"Yes, Captain."

He turned to Rigel. "We have to get to the bridge."

24

Running.

Physical movement: legs crashing against the hard deck, muscles pumping, straining. Material body racing through the halls of the *Alchemon*, endlessly orbiting. Eyes seeing the same corridors over and over, not caring. Mars Lea Frock—satellite of the starship *Alchemon*, fleeing for a lifetime.

Hours? Days? Years?

She stopped before a closed airseal, out of breath, leaned over to grip her knees, sucked down air in great gulps. Above her, twin perpendicular lines—a time/date clock— chronicled her mad dash, showed that less than ten minutes had elapsed since she took flight.

Barely a fraction of a lifetime.

And Rigel Keller was still out there somewhere, coming for her, coming to kill her.

Everything is connected. Everything is a part of the whole.

The concept applied not only to physical entities—to matter, to things that possessed the dimensions of size and shape—but also to the fabric of the temporal. Time was connected too. Time was being shaped, was being made into a part of the whole.

Wheezing, body still desperate for air, she straightened and gazed at the closed airseal, wondered how long she could go on like this. She was not accustomed to such physical exertion.

And from the outer edge of awareness, a presence that would not go away: the consciousness of blue blob.

Enter the blackness, it urged.

It was easier this time. She simply allowed the psionic universe to overwhelm her, to penetrate awareness until the corridor of the ship disappeared into a dark fog.

Again, the bright stars, psionic representations of human beings, linked together by the unnatural web—strands of fire; binding, controlling. Again, the consciousness of blue blob poured through her with sharpened clarity.

The creature that invades your vessel: We call it the Unity.

Mars Lea examined the phrase, cycled it through her mind, tried to arrive at a conceptual understanding of it. The Unity.

It is an actual living creature, said blue-blob, *though not alive as you comprehend life. The Unity exists as an energy web within the physical universe and as a powerful conglomeration of forces within the universe of the Psionic. It seeks to absorb all matter, all energy, all time. It seeks to absorb both universes.*

And Mars Lea knew that blue blob—the alien consciousness who had been struggling to communicate with her all along, the dead creature who now existed solely as thought/energy within the blackness—blue blob and the Unity were mortal enemies.

And what am I?

You are a rarity in the universe. Like myself, you are an entropy junction—a focal point in the endless process of matter/energy degradation.

I'll never die, she realized. *In the psionic universe—in the blackness—I'll exist forever.*

She perceived the glowing rivers of lava that connected the stars, binding them together, making them a part of the whole. She understood. The vast spiderweb of light, enveloping all: This was the psionic representation of a powerful telempathic life form—the Unity.

Abruptly, she felt weak, helpless. *What can I do?*

Comprehend.

She allowed her consciousness to soar outward from a central core, probe further into the endless night. And as she traveled within the blackness, she realized that her movement was carrying her through time as well as space.

She arrived at a point/moment where there was no web. Only three stars existed there, clustered together at the periphery of awareness, floating free in the omnipotent darkness.

Three stars—three of the *Alchemon*'s crew. She tried to move closer, but they seemed to shrink away from her, remaining too distant, too indistinct to make out individual personalities.

She understood. *I'm seeing a future time when only three crew members of the* Alchemon *remain alive.*

Three survivors.

Thoughts raced. *Three of the crew will survive, but they will travel an opposite course from the one that I must take.*

She wondered if Jonomy was one of the three. *Even if he lives, I'll never see him again. We'll be separated forever.*

That was truth, and she recognized it as such. And the truth brought pain.

Pain—a facet of the physical universe, a manifestation of the real world. The blackness receded and she became conscious once again of the *Alchemon*'s deck beneath her weary legs.

Good-bye, Jonomy.

There was nothing left for her to do but continue running, until time ran out.

She smacked her hand against the airseal's manual override switch. It flashed open. And there before her, eyes blazing with anger, stood Rigel Keller. And she understood what the extra arms on his shieldsuit—the two that were pointing at her—were to be used for.

25

Ericho followed Rigel in a mad dash toward the bridge. Their powerful shieldsuit motors provided inhuman impetus as they bounded along the *Alchemon*'s corridor, heavy boots slamming loudly against the deck, harsh clangs reverberating through their helmets.

Jonomy's voice cut through the din. "Captain—that hyperenhanced data flow between EPS and GEL, the massive probability scan of our library. I've discovered that the information is being plotted against an extremely sophisticated technohistorical grid."

Ericho forced patience. "What does that mean?"

"It suggests that the invader is mapping out the history of our culture in terms of technological advancement, and is projecting those Corporeal growth patterns forward, into the future. I'm not certain what purpose this serves, but I do know that the invader is attaching inordinate importance to this scan."

"I'll show you what the fuck's important," snapped Rigel as he halted before another unresponsive airseal.

Ericho perceived madness in that voice, a pattern in the words that went beyond Rigel's usual maledictions.

"Ease up, Rigel." He stopped a few meters behind and watched the tech officer rip open the control panel to engage the manual release. None of the doors were working properly. Ericho was surprised that the corridors still had light and heat, considering the fact that the systems responsible for maintaining those functions were also Level 6, and under the invader's control.

A yellow trouble lume ignited on Ericho's helmet display, followed immediately by a series of gentle beeps. It was an internal environmental alert: Only ten minutes' worth of breathable air remained in his shieldsuit. By purging the cylinders in the natatorium, he had used up most of his supply.

en minutes. Plenty of time. He could stop at any one of
storage closets and retrieve a fresh cylinder.

Rigel tripped the release and the airseal flashed open.
Mars Lea stood on the other side of the portal. She was not
wearing a shieldsuit.

The tech officer raised his fighting arms and aimed them
at her chest. His words chilled Ericho. "You're the bitch
who's responsible for all this, aren't you?"

Her eyes opened wide and she stared at them. She looked
like a guilty child, about to cringe before adult wrath.

"Captain," Jonomy whispered, "we have a Sentinel alert.
Unknown origin."

Rigel went on. "If it hadn't been for you, that goddamned
alien would never have been found. It would never have
gotten aboard this ship." His voice rose. "Elke would still
be alive."

"Warrior pups," warned Jonomy. "The Sentinels activated them—"

"What do you have to say, bitch!"

"Captain! The warrior pups are on their way to your
position. I believe that SEN is reacting to the threat of
Rigel's . . . violence."

Ericho took a step forward. "Rigel! It's not her fault. You
know that. Lower your weapons—"

They came out of the ceiling vents, two of them, floating
through the air with deadly grace. One of them positioned
itself above and behind Mars Lea. The other one halted
next to Ericho, so close that he could have reached out and
touched it.

The warrior pups had their primary weapon systems trained
on Rigel.

Ericho drew a deep breath. "Rigel, I want you to lower
your fighting arms, very slowly. Make no sudden movements."

The tech officer turned sideways, so that Ericho could see
his face. A wolfish grin spread across his cheeks.

"And now the fuckin' ship is protecting her. Can you
believe that?"

"Lower your weapons," urged Ericho.

Rigel's smile went cold. His eyes narrowed, grew distant.
"You know, I always wanted to find out how fast these little
shrimpfuckers really are."

The fighting arms flared upward, one in each direction,
belching mag-projectiles and beams of incinerating blue light.

His two targets fired back: The corridor became a tableau thunder and flame.

The warrior pup above Mars Lea split open under a hail of bullets, spilling a stream of circuitry guts onto her. She cried out, threw her head down, brushed hot shrapnel from her hair. The disemboweled robot, gyros gone, tumbled sideways and with a resounding whack embedded itself halfway through an intercom terminal.

The second fighter sliced downward with a laser, cutting Rigel's left arms off below the shoulder. Fighting arm and real arm parted from his body and Rigel began screaming, half in pain, half in fury. But somehow he managed to whip the other fighting arm over his head and then the warrior pup next to Ericho was coming apart, splattering pieces of itself all over the corridor.

But the pup kept firing. Twin strands of blue light pierced Rigel, one on each side of his chest. The tech officer snapped fully erect, like a soldier coming to attention. For a moment, vacant eyes gazed at Ericho. Then Rigel fell forward, crashed to the deck. Leg servos jerked spasmodically.

The damaged warrior pup exploded into flames. It hung there, a meter above the floor, sizzling and crackling, slowly cooking in its own juices, a miniature ball of orange fire.

Mars Lea screamed. And then she was gone. The airseal separating her from Ericho had snapped shut.

"External airseal alert!" shouted Jonomy. "Maintenance lock D, two seals behind you, Captain—it's opened."

Ericho stared at Rigel's body, too numbed to move.

"Depressurization!" warned the Lytic.

A loud whistling filled the inside of Ericho's helmet. He turned. The two airseals behind him had also whipped open. Fifty meters away, where the corridor made a ninety-degree turn, he should have been able to see the inner seal of maintenance lock D. But all that was visible was a black void, filled with distant stars.

"Vacuum purge!" yelled Jonomy.

Ericho felt himself being lifted into the air and then he was caught in the jetstream, rocketing out of control, feet first, dropping down a tunnel, dropping down into space, being sucked out through the portal that now seemed like the bottom of the ship. White corridor lumes flashed past. The warrior pup, racing beside him, burned a trail of orange flame behind it like a miniature shooting star. The rectangle

blackness expanded rapidly until it filled Ericho's vision,
d then a loud popping noise burst through his helmet.

He shot out into the void. And then there was no sound
at all.

—From the papers of Thomas Andrew Dianaldi

*In a few weeks, I leave Earth again: a nineteen-month
assignment on the* Alchemon. *An exploratory voyage. Up
until a week ago, everything about this upcoming expedition
seemed routine. But there's been a change—a horrible change.*

And Renfro Dackaman was responsible for that change.

*I thought I'd been pretty careful, these past years, as I investi-
gated Dackaman, building my case against him. I can prove
that he's been involved in bribery, fraud, primary data manipulation, and illegal trading. And next time it won't be a
mere board of inquiry that hears about Dackaman, but a
genuine Corporeal Court—a real trial, and one that I don't
think even Dackaman can beat. Right now—today—I think I
have enough hard evidence to send the son-of-a-bitch to
prison for at least five years.*

But I want more.

And that's why I'm going to go on the Alchemon *expedition, willingly.*

*Dackaman's on to me, of course. Somewhere, somehow, I
wasn't careful enough. He found out that I've been investigating
him. But obviously he doesn't think I've got much on him; if
he did, I'm sure he'd try to deal with me in a more direct
manner.*

*He's learned about my high telempathic rating, learned that
"m a gifted receptor. And what better way to get back at me
than to trap me in a closed environment for nineteen months
with a truly powerful Psionic.*

*Pannis is supposed to be very careful about psionic place-
ments. But somehow, Dackaman used his position as a Su-
ervisor to circumvent the rules. He had Mars Lea Frock
assigned to the* Alchemon; *in the process, he no doubt carefully disguised his own involvement. When the Consortium
eventually discovers their mistake, Dackaman assumes he
will not be blamed. Probably some poor Pannis Assignor has
been set up to take the fall.*

But there are some surprises in store for Renfro Dackaman.

I met Mars Lea Frock for the first time yesterday afternoon and she affected me greatly. I could feel things pouring out of her. I experienced a deep sense of tragedy, a feeling that stayed with me for the rest of the day.

That night, I had strange dreams—visions.

I saw an elongated triangular face, a face formed from one endless line. It had a large grotesque mouth and hardly any forehead, and savage eyes located near the top of the skull. That face seemed to float through my mind for the entire night.

When I awoke, I remembered where I'd seen the image. A museum of ancient art—two months ago, as I recalled. Some kind of Babylonian demon.

I don't know what the image means but I do know that it will become very important to me. I know that it will contribute to my insanity.

I'll be spending nineteen months with a powerful Psionic. Renfro Dackaman probably believes that by the time the Alchemon *returns to Earth, I'll be totally insane. Dackaman would enjoy that situation: a crazy man, trying to bring charges against him.*

But you see, I won't be coming back. Nineteen months from now, the Alchemon *won't be coming back.*

That feeling of tragedy that Mars Lea Frock overwhelmed me with made things very clear. I'm going to die out there, light-years from Earth.

I've made arrangements for all my evidence, all my papers, to be turned over to the Corporeal Court. Nineteen months from now, when the Alchemon *doesn't return from Sycamore, the finger of blame will be pointed. Renfro Dackaman will have some explaining to do.*

I believe they'll be able to indict him for the murders of the nine crew members of the Alchemon.

26

Ericho shot into space.

Maintenance lock D dwindled, becoming a rectangle of light nestled within the huge dark slab of the *Alchemon*. Beyond the vessel, rising above it, he could see Sycamore's fierce red sun and the planet itself, a tiny ball of darkness, a virulent speck on the star's horizon. His shieldsuit faceplate automatically selected the proper opaque density, protecting him from the sun's dangerous spectrum of radiation.

A ball of simmering orange plastic—the remains of the warrior pup—floated beside him. Drifting a few meters behind it, enveloped by a collage of instantly frozen body fluids, came the shieldsuited corpse of Rigel Keller. Both objects were traveling at the same rate of acceleration as Ericho, making them appear to be standing still.

He had been ejected in the most fortuitous position—feet first, the air cylinders on his back facing away from the ship, properly aimed for use as decelerators. A quick glance at his helmet display showed less than seven minutes of air left.

He sight-typed a command for a controlled environmental purge, then carefully depressed the thumb trigger, releasing a fluttering stream from the cylinders. Rigel and the warrior pup shot past, shrinking into the void: Ericho had successfully slowed himself down. But a look behind him made it clear that the bulk of the *Alchemon* was still receding. The air purge had not been enough.

Jonomy's voice startled him. "Captain, I have no access to any of the external rescue units. Most of the network is now beyond my control. Level Two is completely gone. However, I did manage to disengage one of the landers from the Lander Interface System shortly before the invader gained control of LIS. June is going to try and make it to that lander hold, pilot the craft out to you—"

"Forget it."

"Captain, she has a good chance—"

222

A harsh laugh escaped Ericho. "Jonomy, I have less th two minutes of air left."

The Lytic did not reply. There was no need. Even if June managed to get to the lander, she would not be able to reach him in anything under ten minutes. At the very least.

I'm alive, he told himself.

But the words seemed devoid of any emotion.

I'm alive, but I won't be for long. I'll be joining Rigel in a few more minutes.

Joining Rigel. Yes!

He took a deep breath and sight-typed a command that disengaged his backpack locks. Reaching one hand awkwardly behind him, he grasped the pack and swung it around to the front. One of the two cylinders read Empty, and the second had only a minute-plus worth of remaining air. It would have to do.

He turned the backpack so that the airjet nozzle faced toward the *Alchemon,* then manually keyed the cylinder's reset computer. The cylinder purged its precious remaining air, rocketing him farther away from the ship in his original line of motion, accelerating him toward Rigel Keller's shieldsuit and its pair of hopefully undamaged air cylinders.

But the purge was not enough; he had used too much air in foolishly trying to slow down and now there was not enough left to compensate. Rigel and the glowing warrior pup were still moving away from him, at a much lessened acceleration differential.

But moving away, nonetheless.

Ericho figured he could hold his breath for another forty or fifty seconds. Then he would have to release it. His lungs would expand again, trying to saturate themselves with fresh oxygen. But only waste gases now remained in his suit.

There was one more chance, a trick he had heard about years ago. Most spacers knew of it and most hoped that they would never have to try it.

Ericho ignited his laser-cutter. Raising his other hand, he pointed the forefinger toward the *Alchemon.* He drew his finger back into the shieldsuit glove as far as possible, then whipped the laser-cutter down across the tip of the extended digit. Blue light sliced through cleanly.

Red trouble lumes flared across the arc of his control panel and a miniature symphony of warning tones erupted in his ears.

...e had just depressurized his shieldsuit.

A jetstream of air—carbon dioxide, nitrogen, other unbreathable gases—poured out through the finger of his ruptured glove. Quickly, before the action proved fatal, he bent the extended finger down into the fist, sealing the breached digit against the palm of that hand.

Cold.

A good deal of heat had also been ejected from his suit at the instant of the purge and tiny icicles were already forming on his lips, and around his eyes and nose. His hand felt like a lump of frozen clay; no sensation remained in his breached forefinger. But right now, quick-frozen flesh did not seem too important. Lack of oxygen would kill him long before frostbite.

But the trick had worked. The intense jetstream that had poured out the tip of his glove finger for that brief moment had provided his shieldsuit with a tremendous kick of acceleration. He was closing in on Rigel now—closing quickly.

If he had misjudged, directed his finger-rocket a few degrees in the wrong direction he would miss the tech officer and become a dead projectile, sailing through the void for millennia to come.

But he had judged correctly.

Pushing aside the icy fragments of blood and tissue that surrounded the tech officer, Ericho caught Rigel's fighting arm. His right hand crushed the gun barrel.

He held on with all his remaining strength, feeling his arm being stretched and pulled—a flesh-and-blood shock absorber trying to compensate between a pair of human missiles possessing diferent inertias. Fortunately, upper torso shieldsuit motors quickly accepted the brunt of the speed differential. Stresses equalized. In a few seconds, he and Rigel were traveling at the same rate of acceleration.

And Ericho's final breath was about to burst out of him.

He had only one hand to work with; if he opened his left fist, the ruptured finger would kill him instantly. Fumbling with his right, he turned Rigel around and in the process received an unwanted glimpse through the tech officer's helmet. Full exposure to a vacuum had boiled Rigel's blood and exploded his flesh. The inside of Rigel's transparent visor was coated with a chunky red film. Ericho almost lost his breath at the sight of it.

But he held on, pinching his lips closed, feeling his own

face turning red under the strain. Another few seconds a
he would have to open his mouth, suck for oxygen that wa
not there.

One of Rigel's cylinders read Empty; it had been pierced
by the warrior pup's laser. The second contained air.

Ericho keyed the tiny resets, ripped the cylinder out of
the backpack, and snapped it onto an emergency intake
module located on his belt.

His breath gave out. Lungs collapsed, expelling at the
same instant his finger ignited Rigel's cylinder.

Air!

He sucked joyously, filling his lungs with great gulps of
fresh oxygen. Bizarre delight shot through him as his helmet
display adjusted to nearly four hours of breathable atmosphere.

Four hours of air! He almost felt like crying.

"Captain?"

"I'm all right," he gasped. "It's all right. I'm coming in."

He had to hold his breath several more times in order to
disconnect Rigel's cylinder and eject air—another series of
controlled purges. And with several minor course correc-
tions, he ended up using almost another hour's worth of
oxygen. But ten minutes later, he was back on the hull of
the *Alchemon;* his frictionized boots gripping the scarred
metal.

He had landed on the underside, below the meter-wide
depression of the main sensor channel, an artificial bound-
ary separating the top and bottom halves of the ship. From
his position, facing the stern, he could just make out the
curving outline of the west storage pod, a dark hemisphere
suspended against the even darker velvet of space, a disk
blotting out the stars.

Looking at the pod made him think of their science rep.
"Jonomy—any contact with Hardy?"

"No, Captain. SPI was Level Four. The Storage Pod
Interface is long gone. If Hardy's still down there . . ." The
Lytic trailed off.

Ericho nodded. If the science rep was still alive, he was
on his own.

"June and Alan?"

"Alan's stable. June has been . . . very quiet since she
arrived on the bridge. And, Captain, there are signs that
Level One is being breached. Navigation, PAQ, our main
power sources . . . . I'm beginning to register multiple glitches."

hen we don't have much time left.

Ericho began walking up the side of the ship toward the main sensor channel. From there he would head north to the bow of the *Alchemon* and the emergency entrance to the northwest lander hold.

"Any problems with life support?"

"No, Captain. The invader has not yet interrupted any of PEH's functions. And we still have geonic stability, even though that system is also now outside my control."

Ericho reached the main sensor channel and turned north, marching along the edge of the miniature canyon.

"Jonomy, that Sentinel alert, with the warrior pups and . . . Rigel—"

He stopped, surprised to find himself suddenly choking on the tech officer's name. The reality of Rigel's death hit home.

He's dead. He's a part of the blackness, now, for all eternity.

At least Rigel had escaped Elke's fate.

Drawing a deep breath, Ericho forced himself to repress his feelings. *Now is not the time for grief. Later I will mourn for a lost friend.*

If there was a later.

"Jonomy, the Sentinels reacted to Rigel's violence as they were programmed to. But they didn't open up that external lock, did they?"

"No, Captain. EAC—external airseal control—is Level Two, and now under the creature's control. I believe it was our invader who ejected you from the ship."

"But it spared Mars Lea."

There was a pause. "Captain, I believe that for some unknown reason, this invader is protecting Mars Lea. I suspect that following Rigel's demise, it perceived you as another possible threat to her. It used the most expedient method for removing you from her presence."

It wants her alive.

Another question occurred to him. "Why didn't the vacuum purge trigger another Sentinel alert?"

"You were wearing a shieldsuit, Captain. The Sentinels did not consider the purge a life-threatening situation."

A shadow suddenly crossed Ericho's path: a figure, approaching from above, walking down the hull on the other side of the sensor channel.

A cyberlink robot.

Its frail-looking arms were extended, supporting a tubular conglomeration of some sort. A mass of power conduits trailed away from the device, vanishing beyond the horizon of the ship.

Ericho ignited his laser-cutter, preparing for confrontation.

But the robot ignored him. When it reached the two-meter-wide sensor channel, it bent forward and stepped over the lip. Power conduits trailed into the darkness as the robot walked down the side of the canyon, disappearing from view.

Ericho moved closer. He peered over the edge. Three meters below, the floor of the channel bustled with movement, activity.

There were several other cyberlinks, at least a dozen pups, and one shieldsuited figure, with its back to Ericho. Clusters of unidentifiable equipment and boxes of power tools floated in the dark cavity, all linked to the hull by safety lines.

"Hardy?" Ericho called softly to the shieldsuited figure. He felt his throat going dry with fear even as he uttered the name.

The figure did not respond.

"Captain, you're at the main west junction of the Loop system. Those robots are working on the spatiotemporal coagulators—"

"Hardy?" Ericho whispered again, knowing that it wasn't Hardy, that someone or something else was inside that shieldsuit.

"Captain, I've been picking up internal alterations to SCO as well. The entire Loop system is being changed . . . modified. And that earlier data flow between EPS and GEL—the probability scan of our library—all that information is now being fed directly into SCO."

The shieldsuited figure turned to reach into an open toolbox. Ericho saw its face.

Inside the helmet, floating within a colorful mass of gelatinous nutriments, was a small pup. The tiny robot blinked its running lights—a coded sequence of some sort. The pup was relaying messages to the suit's sight-typer, ordering the shieldsuit to perform the necessary duties.

Ericho felt a sense of revulsion. The combination of

eldsuit, pup, and nutriment chemicals was, in its own ay, as perverse as what had happened to Elke.

He had seen enough. He turned away, continued his trek to the northwest lander hold.

Somehow, the invader had to be stopped. It could not be allowed to reach Earth. Ericho began considering options, ways of dealing with the monstrosity, courses of action that Jonomy might have overlooked, rejected because they were too dangerous.

"Captain, I believe I understand what the invader is trying to do. The SCO system, the probability scan—everything fits. Those projected Corporeal growth patterns I spoke of—the invader has now obtained specific data. The creature has calculated that social and technological advancement will continue unabated for at least another three hundred and fifty years."

The Lytic's voice grew very quiet. "It's going to take us there, Captain. That's why the SCO system is being modified; that's why all this activity is taking place on the hull. We're going to shortly undergo a controlled chronomute— an accomplishment that our present-day Corporeal science has not yet been able to achieve. We're going to be thrust forward in time—three hundred and fifty years into our future."

Ericho accepted the news silently. By the time he reached the airlock, he knew what had to be done.

The manual resets functioned properly and the outer seal slid noiselessly open. He entered the lower deck of the northwest hold, a narrow corridor running beneath the lander. The door closed and he waited silently for the shaft to repressurize.

That the invader had permitted him to reenter the ship so easily came as no great surprise. Out in space, dead or alive, he was of no use. In here, he could be connected, made a part of the whole. For now, that meant he had a chance to fight the invader. *As long as I stay away from Mars Lea.*

The inner seal opened and Ericho entered the corridor leading to the bridge.

"Controlled chronomuting," continued Jonomy calmly, as if he found the whole process an interesting field of study. "The invader understands the complexities of spatiotemporal technology, Captain. It knows what modifications had to be made to our Loop systems. It knows how to chronomute forward to a specific era."

Another airseal obediently parted. Ericho entered the last section of corridor.

"Three hundred and fifty years forward," repeated the Lytic. "We're going to be returning to an Earth when the Corporeal will be thousands, perhaps millions of times larger and more powerful than it is today.

"Think of it, Captain. A network consisting of billions of computers, rather than millions. Our civilization—larger, more complex, perhaps spread throughout half the galaxy. Why should the creature return to our own time when it can go forward into a future that offers so much more."

Ericho nodded. *The invader will link everything together— humans and animals and plants and machines and computers.* All would become a part of the whole. One creation spreading out to encompass the universe.

It had to be stopped.

The final airseal opened. Ericho walked onto the bridge.

Jonomy sat at the far side of his data circle, the umbilical trailing from his forehead. His eyes were closed, the pale face drenched in sweat.

Near the center of the room lay Alan's sealed medbed, fastened to the floor with acceleration straps. Next to the medbed, in the lieutenant's chair, sat June. She was staring into the holographic display orb.

The crewdoc's vacant eyes were locked on the HOD's three-dimensional representation: a triangular face, formed of one unbroken line. It was the image of the ancient Babylonian demon, Humbaba.

Erico turned to the Lytic. "Jonomy, I want you to disconnect from the umbilical."

Eyes flashed open. "Captain, until Level One is completely overrun, I can still monitor—"

"It's over."

Jonomy stared at him.

"Disconnect," Ericho repeated. "Remove the umbilical. That's an order."

"Captain—"

Ericho ignited his laser-cutter and moved two steps closer to the Lytic. "If you don't disconnect, I'll cut the cord."

A frown creased Jonomy's forehead. Age lines streaked out from both sides of the umbilical. The Lytic hunched ward and his face began shifting through a range of expressions, from pale anger to disbelief.

Ericho raised the laser-cutter.

Abruptly, Jonomy's face relaxed, as if he had just made peace with some inner turmoil. He reached up, snapped the umbilical out of his forehead, and let it drop to the deck.

"Get into a shieldsuit."

Without a word, the Lytic rose and crossed stiffly to one of the storage closets. Withdrawing a suit, he began a silent examination of its circuitry.

Ericho turned to June. "Can you hear me?"

Behind the faceplate, her eyes fluttered.

"June—snap out of it!"

She peeled her face away from the HOD's entrancing image and stared up at Ericho. She looked incredibly sad, like a lost child.

"June, I want you and Jonomy to take Alan to that lander . . . the one that was disengaged from the network. I want the three of you to assume a safe orbit around the *Alchemon* and wait there until you hear from me."

"Humbaba," she whispered. "I know what it means."

He nodded. "Yes. I know too."

She shook her head. "I know why Tom was so fascinated by it. I know what it meant to him."

He reached down and helped her to stand.

"It was his symbol," she said grimly. "It was his symbol for what he could not comprehend. Humbaba—mythological demon. Humbaba—the creature that Tom knew would annihilate him."

"You have to go," Ericho urged gently. "You have to help Jonomy carry Alan to the lander. The three of you have to blast out of here."

Her eyes widened. "The demon represented Tom's fears. This artistic representation was the closest that Tom could come to contemplating the nature of his own end. It was his very own ghost, his very own personalized demon. Humbaba was his angel of death."

"You have to leave," Ericho repeated. "You . . . all of us . . . we have a chance of making it back to Earth."

Jonomy scowled. "In a lander?"

"Yes. Four and a half months should get the craft to the Sycamore terminus of the Loop. There should be enough air and supplies—"

"For what purpose?" Jonomy interrupted. "We can't take a lander through the Loop; we need the ship's engines for that. And policy dictates that Pannis won't send out a rescue team until at least a year after we're declared overdue."

June nodded her head slowly. "He's right. We won't have enough air and supplies to last that long."

"You won't need them," said Ericho. "Everyone will be vegetated."

Jonomy frowned, as if disturbed by the fact that he had not thought of the possibility.

The crewdoc licked her lips. "It might work."

"Get to the lander," Ericho ordered. "I'll call you from the west storage pod. I'm going down there to get Hardy."

They both stared at him.

"Don't be ridiculous," snapped June. "You can't help—"

"I am the captain of this ship," he said calmly. "The crew is my responsibility."

"But—"

June, right now, my being the captain is more important than you can imagine. Do you understand?"

She glanced uneasily at the image of Humbaba in the HOD, then turned back to Ericho with a frown. She shook her head, refusing to accept his decision.

"You have to come with us," she demanded.

"No."

"But—"

"No," he said firmly. "My mind is clear on this. It's something that I must do."

Jonomy finished suiting up. A sharp hiss sounded in Ericho's helmet as the Lytic pressurized.

Ericho helped them lift the medbed. They carried Alan over to the door leading to the northeast lander hold. The airseal opened properly. Jonomy and June, with their burden, stepped out into the corridor. Ericho remained on the bridge.

June's eyes pleaded with him. "Ericho, please—"

"No. I have to rescue Hardy. Remember: If you make it to the lander, get into a safe orbit and wait for my signal from the west storage pod." He met the Lytic's piercing gaze.

"Jonomy, you do understand, don't you?"

And suddenly, Jonomy's eyes widened. He swallowed. "Captain . . . I—"

Ericho cut him off. "It shouldn't take long to rescue Hardy."

"No, Captain."

Ericho forced a smile. "Just wait for my signal."

"We will wait, Captain, for your signal."

The airseal snapped closed, leaving Ericho alone on the bridge.

Jonomy understood.

The Lytic realized that this nightmare could not be allowed to return to Earth—not now; not three hundred and fifty years from now. It had to be stopped. Ericho did not think that he could kill the creature, but he could strand it out here in the void. For how long, he did not know. Certainly not for all time.

But maybe for a few thousand years.

He crossed quickly to a closet and replaced his damaged glove. Some feeling had returned to his nearly frozen hand, but the forefinger remained numb. He might lose it.

The thought brought on a huge grin. With a chuckle, he sealed the new glove.

His suit repressurized and he exited the bridge through the southwest airseal. He headed for the west storage pod.

Down there, underneath the ship, was where the chain reaction would begin. Down there, where he was ostensibly going to rescue Hardy. Down in the storage pod, where the mass of fusion batteries was stored.

His laser-cutter needed to pierce only one cell. The chain reaction would ignite the rest, and within microseconds enough raw energy would be released to vaporize most of the ship.

With luck, Jonomy, June, and Alan would make it to the lander. From a safe distance, they would watch as the starship *Alchemon* was engulfed by the indomitable energy of a total melt.

That would be their signal to head for home.

27

It seemed as if it was over before it began.

Time accelerated, or decelerated—Mars Lea was not sure which. Multiple temporal paths seemed to flow simultaneously. One part of her mind registered the passage of nanoseconds within the physical universe, another grew cognizant of dissimilar time lines existing within the blackness. Yet she remained outside of chronological influences, a traveler skating on the edge of eternity.

She recalled the airseal sliding open. Rigel Keller, standing on the other side, his shieldsuit brimming with deadly weapons; the captain, a short distance behind him.

And then she was . . . going away, simultaneously retreating into herself and into the blackness. A sensation of incredible speed, racing along the event horizon separating the physical from the psionic universe. She could sense everyone and everything, throughout time and space, and she knew that she was experiencing, for the first time, the true state of *Ta-shad*—concurrent consciousness of both universes.

From the event horizon—from this new perspective— Mars Lea could see odd constructions taking shape within the blackness: triangles and squares and rectangles of brilliant light, churning with their own logic, flowing along the darkened edges of an enormous enclosed space, leading her toward its center. She plunged into that vast geometry of light and form, saw gridworks expanding in complexity; triangles bursting out of octahedrons, cubes mutating into wild geodesic configurations, blistering symmetries, alien, yet engagingly familiar.

A school of Platonic solids—dodecahedrons and cubes— flying past her, sailing down some invisible line of motion, disappearing into a vortex of dark cavities far below. A great inverted retrosnub icosidodecahedron, gleaming like some fantastic ancestor of all snowflake crystals, spiraling

ong multiple axes—a visual impossibility—throwing beaded
streams of purple light against a thousand targets.

More exotic geometrical solids tumbled through the gridwork: a quasirhombicuboctahedron, a second stellation of
the cuboctahedron. She knew each of the solids by name,
identified each merely by looking at it, and that fact alone
struck her with wonder. But she remained confused about
exactly what this vast gridwork—this quantified lunacy of
exotic shapes—represented.

And then a sphere of hot yellow luminance appeared, in
three . . . four . . . six locations at the same time. And Mars
Lea knew that this orb of golden light possessed superluminal
powers similar to her own: the ability to exist outside the
normal channels of time. And as she looked at it, she knew
what it was.

A Sentinel.

I am inside the ship.

Somehow, her consciousness was flowing through the circuitry of the computer. By entering the true state of *Ta-
shad*—by bringing together the psionic and the physical
universes—she had finally become aware of the vast network that had surrounded and enclosed her for the past ten
months. Just as human beings existed as bright stars within
the blackness, so too did the starship *Alchemon* occupy
psionic space, represented by this incredible constellation of
glowing geometries.

The voice of the alien consciousness—of blue blob—flowed
through her. *You have taken another step as an entropy
junction, Mars Lea. Now you must extend yourself, feel the
power that surrounds you, become what you were meant to
be.*

"What I was meant to be," she whispered to the empty
corridor. A sense of revulsion overcame her. *I'm a monster.*

The time has come for clarity, said the alien. *A temporal
storm is brewing and you can deny yourself no longer.
Accept what you are, Mars Lea Frock. Accept, or the Unity
will control you and your species for all eternity.*

I'm a monster, she repeated.

Yes, said the alien. *By the standards of your race, you are
a monster—a freak—an accident of nature. But you are also
their only hope.*

Mars Lea knew it was true.

She returned to the vast geometry of complex forms—the

ship's computer—focusing awareness on the gridwork of exotic shapes. She began to perceive their nature more clearly.

A pair of white cubes, spinning in tandem, represented the *Alchemon*'s Level 6 Luminosity System, injecting the control pulses that provided the vessel with steady lighting. A denser shape, a sharp-pointed stellated octahedron spouting shafts of green lightning, monitored and regulated Level 3 Hydroponics. Sixteen great icosahedrons orbited the central body of the simplest Platonic solid, a four-sided tetrahedron. This complex arrangement guided a matrix of lesser shapes, together overseeing the powerful Primary Quantizer of Level 1.

She looked deeper, became aware that each geometric form, no matter how complex, had faint white lines connecting it to a dark opening situated high above. Soaring upward, she headed straight for that nexus of systems.

A growing unease stopped her, prevented her from entering that dark hole in the gridwork. From a distance, she stared at the converging white lines. Sadness enveloped her.

With all her soul, she desired to become one of those faint lines, to flow into that nexus with the rest of the *Alchemon*'s systems. But if she allowed that to happen, if she permitted her feelings full sway, if she plunged into that conglomeration of data, it would be the end of her.

There was a temporal storm brewing. She could sense it—a chill wind, howling in the darkness, irresistibly approaching. But she would not survive that storm by running away and hiding, no matter how reassuring the hiding place might appear.

That nexus of faint white lines was the umbilical, the entrance port into Jonomy's cybernetically enhanced brain.

It was hard to say good-bye to him a second time. But she did it. She turned her back on that gateway to Jonomy's mind.

And here, from this perspective, adjacent to the Lytic's terminal, the entire gridwork lay spread out beneath her, like a blazing nighttime city seen from a mountaintop. This psionic symbolization of the starship *Alchemon*, this symmetry of jewels, taunted her with its ethereal beauty. It beckoned to her.

But a pulsing sheen disturbed the purity of the glittering metropolis. From this distance, the surfaces of the geo-

tric forms seemed to sparkle unnaturally. And looking
oser, she saw that each cube and octahedron, each complex shape, was alive with a million tiny fireflies. She sensed
wrongness: This was not the way the *Alchemon* was supposed to be.

Each of those tiny fireflies had the characteristics of a
Sentinel, their sparkling caused by constant disappearances
and reappearances within the gridwork. They were superluminal travelers, controlling the destiny of the ship. They
were aspects of the Unity.

The computer was almost completely overrun with them.
A feeling of hopelessness touched her.

It's everywhere! Nothing seemed to be beyond the reach
of this creature. It was unstoppable. *Why doesn't it just kill
me and be done with it?*

The alien consciousness responded: *Because the Unity is
using you, Mars Lea. You are an entropy junction, in the
prime of your power, and you inject a randomness into both
universes. The Unity's lust for you is too great. And even if
it did not desire you, it would still hesitate to kill you for
fear of what you might become as a pure psionic entity. But
it brews a temporal storm and if you are not prepared, that
storm will weaken you. The Unity is attempting to break the
bonds of space/time, hurtle this vessel—this starship* Alchemon—*three hundred and fifty of your years into the future.
If that occurs, and you are not ready, your essence will be
stretched across the centuries. You will lose your ability to
focus upon the moment. You will become a shadow of
yourself, forever lost, a blurring of energies, an entropy
junction stripped of its central core, spread out over a three
hundred and fifty year time span. If that happens, the Unity
will have you within its power forever.*

Then help me! Tell me what you want me to do!

I cannot. You must do for yourself.

Damn you.

With a burst of rage, she reached out toward the alien
consciousness, trying to strike at it, trying to hurt it. But the
alien was dead. There was nothing Mars Lea could do to
cause it pain. Her anger succeeded only in bringing her
closer to its center.

Wet flowers on a muggy riverbank.

Again the smell carried her to the creature's homeworld,
and to the terrible tragedy that had enveloped the alien's

race. Mars Lea sensed a world losing all identity, bein absorbed, connected, all life being shaped into a part of the whole.

A planet destroyed; absorbed by the Unity. But now she perceived that there had been survivors: a glfted few, the most telempathically powerful, able to weather the psionic storm. And those orphans did not run away and hide. Instead, they found a way to save other worlds, other species, from a similar fate.

A deep dread settled within Mars Lea, an agony that she could not identify, only feel. Cold sweat erupted on her skin from head to toes. She grew dizzy. The event horizon blurred. Time and space seemed ready to disappear into a vortex. *Ta-shad* began to slip away.

But she held on. The incredible bravery of the alien's compatriots inspired her; their courage planted a seed, a kernel of buried determination, growing with abandon, filling her consciousness with a raging fire.

I will not run away.

The feeling of dread lessened, grew bearable. Like her earlier virgin crossing into the blackness, the fear of the thing proved far worse than the thing itself.

She had passed another barrier, although she was still not certain of what the barrier was: The core of her dread remained vague. But she had proven herself, proven that she would no longer retreat. And the alien, sensing her resolve, now opened its consciousness.

Our species was ancient compared to your own, Mars Lea. We had achieved a peak of evolutionary mutation and there was nowhere left to explore, no aspect of this universe left untouched. As a species, we had grown into a supreme form.

The realm of the physical universe provided no more challenges. So we looked into the blackness, seeking new avenues of exploration. But all we found there was dissolution.

As an intelligent species, evolving for billions of years, we refused to accept the ultimate truth—that we remained mortal, that death still awaited us. No matter what level of greatness we achieved, the dialectic of life/death still determined our destiny. Against the vast nothingness of the psionic universe, we remained, in essence, children.

As a species, we could not accept this. We could not accept death as the final termination. We felt that there had be more. Billions of years of expanding intellect refused ~~me~~ the blackness as our ultimate destiny.

And so we succumbed.

Evolutionary mutation is random. Organic intelligence is structured, coherent, logical. The force of organic intelligence forms a natural dialectic with the force of random mutation.

Our species ignored that dialectic. In an attempt to create a new synthesis, in an attempt to escape the fate that awaited us within the blackness, we merged the organic intelligence of our species with the power of random mutation.

In effect, we interfused with the very force that had first created us: We performed incest with our own cellular structures. We closed a great circle, brought endings into beginnings. In the process, we destroyed one of the universe's governing dialectics.

By merging into the very force that had created us, our species altered a natural balance. An equation, binding together space and time, was dissolved. That equation became the Unity.

A few of us saw the danger, refused to take part in the great merging. We chose to remain free individuals, accepting death as our natural end. We rejected the Unity, rejected the concept of a single power absorbing the randomness of creation.

The Unity destroyed or absorbed most of us. But I, and a few others, survived.

Like yourself, Mars Lea, I am a being without temporal limits, an entropy junction. Within the psionic universe, I am immortal.

I placed myself in the path of the Unity. I permitted it to use me. Through me, it was able to explore eternity. The Unity was already capable of absorbing physical and psionic energies; in my presence, it gained the ability to achieve a higher dimension, to ravage time as well as space. By granting it this power, I became precious to it.

The Unity grew drunk on me, wild with temporal freedom, mad with its lust to connect everything together. I drew its central core into the psionic universe and then I closed the event horizon, trapped its primary essence within the blackness. In the physical universe, I absorbed its energy web within the very cells of my body, thereby sacrificing my own shape and form. To give the Unity as little freedom of movement as possible, to strip it of sensory functions, I de-evolved my physical body into the gelatinous mass that your exploration team discovered.

The other survivors of my species took me to Sycamore, a rare planet: a world of random energy mutations that could help camouflage my presence. It was hoped that I could hide there, with the Unity as my prisoner, until the natural end of our cosmos, ages hence.

All this occurred over half a million of your years ago.

But all plans carry imperfections: the seeds of failure. The Unity, in those moments before I trapped it, when it was saturating itself with currents of temporal ecstasy, managed to reach into the future and perceive another entropy junction: you. In terms of space and time, you were very close—a mere eight light-years and five hundred thousand years away.

Even trapped within the blackness, trapped within my body, the Unity remained powerful. It was able to reach out across time and space and influence the development of your species. It created coincidences. It arranged matters so that you would someday journey to Sycamore.

Mars Lea acknowledged what she had always somehow known. *I was being manipulated even before I was born.*

Yes, your great power doomed you ages ago. You were destined to come to Sycamore and find the Unity.

The Unity also permitted small microorganisms to escape from my body and adapt themselves to the violent habitat of Sycamore. Merely another part of its plan, a structured coincidence that would help your exploration team locate me.

Mars Lea understood. *One entropy junction to trap the Unity; another to free it. I was brought to Sycamore so that it could engineer its escape from you.*

Yes. Mars Lea Frock, an entropy junction almost completely unaware of her own great powers. You served the Unity well, remaining essentially blind to its manipulation. The core of your being was a twisted mass of primal pains, created by a lifetime of social rejection. Your Corporeal made you into exactly what the Unity desired: a malleable entropy junction.

Events transpired just as the Unity always intended they would: the Sycamore storm that freed my body from a tomb of coagulated rock, the journey to your vessel, the telempathic destruction of your lieutenant. And finally, the melt in your

*ntainment lab, which ended my existence as a living crea-
ure, consigning me to the blackness forever, and thereby
freeing the Unity's physical essence.*

*And now, Mars Lea Frock, the Unity is drunk on your
power.*

"I will not run away," she answered grimly, surprised to
hear her own voice in the corridor of the *Alchemon.*

But against the chill wind of the coming temporal storm,
her words seemed as powerless as echoes.

28

Marching through the *Alchemon*, Ericho wondered what it must be like to lose your identity.

He wondered whether the ship could sense the decimation that was taking place throughout it, whether some barely conscious facet of a Level 1 system was actually *aware* of the incredible transformations that were taking place. He recognized the inherent fallacy of his thoughts: starship *Alchemon* was not alive, at least not in the human sense. It was only a machine, vast and complex, ruled by the binary logic of basic circuits. But still, somewhere in the network, the ship had to sense that things were wrong.

Updeck west—a corridor that he must have trekked through at least a thousand times in the past ten months. All of the landmarks, usually ignored by the eye because of their blatant familiarity, had provided constant subconscious reassurance that this miniature world—this human-created ecosystem—remained at peace with itself.

But now, the walls were stained with the brown and amber molds. And a dark liquid with the viscosity of heated molasses was dripping from several of the air ducts, forming tiny rivulets and puddles in a manner that suggested that the ship's simulated gravity was no longer plumb.

The natatorium had been the breeding ground for these mutations. Now they were spreading, infesting the rest of the ship.

He reached the end of the hall and entered the elevator. The airseal snapped shut. Ericho descended into the west storage pod.

Mars Lea found herself standing before the entrance to the dreamlounge. She did not know why.

She knew only that she hated and feared this place.

The seal parted and she stepped into the middle of a raging storm.

*   *   *

In the pod's dim lighting, Ericho could see no obvious changes. It appeared that the mutations had not yet reached this middle level. Everything still looked normal.

He eased himself out of the elevator, inched across the dirty metallic floor toward the sealed ecocabinet and the small research station set up beside it.

"Hardy?"

No answer.

The work area was illuminated by a bright circle of light, a gridwork of hastily arranged ceiling lumes suspended overhead. But the rest of the huge space remained locked in shadows.

The largest batch of fusion cells was stored at the opposite end of this level, in the darkness beyond the work area. Ericho gripped his laser-cutter tightly and moved forward.

A loud yet somehow muffled voice cut through his helmet. "Captain Brad—more stimuli, please!"

Ericho stopped. "Hardy? Where are you?"

"More stimuli, Captain. It is a necessary adjunct to the experiment. Patience is not a quality worth bearing, at least not gracefully. Intrinsic elements conspire for the uniting. It must be done. We must be undone."

Ericho inched across the deck, sweeping the laser-cutter in a slow arc, ready to ignite it at the first sign of movement. The science rep's words had a familiar quality to them. Hardy sounded as Tom Dianaldi had sounded in those final weeks.

"The rights of the unborn, Captain Brad—precedence and preference—a state of mind illuminating the fingers of coincidence. We must be ready to adapt. We must work to yield, something that a culture overlaid with pragmatism cannot respond to. We must desecrate, but only to conceive."

Ericho turned on his suit headlamp, panned it through the darkness that surrounded him. Storage racks were illuminated, then fell back into shadow. There was no sign of Hardy; the pod offered a wealth of hiding places.

"Fields of space/time, Captain Brad, focusing energies of magnitudes greater than the sun of suns. In the true outline of the cosmos, zero and infinity are numerically identical. That resonance ensures the fluid nature of all life and all death."

Ericho passed in front of the sealed ecocabinet. A glance through the window rooted him to the spot.

"Hardy," he whispered.

The science rep was inside the ecocabinet, stark naked, sitting in the lotus position atop the radioactive remains of blue blob. Hardy's arms were folded across his hairy chest and his head was encased in the isolator hood. Cables, trailing from the bizarre helmet, were attached to a ceiling-mounted instrument panel. A microphone was connected to a chinpiece and Hardy's voice emerged from the unit's speaker.

"It is time for clarity, Captain Brad. I journey to a place beyond the dissonance of the present."

As Ericho watched, Hardy carefully lifted his right arm and, without disturbing the positioning of his head, picked up a thin-bladed lab knife from the floor. He raised the blade above him and smiled through the glass at Ericho.

"Captain Brad, the purity of the experiment requires dedication. And dedication requires purpose.

"I am not insane. My mind is merely afloat within a sea of organic possibility. Awareness is being retrofitted to the climax of the moment, to the climax of each moment, to the remotest strands of space/time.

"I am learning what Mars Lea knows naturally. I am following her example, following her royal path toward the absolute pinnacle of knowledge. She has taught me well.

"Pain is the entrance, Captain Brad."

Hardy brought the knife down into the flesh above his knee, burying the blade almost to the hilt. A piercing cry echoed through the storage pod.

"Pain!" Hardy screamed. "I see it all, now! I see it all!"

Blood erupted from the science rep's leg and his face suddenly twisted into an ugly grimace. He glared at Ericho.

"I know why you're here!" he raged. "You still seek to hinder my experiments! You do not understand! But I understand you, Captain Brad. I understand the twisted convolutions of your mind.

"You are here to destroy us, to ensure that the mission ends in failure. You are here with your laser-cutter, hoping to ignite the fusion cells! I can see your intentions: You cannot hide! Pain has shown me your thoughts!"

Ericho drew a deep breath and willed himself to turn his back on the scientist.

I must end it. I must destroy the Alchemon *so that this monstrosity is left out here in the void. There is no other way.*

But as Ericho started to turn around, he felt something behind him. Through the ecocabinet window, he watched Hardy's face dissolve into a countenance of terror.

Ericho knew that whatever was poised at his back was neither human nor machine. He spun around, and in a moment of terrifying clarity, gazed into the face of madness.

A shapeless glitter emerging from the shadows.

The invader.

I like storms.

Mars Lea remembered saying that once to a Pannis Assignor. She could not recall the details of their conversation, or why she had uttered such foolish words. Then, it had seemed important. Now, it was just another event that had occurred during a time when she had been less conscious.

But here and now, in this place known as the dream-lounge, in this bidirectional slice of space/time that flowed outward from both sides of the event horizon, engulfing both the physical and psionic universes, in this place, Mars Lea Frock had entered the nexus of the ultimate storm.

She stood in the middle of an enraged ocean, white-capped breakers crashing down all around her, salt-sea smell in the damp air. Dark clouds filled the sky, stabs of lightning blistered the horizon, and a heavy rain splattered unpleasantly across her face. Thunder shrieked.

It was impossible to tell where reality ended and dream-lounge illusion began. In fact, it no longer mattered.

You are trapped in a focal point of matter/energy degradation, explained the alien consciousness. *This is your moment, your time. You are at the center of both universes.*

As the thoughts wafted through her, Mars Lea raised her head and gazed at the splitting heavens, and she saw the strands of the web, breaking through the sky, outlining the storm, controlling it.

The Unity.

Cold wind whipped at her hair. The storm grew, howling in fury: the madness of two universes melting into one. The dreamlounge collapsed around her, a core of violence shrinking toward infinity. But she remained calm.

I am the eye of the storm.

You are entropy, agreed the alien. *You are an undilate.
force.*

Mars Lea felt sadness wash over her. *I never tasted human
freedom. I never knew what it was like to choose. My entire
life has been lived as a slave to other forces.*

She could feel the alien agreeing with her. But then it
said: *Here, in this moment—in this space and time—here.
Mars Lea Frock,' you have a choice.*

A choice, she thought bitterly, knowing it was true. But
such a choice offered little consolation. *I can choose to
control or I can choose to be controlled. But I cannot choose
to be free.*

Accept, urged the alien. *Accept before it is too late.
Become what you are.*

I am a martyr.

She thought of Jonomy then, and the times they had
experienced together. She realized that those moments with
the Lytic were the closest she had ever come to being truly
free.

And Jonomy was still alive.

He was out there somewhere, still able to make choices,
still able to chart a course as he glided through the realm of
the physical. And in the realm of the psionic he was a
burning star, a fiery beacon, fighting entropy until the final
dissolution of the blackness came to cloak his spirit.

"For you, Jonomy!" she cried out.

For him, she would become the web of time. For Jonomy,
she would bind the universe.

It floated directly behind Ericho, within the physical boundaries of the storage pod yet distinct from the room, as if it
were out of sequence with the rhythms of this place and
time. He could see it, but he could not see it. It was there,
but it was not there.

It was everything and it was nothing.

His eyes perceived a dense cloud of darkness, a drifting
sphere, full of indescribable color, drenched with smells,
pounding with noise.

He looked into the nothingness and he saw himself, three
hundred and fifty years in the future, returning to Earth in
the lander, diving down through the atmosphere, a rainbow
display of energies outside the window, guiding and protecting the craft from a dangerously fast reentry.

It was his dream. It was the place his mind had created in order to maintain its sanity. He held onto it, held onto the reality of that dream, imagining the beautiful desert sunset as the lander plunged beneath that final cloud cover and glided in for a touchdown.

The dream is all I have.

He tried to close his eyes, tried to deny the floating monstrosity of nothingness drifting toward him. But he could not turn away. The spherical cloud seemed to contain all of creation. It both repelled and captivated him.

Hardy's voice filled his helmet, senseless words, yet simultaneously imbued with deep meaning: "The shape of destiny convolutes us. The outlines of our fate retreat from us. The onslaught of emblems too weak to conceive mutate into fabrics of all creation. We adhere to the now so that the past and future do not intrude."

Ericho understood everything Hardy was saying and he understood none of it.

He remembered the laser-cutter in his hand and his reason for coming to the storage pod. He thought of the batch of fusion batteries, only meters away from where he stood.

He thought of death, in the here and now, and he thought of life, glowing beneath a desert sunset, three hundred and fifty years in the future, and he realized that he had absolutely no choice as to which of those fates would encompass him.

He could not move. He was powerless, an observer of events that seemed to be occurring beyond some distant horizon. There was simply nothing he could do that would make the slightest difference. He could bear witness—nothing more.

The Unity moved. A scream erupted from Hardy.

Ericho felt a weird sensation, a fluttering deep within his flesh, as if his very muscles were vibrating in tandem to some force that defied understanding. The sensation spread quickly throughout his whole body. From the pit of his stomach to the bottom of his toes to the strands of hair atop his head, the energy of displaced temporal currents shattered his cells.

He had never before experienced such strong sensations, but he knew exactly what they were. Ingested psychedelics usually camouflaged the side effects of looping, but anyone who had ever traveled through a transpatial corridor knew

what those indescribable yet unmistakable sensations re
resented. Those who passed through Loop space knew how
it felt to cheat time.

*We've been chronomuted—plunged forward in time. We've
just traveled three hundred and fifty years into the future.*

Mars Lea spread her arms and reached toward the sky.
The storm split apart. Thunder, lightning, and savage rain
disappeared into blackness. A wild universe took shape in
the damp air, unfolding like a larva wriggling from its cocoon.

Fear—a pure unmitigated torrent of it—poured out of the
blackness and blasted into her mind, seeking to disrupt her
consciousness, seeking to control.

But she ignored the fear. And unacknowledged, it vanished into dreams.

*I know who and what I am. There is no longer anything
you can do that will make me afraid.*

She sensed the Unity becoming enraged by her show of
will. A wave of anger descended on her. The Unity realized
it could no longer manipulate her unconscious mind. Now it
sought to destroy her.

The last of the *Alchemon*'s warrior pups swept into the
dreamlounge. No Sentinel controlled the fighter this time; it
was being guided by the Unity. Something was keeping the
Sentinels occupied.

The tiny robot approached from above, firing its lasers. A
volley of mag-projectiles erupted from its cannons. At precisely the same instant, Mars Lea felt the *Alchemon* begin to
shift in time, uproot itself from the continuum of the moment, hurtle forward.

She understood. The *Alchemon* was being chronomuted.
And the Sentinels, obeying their primary directive, were
racing through the ship's circuitry, trying to prevent the
temporal odyssey. To SEN, saving the ship from an attempted chronomute was more important than saving the
life of a crew member.

Analysis/abstraction of the situation occurred with superluminal swiftness. There were two paths open to her, two
courses of action. But it was a mockery of a choice, for both
paths would lead the Unity to complete victory.

She could remain passive—do nothing—allow herself to
be chronomuted forward, shifted into the future along with

e ship. But if she chose that course, the warrior pup would destroy her body in those microseconds of temporal transition.

Or she could preserve her physical essence by fleeing into the event horizon, that borderline between the psionic and physical universes: *Ta-Shad*, a timeless haven where no harm could befall her, where she could exist in a state of constant acceleration, forever racing away from the events of the real world, forever retreating from the attacking warrior pup, forever an observer on the rim of eternity.

But if she escaped into the event horizon, she would lose her focus, lose her vantage point of being at the center of both universes—the eye of the storm—and in that instant, the Unity would overwhelm her. It would trap her within that state of *Ta-Shad*, dilute her power across a timeframe of three hundred and fifty years. She would be forever enmeshed in the Unity's web, forever under its control.

She was being forced into making an impossible choice. *No. I refuse.* Anger solidified into resolve.

I am an entropy junction. I will make my own path.

She hurled her consciousness into the blackness and projected herself backward in time, to an instant several seconds before the warrior pup ignited its weapons.

"Sentinels obey," she commanded, knowing now why those words carried such import. They were the last human sounds she would ever utter.

The Sentinels came. From the bowels of the *Alchemon* they emerged, from hidden circuits within all six levels of the network; from the psionic representation of the ship they came, from the vortex of complex geometries, the swirling Platonic solids and great inverted retrosnub icosahedrons.

Sentinels obey.

They coursed through the ship, under her command now, miniature extensions of Mars Lea's very consciousness, superluminal linkages, aligning themselves to the telempathic pathways of her will.

The Unity reeled, its consciousness overwhelmed by the sudden onslaught. One of her Sentinels took control of the warrior pup at the precise instant the robot fired its weapons. Under Mars Lea's will, the Sentinel physically moved the robot forward in time and space, positioning the pup directly in the path of its own mag-projectiles and lasers. Caught in a temporal paradox, the warrior pup attacked

itself. Shrapnel exploded into the blackness as the r͟o̶
literally blew itself apart.

*I am an entropy junction. I am alive throughout all tim͟e̶
and space.*

She shifted forward along the axes of time, flowed into
the future along with the Unity and the ship. All sensory
remnants of the dreamlounge vanished. Nothing remained
but the vast energy web, attempting to connect the disparate
elements of the universe into a whole: the stars, the blackness, the psionic geometries of the *Alchemon,* the physical
structures of plastic and metal, the matrix of all living
creatures.

But the Sentinels were a part of Mars Lea now, and they
relentlessly drove the invader out of the ship, drove it from
the blackness.

All around her, Mars Lea perceived the Unity's handiwork perishing. In the corridors, brown and amber molds
shriveled and died, circuits altered by alien logic burnt themselves out, the maelstrom in the pool dissolved into a lifeless
mass. The *Alchemon*'s biosystems reassumed control, began
to flush the contamination from the vessel.

The Unity perceived its destiny. It tried to escape, tried to
crawl forward along its own web into some future era, into
some place where Mars Lea could not follow it.

She opened her consciousness and lunged outward. Like
the gaping jaws of some impossible psychic predator, she
absorbed the Unity, swallowing it whole. She merged the
creature into the very cells of her body, molded its energy to
the contours of her soul.

And then she was back in the dreamlounge—a plain white
room, devoid of images. She could feel the creature inside
her, already probing and searching along the molecular structure of her tissues, seeking a way out of its new prison. The
Unity would not be a submissive captive. Eventually, it
might succeed in finding a way to escape.

But not for a long, long time.

Ericho felt as if he had just been released from a nightmare.

The invader vanished. One moment it was there, the next
it was gone. The cloud of darkness disappeared, and not
just from the storage pod. It vanished, period.

Something had happened.

The Alchemon had been chronomuted into the future; of

Ericho was certain. But now the ship felt . . . different . somehow more free.

He knew such thoughts made little sense, yet there was no denying what his feelings were telling him.

The ship had passed through a violent storm, and it had been terribly mutated and battered. But it had survived.

Ericho had survived.

He turned around to check on Hardy, but the science rep had not been so lucky. For a brief time, Ericho stared sadly through the window of the ecocabinet.

Everyone needed a place to go when things got too bad—a retreat, a dream, a concept to hold onto until reality again became bearable. Every human being needed a hole to crawl into when the dark times came.

Hardy must never have known about such places.

The science rep had apparently pried the lab knife out of his leg. His second self-mutilation offered no chance for survival. The knife handle stuck out of Hardy's forehead, directly above the bridge of his nose. Dead eyes, streaked with blood, leered into the darkness.

Ericho turned away and walked toward the elevator.

"Jonomy?"

"Yes, Captain, we read you. We never made it to the lander. We're still on the *Alchemon*."

That was a relief. If the ship had chronomuted with the lander far enough away from it, Ericho would have had to face spending his future alone.

But now he would have company.

I am a vessel of containment. I am no longer a human being.

For a time, Mars Lea wondered where she would go with her prisoner. She considered the idea of trying to find the other members of the alien's species: the ones who had consigned Mars Lea's predecessor to the planet Sycamore. But that event had occurred over half a million years ago. If those creatures remained alive, a search for them could take forever.

Of course, within the blackness, that would be more than enough time.

She was truly alone now; even the alien consciousness had removed itself from her path. But being alone did not frighten her.

I have infinity to keep me company.

She chose her course of action.

I will take one of the Alchemon's *landers and I will launch myself into space. I will become a mobile prison, drifting forever through the galaxy. I will explore the stars.*

The stars.

She gazed into the blackness—into the future—and watched as the three surviving crew members piloted the *Alchemon* back to Earth.

But something was wrong. Confusion struck her.

In the psionic world there are three survivors. Yet in the physical world, there are four—Jonomy, June, the captain, and Alan.

Mars Lea scanned the *Alchemon*'s computer and discovered the solution to the dichotomy.

There are four survivors. But within the psionic universe, only three of them are visible to me. The fourth—Alan—has no telempathic powers. He has no star.

And that fact filled Mars Lea with pure joy.

Alan cannot be detected within the blackness! Even the Unity cannot perceive him there!

Despite the Unity's powers, there remained forces within the universe that lay forever beyond its scope.

Always, there would be things that were unknowable, disconnected from the rest of creation. Always, the future would be tinged by a bit of uncertainty.

That was good. It meant that there would always be hope.

Epilogue

At first they thought she was going back to Sycamore. The lander's course pattern diverged only a few degrees from an orbital heading, and a final correction could always be made once the craft entered Sycamore's gravitational field. But at the last possible moment, the lander's retroengines fired, turning the vessel away from the planet. Jonomy calculated that if she held to her new course, she would not approach any known spatial objects for the next twelve and a half million years.

In the end, Ericho had been the only one actually to see her. After the *Alchemon* came back under their control, he and June had begun to search the ship. The crewdoc had gone straight to the medcenter, but something had prompted Ericho to check the northeast hold and the lander that Jonomy had disengaged from the network.

Mars Lea was there, sitting in the pilot's chair, her eyes closed, her hands folded gently on her lap. Ericho had stood quietly in front of the lander and stared in at her through the thick glass of the viewport.

Maybe it had been the tension of the moment, or perhaps the relief of tension, after so many days of madness. But Ericho felt that he had never before gazed upon a face so restful, so at peace with itself.

The dark hair cascaded to her shoulders and curled up under her chin. The lips were gently parted, the cheeks softened into the vaguest hint of a smile. Lines that had creased her forehead were gone.

She had the look of a child.

He had stood there in front of the lander, unable to tear his eyes away from her, even after the hold's sirens warned of imminent depressurization. He had even thought of calling Jonomy, ordering the Lytic to do something, prevent Mars Lea from leaving the *Alchemon*, prevent such beauty from deserting them.

And then she had opened her eyes.

Deserts swirled, vicious storms blanketed whole planets, razors of dark light leaped out to thrash the cosmos. The madness of the universe lay behind those eyes and it pulled at Ericho, yearned for him, a desperate force trying to suck consciousness into a maelstrom of endless possibility.

Mercifully, she closed her eyes, sealing off the terrifying vista. Once again, her face assumed a pattern of tranquillity. He considered thanking her, but it would have been a senseless gesture. Mars Lea, better than anyone, understood what was left unsaid.

Ericho retreated from the lander hold without uttering a word.

Slowly over the next few days, the *Alchemon* returned to normal. In fact, most of the major systems came back on line immediately after Mars Lea's lift-off. The rest of the network, including the badly damaged natatorium, required more time for internal correction and repair. Eventually, though, with Jonomy's help, the network restored itself.

There were anomalies. The dreamlounge system was in shambles—unrepairable, according to the Lytic. Whatever had occurred in there had literally incinerated all of the primary and secondary circuits. Nothing remained but a plain white room, incapable of ever again supporting illusions.

But the strangest anomaly of all regarded the Level 1 Sentinel network. Although Jonomy searched and scanned for days, although he triggered complex feedback loops and staged mock emergencies, although he prodded and cajoled and threatened whole portions of the network with physical harm, SEN did not react.

The Sentinels were gone. Not a trace of them remained.

"What do you think it's like for her?" Ericho asked.

June, sitting across the cramped diner table from him, hunched forward and poured herself another glass of water. She shrugged.

"Who knows? And to tell you the truth, Ericho, I'd honestly prefer not to think about Mars Lea anymore. She's gone and that thing is gone with her."

"I believe she saved our lives," Ericho said quietly.

"I believe you're right. But I'd also like to believe that she'd want us to try and forget about her, concentrate on living our own lives. If there's any testimonial we could make to Mars Lea Frock, that would be it."

He smiled and changed the subject. "How's Alan doing?"

"Good. He's conscious and he should be up and about in a few weeks." She took a sip of water and studied him intently. "And how are you doing?"

Ericho wagged his bandaged forefinger at her. "My frostbitten digit and I are doing just fine, thank you."

"That's not what I meant."

"I know." He sighed. "Don't worry. I'll be all right. Even if our new world doesn't have starships or captains anymore, I'll find something to keep me busy."

June shook her head. "Three hundred and fifty years. There will have been some drastic changes."

"We're survivors," said Ericho. "Whatever our new world has in store for us, we can handle it." He frowned. "But there is one thing that worries me a bit. My dream. It's gone; I haven't had it since Mars Lea left. And that makes me feel as if I've lost something important."

"You haven't. You've merely transferred something that was fantasy into something that is real."

She stared into her glass. "I believe that we'll land in that desert of yours, at the end of a golden day, under a beautiful violet sunset. And when the following day dawns, I think that we'll be ready to begin our new lives."

"Have you had the dream too?"

She shook her head. "No. But I feel as if that's the way it's going to happen. It just seems . . . proper."

The crewdoc hesitated. "There is one thing that's troubling me, though. Jonomy. Our Lytic's going to have more problems adjusting than the rest of us. He was designed to interface with a machine culture that probably no longer exists. He's the epitome of human specialization, firmly grounded in the timeframe that created him. I don't think he'll be able to adapt to new circumstances as well as the rest of us."

"And he's lost a lover," Ericho pointed out.

June shrugged. "Has he? I don't know. I'd like to believe that he was in love with Mars Lea, but somehow I can't quite escape the idea that their entire affair was a carefully orchestrated cybergenetic plan, from day one.

"I think Jonomy conceptualized the psionic dangers before any of us realized the *Alchemon* was in trouble. I believe he set about seducing Mars Lea in order to dampen—control—her telempathic output. I think that he made love to her out of a sense of duty—because he felt that a good Lytic was ultimately responsible for his ship and crew."

"Maybe," said Ericho softly. "But maybe he actually fell in love with her."

June smiled. "I suppose anything's possible. Whatever the case, I still think that he's going to have a lot of trouble adapting to the world of the future."

"Who knows?" said Ericho. "Perhaps he'll find some totally new occupation."

"Historian, perhaps," mused June.

"Or poet."

ABOUT THE AUTHOR

CHRISTOPHER HINZ is the author of *Liege-Killer*, winner of the Compton Crook Award for Best Science Fiction Novel of 1987. He is currently technical director of Berks Community Television in Reading, Pennsylvania, where he lives.